Seven Lively Suspects

Also by Katy Watson

The Three Dahlias
A Very Lively Murder

Seven Lively Suspects

Katy Watson

CONSTABLE

First published in Great Britain in 2024 by Constable

1 3 5 7 9 10 8 6 4 2

All characters and events in this publication, other than those clearly in the public domain, are fictitious and any resemblance to real persons, living or dead, is purely coincidental.

A CIP catalogue record for this book
is available from the British Library.

ISBN: 978-1-40871-648-9 (hardcover)
ISBN: 978-1-40871-649-6 (trade paperback)

Typeset in Adobe Garamond by Hewer Text UK Ltd, Edinburgh
Printed and bound in Great Britain by Clays Ltd, Elcograf S.p.A.

Papers used by Constable are from well-managed forests and other responsible sources.

Constable
An imprint of
Little, Brown Book Group
Carmelite House
50 Victoria Embankment
London EC4Y 0DZ

An Hachette UK Company
www.hachette.co.uk

www.littlebrown.co.uk

To Gemma, for everything

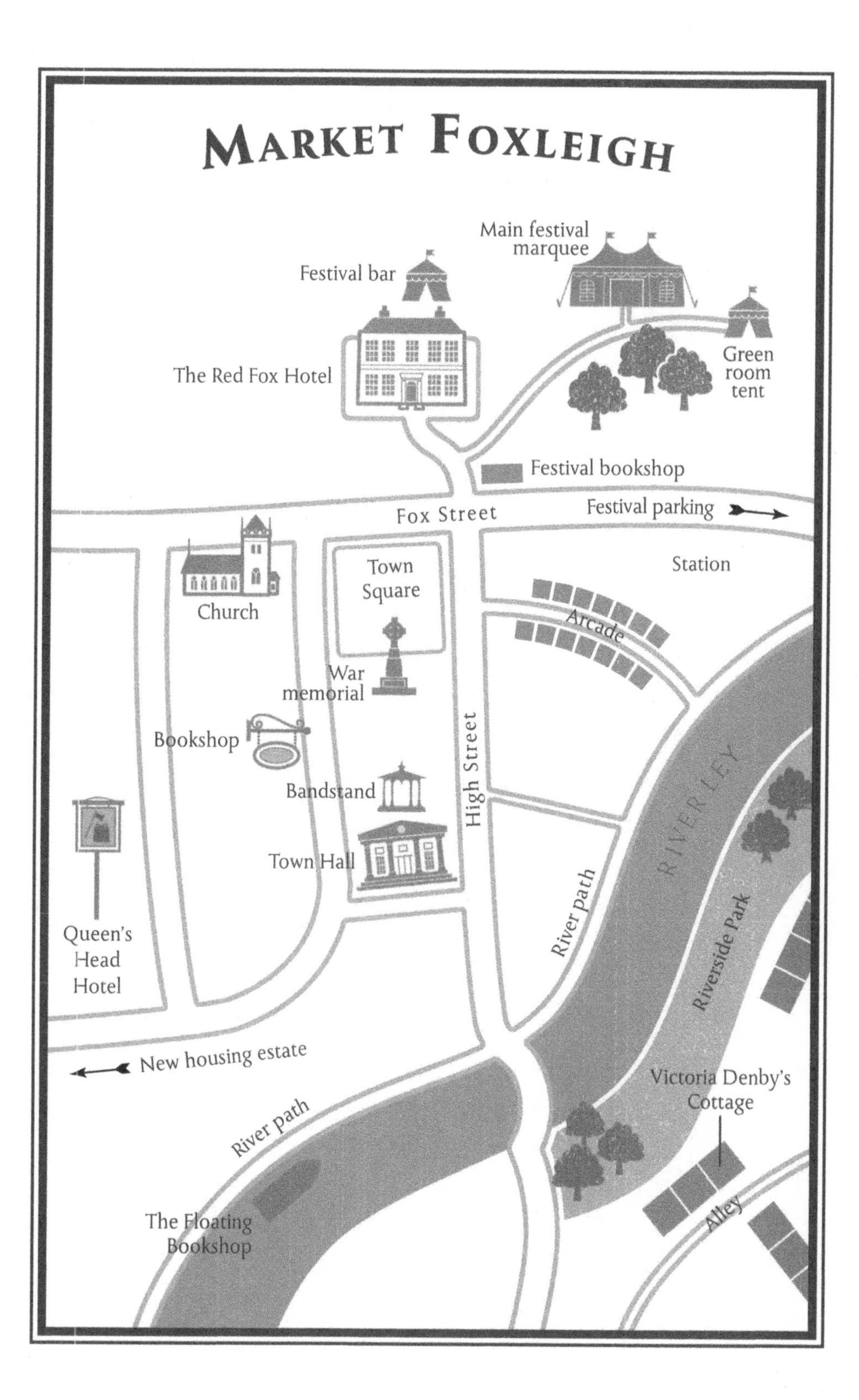

MARKET FOXLEIGH
Main festival marquee
Festival bar
The Red Fox Hotel
Green room tent
Festival bookshop
Fox Street
Festival parking
Station
Church
Town Square
Arcade
War memorial
Bookshop
High Street
Bandstand
RIVER LEY
Town Hall
River path
Riverside Park
Queen's Head Hotel
New housing estate
Victoria Denby's Cottage
River path
The Floating Bookshop
Alley

Cast List

Members of the Market Foxleigh Writing Circle
(at time of murder)
Victoria Denby (founder)
Scott Baker
Sarah Baker
Iain Hardy
Milla Kowalski
Danny Whitlock
Rachel Cassidy (now known as Raven)
Hakim Malik

Also attending this year's Market Foxleigh Crime Writing Festival
Caro Hooper, author of *The Three Dahlias* (headline guest)
Rosalind King (guest of Caro Hooper)
Posy Starling (guest of Caro Hooper)
Charlotte, Caro's editor
Jemima, Caro's publicist
Petra Wren, Caro's agent
Eleanor Grey, podcaster and TV broadcaster
Will Pollinger, TV actor-turned-author
Melody Kane, reality TV celebrity-turned-author

And a very special Surprise Guest Star Author . . .

Chapter One

'We could go see a movie,' Johnnie suggested. 'One of the new talkies, even. If you wanted.'

Dahlia sighed. 'Oh, all right. But only because there aren't any good murders that need solving right at this minute.'

Dahlia Lively *in* Murder Looks Lively
***By* Lettice Davenport, 1933**

Caro

Caro Hooper took her date's hand and stepped out of the car onto the red carpet. 'Anton must be positively seething somewhere, watching this.' Her words were almost lost in the noise of the crowd gathered in Leicester Square, but Kit was close enough to hear them.

He chuckled. 'If you attending this premiere as my date is the only thing our esteemed director is worrying about tonight, then I reckon we're doing okay. Don't you?'

Given the long road it had taken to get them there – metaphorically, rather than the journey from the London townhouse she shared with her wife, Annie – Caro had to agree.

Against all odds, the movie reboot of *The Lady Detective* had been completed, and very soon the world would be able to watch it. Posy Starling had officially taken her place in the detective pantheon by starring as the lady detective herself, Dahlia Lively. And the *original*

Dahlia, Rosalind King, had also managed not only to appear in the latest movie, but also survive the experience – which hadn't seemed such a sure thing eighteen months earlier.

They'd had to recast and relocate after the murderous events of the original film shoot in Wales, but filming up in Scotland instead hadn't been such a bad thing. For instance, the handsome laird whose family owned the estate they'd filmed at had taken a considerable shine to their scriptwriter, Libby McKinley. Caro smiled as she watched Libby and Duncan make their way along the carpet ahead of them.

'Our turn.' Kit tugged her hand through the crook of his arm, and they stepped forward together. He really was an old-fashioned gentleman – even though Caro knew she wasn't the Dahlia he *actually* wanted on his arm tonight.

Annie had laughed when Caro told her that Kit had invited her to the premiere as his date.

'Which one of them do you suppose put him up to that?' she'd asked. 'Posy or Rosalind?'

'Probably both,' Caro admitted. 'But Anton can't really complain if it's Kit taking me, not them.'

Kit Lewis was a rising star whose brightness was starting to eclipse the rest of them. If Anton wanted him back on set for the sequel, starring as DI Johnnie Swain once more, he couldn't afford to offend him. Which worked out nicely for Caro.

Anton hadn't wanted her on set in Wales, and he *certainly* hadn't wanted her on set in Scotland, but in the end he hadn't had much choice in the matter. Caro wasn't about to start letting men – or anyone – tell her where she could and couldn't go at this point in her life. And besides, Anton knew she was writing a novel based on their first murder investigation at Aldermere – the investigation that had turned Rosalind, Caro and Posy into the Three Dahlias, each of them as famous now for solving murders as for playing fictional detective, Dahlia Lively, on screen. Given his part in the events that transpired at Aldermere . . . Anton really did need to stay on her good side.

Which didn't mean he had to like it. Caro glanced around the gathered celebrities and film people on the red carpet to try and spot him, intending to give him a rather smug smile, but he must have already headed inside as he was nowhere to be seen.

It had been a long time since Caro had been on display like this. Ever since her TV series, *The Dahlia Lively Mysteries*, had been cancelled, she'd not exactly been in high demand for premieres and parties – or for parts, either, as it happened. The lack of roles for forty-something women in TV and film was just one of the reasons she'd turned author.

But she hadn't forgotten how this all worked. She smoothed down her green silk dress, smiled her brightest smile, and raised a hand to wave to the crowd as they walked towards the cinema entrance, and the photographers and reporters waiting for them. Tomorrow, her photo would be in the papers beside Kit's, forever connected with Dahlia Lively and this movie – and there was nothing that Anton could do about it.

Revenge really was a dish best served cold.

'Not that I don't appreciate you inviting me,' she said to Kit as they walked. 'But can I assume that you'll be going home with a different Dahlia tonight?'

Posy had been frustratingly cagey about her relationship with Kit – whether it was on, off, serious or imaginary was the subject of much gossip online *and* on the film set. The fact that Kit had spent so much time out of the country filming new projects over the last year couldn't have helped matters, though.

Posy was very protective of her privacy – and for good reason – but *really*. She could at least put Rosalind and Caro out of their misery and give them the details. Even Rosalind shared the basics of her developing relationship with her old friend, ex-detective inspector Jack Hughes – although she'd just smiled beatifically when Caro had asked her how the sex was.

If Posy would give her the same, Caro wouldn't have to interrogate Kit for the gossip.

As it was, he just shook his head. 'That's entirely up to her.'

'Hmm.' Caro cast a glance back over her shoulder to where Rosalind and Posy were making their way along the red carpet, both looking utterly stunning in their own ways, as usual. 'Well, if she doesn't, she's a fool.'

Kit squeezed her hand in gratitude for her support. 'Not a fool. Just . . . cautious.'

It would do Posy no harm at all to throw caution to the wind every now and then, in Caro's opinion. But then, she hadn't been around for the period of Posy's life where she'd had no caution – or common sense – at all, so what did she know?

Still, the most rebellious thing Posy had done in a while was to buy a flat in an area of London that might – or might not – be on the cusp of regeneration. Caro hadn't had the opportunity to visit yet, but she was bracing herself, all the same. Rosalind, she knew, had continued sending Posy listings for flats long after the sale had gone through.

Kit stopped for photos and to sign autographs for many of the fans who'd waited probably hours to see him. They waved their phones and notebooks, and Kit just smiled and posed, camera flashes brightening the summer evening around them. One or two of the fans wanted to catch Caro's eye, too, which was gratifying.

They'd barely made it halfway along the red carpet when she heard another voice calling her name – this one with rather more insistence than the others.

'Caro! Caro Hooper!'

Best smile in place, Caro turned to try and find the fan, scanning the crowd.

When she saw her, Caro knew in an instant that the woman wasn't there for an autograph, or a selfie. She wasn't even there for the movie.

She was there for Caro. Her own past coming back to haunt her.

'Caro!' the woman called again, waving wildly.

It was the eyes she recognised first. The pale blue eyes so like her brother's. She was older now, of course – it had been over four years since Caro had seen her, across the courtroom, staring accusingly at her.

Her fluffy blonde hair hung around her shoulders, the summer evening sunlight making it glow like a halo. She'd pushed her way to the front of the rope line, so Caro could see she wore a long, embroidered dress with flowers on it. And this time, there wasn't accusation in her gaze.

There was hope.

Caro turned away.

'Everything okay?' Kit murmured, as he tucked her hand through his arm again. At the front of the cinema, the security team were starting to beckon them in.

'Fine,' Caro lied. 'Your fans done with you?'

'For now.' Kit gave her a wink. 'What about yours?'

'Oh, this is your crowd, not mine,' she said, as casually as she could. 'I'm saving my hand strength for all the books I'll need to sign at festivals and such this summer, now *The Three Dahlias* is published.' The release had been cunningly timed by her publisher to coincide with the premiere of the new movie, and she'd held her launch event the night before.

'Probably a good idea. From what I've heard, it's going to be a huge hit.'

'That's the idea.'

As they stepped towards the foyer, Caro comforted herself with that thought. Soon her name would be back on everyone's lips, not because of a film she didn't even appear in, but because of something of her own. A book she'd written, herself, and a murder she'd solved – with a little help from her friends.

This was going to be her year, and no face from the past was going to change that.

Behind her, she heard the desperate voice call again.

'Posy! *Dahlia!* Please! I need your help.'

A chill settled in Caro's chest, despite the summer evening, and her steps slowed. She didn't turn, though. Just listened.

'He didn't do it! You have to help me prove it.'

Of course he did it. Who else could have?

'Caro?' Kit asked, frowning.

She waved a hand to shush him. 'One moment.'

Reluctantly, she twisted halfway round. Behind them, her fellow Dahlias had almost reached the doors, too – Posy sparkling in the silver dress from some up-and-coming London designer, and Rosalind elegant in a russet gown that looked too warm for the British summer but perfectly fitted her classic brand.

They'd stopped on the red carpet, staring out into the crowd at the rope line. And Caro knew exactly who they were looking at.

Sarah Baker.

The security team were ushering Rosalind and Posy inside now. But Sarah's last words echoed in behind them.

'The real murderer is still out there. You have to help me find them!'

Caro grabbed Kit's arm and started walking again.

She might be a part-time private detective and part-time crime author now, but the case Sarah Baker was talking about wasn't one she had any interest in revisiting.

Ever.

Rosalind

The movie was good.

No, it was better than good. It was everything Rosalind had hoped it would be.

She'd seen snippets before the premiere, of course. But she hadn't wanted to watch anything much until it was the finished article, complete with the music score and credits and everything. The way audiences would watch it, around the world.

And they were going to love it.

She smiled as she considered the individual performances. For herself, her turn as Aunt Hermione came across well – at least well enough to forestall having to move into voicing funeral-plan adverts any time in the near future, she hoped.

But more importantly, Posy's performance as Dahlia Lively *shone.* Oh, she wasn't the Dahlia Rosalind had been, or even the Dahlia that Caro had embodied. She was her own Dahlia, a Dahlia for *now*, and she was perfect.

Which, Rosalind had to admit, was a relief. Not least because it meant Posy might stop squeezing her hand so hard now the credits had rolled.

'It was good,' Rosalind murmured to her, while around them the theatre burst into cheers and applause. 'You were perfect.'

Posy let out a long breath, as if she'd been holding it for the entire one hundred and ten minutes. 'Thank God for that.' She looked up at Rosalind with a shaky smile. 'Now we just have to make it through the after party.'

Because, of course, the film was only the start of it.

Rosalind hadn't planned to attend the premiere alone, but Jack had little to no interest in being photographed on the red carpet and, besides, he had some sort of plumbing or guttering emergency to deal with back at his cottage in the hills of Llangollen. Rosalind might have finally learned to say the name of the town where he lived, but she drew the line at assisting with home maintenance when Jack could easily have paid someone else to fix it. But he liked to believe he was still a jack of all trades, so she ignored the fact it was clearly an excuse to avoid the cameras and went without him.

It did occur to her, as she travelled home from Wales, that there were rather a lot of things they were ignoring in their fledgeling relationship – like the two hundred miles that separated them most of the time, and kept the relationship perpetually in those early stages, even more than a year after their first official date.

Posy probably would have come with Kit, Rosalind assumed, if he hadn't been bringing Caro. It was fun to see Caro on the arm of the hottest young actor on the block, though. Rosalind imagined Annie was in stitches, watching at home.

They were led out of the cinema, past more fans and more cameras, to the cars waiting to take them to the after party. Rosalind had hoped to catch up with Caro, to see what she'd made of it, but she and Kit were too far ahead, and there were more autographs to sign, anyway.

She saw Posy scanning the crowd, and guessed what she was looking for – the woman who'd called out for Dahlia's help before the movie started. Heaven only knew what that was all about. These days, the three of them were almost synonymous with amateur murder investigations – although whether that was because they'd solved two genuine murder cases together, or because they were famous for playing Dahlia Lively, Rosalind wasn't entirely sure. Either way, the papers had enjoyed coming up with pun-filled headlines for both.

'Any sign?' she asked.

Posy shook her head, without Rosalind needing to elaborate. 'She must have gone.'

'Perhaps.' Except, why would she leave after so desperately calling for their help, when she knew they'd be coming back out this way again?

Probably just a crank, Rosalind decided. Or a ploy to get their attention for a photo or autograph. Nothing to waste time worrying about.

She ignored the strange feeling in the pit of her stomach that suggested otherwise.

The after party was being held at a museum space not far away, and sprawled over several floors and rooms, all well stocked with champagne and canapés. The museum itself seemed to specialise in crime memorabilia, which was presumably why it had been chosen, but Rosalind wasn't entirely sure that *all* of the rooms really fitted with the Dahlia Lively vibe.

Almost as soon as she was through the door she was collared by an old acquaintance for a chat, and lost Posy in the melee. It was a very boring five minutes before she was able to escape and explore the rest of the party.

She spotted Posy looking cosy with Kit in a far corner as she passed through one of the side rooms, and the sight made her smile. She was about to move on through the archway to the next exhibit space when Posy looked up and noticed her. She placed a hand on Kit's arm, murmured something to him, then broke away to head towards Rosalind – only to recoil at the exhibit she had to pass close by to reach her.

Looking at it even from a greater distance, Rosalind didn't blame her.

'Okay, I could have lived without ever seeing that,' Posy said, as she stepped around the display of a murder victim's severed head rendered in alarming – and hopefully not authentic – detail. Really, the death and gore theme didn't go so well with the designer dresses and diamonds filling the rooms.

Rosalind tugged on her arm and led her back through to the main atrium, where the displays were less, well, niche. 'Come on. I want to find Caro.'

'Me too.' Posy worried at her lower lip with her teeth. Rosalind had a fairly good idea what was bothering her.

'Stop worrying. She'll have loved you, too.'

'Then where is she?' Posy murmured, as they moved through the crowd.

Rosalind didn't have an answer to that. She'd expected Caro to be waiting at the door, ready to congratulate their Dahlia protégée on a stunning performance – just like they'd both been there at Caro's book launch the night before, to celebrate with her. But so far, their third Dahlia was nowhere to be seen.

The problem with a party like this one, especially when in the company of the star of the movie, was that it was almost impossible to get anywhere quickly. There were too many people who wanted to stop and chat – to pay compliments or, more often, fish for opportunities. Several women stopped Posy under the pretence of asking who had designed her dress, when they had to know that information would be on the gossip sites the next morning. Still, Posy took the chance to promote the work of Kit's up-and-coming designer friend, and Rosalind kept a fixed smile on her face as they made their way around the gathered horde.

Ignoring the waffling of a film critic who was apparently trying to suck up to Posy with some barbed backhanded compliments about other actresses, and occasionally Posy herself, Rosalind scanned the crowd again. She didn't find Caro, but she did spot someone who put a real smile on her face this time.

Across the marble hall, Libby McKinley waved from the sweeping staircase, and her companion gently grabbed her arm to stop her from slipping.

'Sorry, you must excuse us,' Rosalind said, not really caring she'd cut the critic off in the middle of a sentence. She slipped a hand through Posy's arm and led her towards the stairs.

'Libby! And Duncan. It's so good to see you both!' Posy leaned in to hug both Libby and her Laird-of-the-Manor boyfriend, and seemed genuinely relaxed and happy for the first time that evening.

Rosalind gave them her own embrace, then stood back. 'So, how did it feel, Libby? Seeing your story up there?'

Libby laughed. 'It's hardly my story, Rosalind. It will always be Lettice's.'

'Your interpretation, then.' Rosalind thought that the scriptwriter wasn't giving herself enough credit. Yes, she might have adapted the story from Lettice's original novel, but she'd certainly made it her own, adding touches and twists that brought it up to date for a modern audience. And that was before she got started on Anton's request for five possible endings.

In the end, Rosalind suspected that everyone would be satisfied with the one he'd chosen for the final cut. Libby certainly seemed to be; she was glowing as she gushed about how good they'd both looked up on the screen, how beautiful the cinematography was, and how the cast had brought her script to life.

Or maybe that glow had to do with something else.

Rosalind reached out to grab Libby's left hand as she waved it around for emphasis as she talked. 'Never mind the film – tell us about this!'

'This' being the giant diamond sitting on Libby's ring finger. Posy gasped and wiggled closer for a look, while Libby blushed a delightful shade of pink.

'Oh, well, yes. I wasn't going to steal anyone's thunder by announcing it tonight but . . . invitations will be in the post!' Libby smiled up at Duncan soppily, and even Rosalind's creaky old heart was warmed by the look they shared.

'We're thinking of a Christmas wedding, up home in Scotland,' Duncan added.

'It sounds perfect,' Rosalind said, approvingly, wondering how Jack would feel about spending Christmas in Scotland. 'And I want to hear all about it later. But first . . .'

'Have you seen Caro yet this evening?' Posy finished for her.

'Oh, she was just upstairs in the detective fiction display room,' Libby said, waving a hand in the general direction of where she'd last seen Caro.

'Of course she was,' Rosalind muttered. 'Probably looking for an exhibit about her personally. We'd better go find her before she starts giving tours to the guests. Congratulations again, you two. Come on, Posy.'

From the balcony level at the top of the main staircase, Rosalind could see out over the whole party. Camera flashes sparkled off champagne glasses, and the volume of the conversation rose well above whatever music was being played over the speakers. But the buzz was good. The buzz spoke of a successful movie, one everyone had enjoyed. Even the producers and the investors were looking relaxed.

Only Posy still looked tense. And Rosalind was sure that as soon as they found Caro, and the other Dahlia told her she'd done a good job, Posy would unclench.

'*There* you are!' Caro emerged from a side room, glass of champagne clutched in one hand, beaming as she leaned in to kiss Posy's cheek. 'Kiddo, you were amazing.'

Rosalind bit back a laugh as she watched Posy's shoulders visibly relax at her words.

'You weren't bad either,' Caro continued, as she embraced Rosalind.

'For an ageing relic?' Rosalind asked, pointedly, one eyebrow raised.

'For a national treasure,' Caro countered.

'What are you doing up here, anyway?' Posy asked, looking around them at the mostly empty balcony.

Rosalind frowned as she followed suit. There were a few small clusters of people up there talking more quietly than the raucous conversations downstairs, but this definitely wasn't where the party was.

And Caro was always where the party was.

'Oh, just checking out the amateur detective display, to see if we're mentioned,' Caro replied, too casually.

Posy clocked it, too, if Rosalind read her look right.

Something was going on with Caro. But finding out what it was would have to wait until after the party, she decided, as Anton was moving purposefully in their direction.

'And here they are. Our three Dahlias.' Posy and Caro both turned as one at the sound of Anton's voice behind them. He gripped hold of the banister as he took the last two steps, followed by three women – one Rosalind recognised, and two she didn't. 'I've got some people who'd like to talk to you three.'

Rosalind glanced across at her friends, and saw all the colour drain from Caro's face.

Maybe they wouldn't have to wait, after all.

Chapter Two

'In my experience, there's nothing so dangerous, or more insidious, than an open-and-shut, cut-and-dried case,' Dahlia said, slamming the file closed. 'They're always the ones that turn out to be far more complicated than anyone expected.'

Dahlia Lively *in* A Secret To Tell
***By* Lettice Davenport, 1959**

Posy

Posy stepped forward, her hand out, conveniently blocking Caro from view as she greeted the women. She cast a hurried glance at Rosalind, but from her barely perceptible shrug she had no idea what was going on with Caro either. Which meant they'd just have to distract Anton and his friends from her strange reaction until they were alone and could quiz her properly.

All Posy knew was, this wasn't the Caro she'd expected this evening – or the one who'd spent a fair portion of her own book launch the night before fishing for details about what was going on with her and Kit, and why he wasn't there. She didn't recognise *this* Caro at all.

She *did* recognise the first of Anton's companions – a twenty-something black woman in a stunning scarlet dress.

'Posy Starling,' Posy said, shaking the woman's hand. 'And you're

Eleanor Grey, right? I watched your recent TV programme on . . .' Dammit, what had it been on?

'The Devonshire Ripper Theory,' Eleanor finished for her. 'What did you think?'

'It was . . . a fascinating theory,' Posy said, diplomatically. In fact, as far as she could tell, there was practically no genuine evidence linking the series of eighteenth-century murders across Devon to one serial killer, but what did she know? She had enough to worry about solving crimes that happened on her watch, without travelling back in time to solve ones where the murderers were already long dead too.

She'd only watched the documentary in the first place because she'd been alone for the weekend and determined to chill out and not leave her tiny, new London flat unless absolutely necessary.

But Eleanor, with her intelligent brown eyes and engaging manner, had been strangely compelling to watch, as she linked the cases across the county. Even if Posy hadn't quite believed it, the presenter had made her *want* to believe, which was quite an achievement in itself.

'It was a stretch,' Eleanor admitted, with a self-deprecating smile that made Posy like her more, all of a sudden. 'But it made a good story.'

'It definitely did that,' Posy agreed, turning to Eleanor's companions.

The second woman she didn't know at all. She was of an age with Eleanor, wearing a simple black dress with heels, classic rather than standing out. She kept a comforting hand on the back of the last woman, who Posy felt somehow that she *should* know. She was a few years older than the others, white, slender, and with fluffy blonde hair that fell to her shoulders. But in the end, it was the embroidered dress she was wearing that Posy recognised.

'You were in the crowd earlier,' Posy said, holding out her hand again with a little less certainty this time. 'Did you come to see the film?'

The blonde smiled. 'I did. I loved it – you were great. And it was such a treat for me – my husband always falls asleep in films so I never get to go to the cinema.' She was babbling. Nervous, Posy guessed.

'Then I'm glad you enjoyed this trip,' Posy replied. 'I'm sorry, I didn't catch your name?'

'Posy, this is Milla Kowalski and Sarah Baker,' Eleanor said. 'Milla, Sarah, I'm sure you both know Posy Starling, and Rosalind King, and—'

'Caro Hooper,' Sarah finished for her, her eyes narrowing just a little as she looked over Posy's shoulder at Caro.

Oh. Maybe Caro hadn't been avoiding them because of the film, because she thought Posy wasn't a good enough Dahlia.

Perhaps *this* was what was going on with Caro.

Was it wrong that Posy felt kind of good about that?

It probably depended on what *this* turned out to be.

'Sarah,' Caro said, her voice chillier than Posy had ever heard it before. 'I'm surprised to see you here.'

'Eleanor was just telling me all about her podcast series, and mentioned that she'd hoped to meet the three of you tonight to discuss it with you,' Anton explained. 'Obviously, I did the chivalrous thing and offered to make introductions. And now I've done that, I'll leave you all to it.' He nodded a goodbye, then jogged away down the stairs back to the party proper.

Leaving them to try and figure out the rest themselves.

'A podcast?' Rosalind said. 'What about? Women in the arts? Roles for women over forty?'

'Murder,' Eleanor said, succinctly. Because of course it was.

Posy sighed. 'Why don't we all go find somewhere to sit down, and you can tell us all about it.'

The best place to sit in the entire museum, according to their new acquaintances, was a tiny cinema set up in one of the side rooms. It was really just four rows of old flip-up cinema seats, set up in front of a large screen playing some sort of documentary about murder investigations on stage and screen through the ages. Fortunately for them, the sound was off, with subtitles scrolling across the bottom of the screen instead.

'This is perfect,' Milla said, flashing a smile at Sarah before stepping away. 'I'll go get things set up.'

'Get *what* set up?' Posy asked, but Milla was already gone, her black heels clacking against the floor as she hurried towards the door at the back of the room.

The rest of them took seats in the back two rows. It was awkward, with Posy and Caro having to twist round to see the other three in the row behind them. But it was still better than having this conversation out on the balcony. Especially given the way that Caro *wasn't* turning around, not all the way. As if she didn't want to look at Sarah or Eleanor at all.

'You mentioned to Anton that you wanted to talk to us about your podcast?' Rosalind prompted.

Eleanor nodded. '*Writing A Wrong.* It's been going for three seasons now, and has a dedicated audience supporting it.'

'You re-examine unsolved cold cases, right?' Posy wasn't sure exactly what that had to do with them, since both cases *they'd* been involved with they'd solved.

'That's right.' Eleanor's gaze slid left towards Sarah. 'At least, usually.'

'I approached Eleanor with a different sort of case I'd like her to look at,' Sarah explained. 'Milla . . . she's my best friend, the only one who stuck by me after everything that happened, but she was also friends with Eleanor at university, and she put me in touch with her. Sort of a last roll of the dice.' She glanced over at Eleanor with a small smile, the sort of thankful smile that said she still couldn't quite believe her luck. 'We knew it was a long shot, but Eleanor agreed to help us—'

'With conditions,' Eleanor put in, leaving Posy wondering exactly what those conditions were. She suspected *that* was where they came in.

'And she got us in here tonight to talk to you three,' Sarah finished.

The room suddenly darkened. Posy glanced over her shoulder and saw that the dry documentary that had been playing had disappeared from the screen, leaving it black.

Then suddenly it burst into life again, only this time the image was something different entirely. Now, it showed a man – maybe late twenties, or early thirties – with very close-cropped, pale blond hair and tired blue eyes. He was frozen, waiting for someone – Milla, Posy assumed – to press play.

She didn't recognise him, but beside her, Caro stiffened.

'This is Sarah's brother, Scott. Four years ago he was convicted of the murder of Victoria Denby.' Eleanor pulled a thick file from her black leather shoulder bag and rested it on her knee. 'You might remember the case? She was the daughter of Charles Denby, the famous essayist and author, so it got quite some attention – for that and, well, other reasons. The important thing is, Sarah and Milla believe that Scott was *wrongly* convicted, that the police screwed up the investigation and prosecuted the wrong man.'

'And they want to use your podcast to prove it,' Posy surmised.

'He didn't do it,' Sarah said, fervently. She had the conviction of a true believer, Posy had to give her that. She could see it in her eyes – the same blue as her brother's, up on the screen. Now that she knew the connection, the similarities were there to see – even if it looked like only one of them had any fight left. 'I know he didn't. He couldn't. Scott . . . you'll see. He wouldn't hurt anyone, not ever.'

'But the police obviously thought he did, and so did the jury, if he was convicted. So I assume you have new evidence, if you're making such a strong accusation?' Rosalind said, one eyebrow raised. Posy hid a smile. She'd been spending too much time with Jack, lately, if she was rising instantly to the defence of the police.

'That's where my conditions come in,' Eleanor explained. 'This would be a big shift for my podcast, but I think it could be a good one – if it works. But I'm going to need more to convince my bosses to go with it. My podcast's not one of those 'recorded in my basement conspiracy theory' types. It's serious broadcasting, and we need to know where the investigation is going to go before we start recording. We need evidence – and we need proof of public interest.'

As she spoke, Milla re-emerged from the back room, a small remote control in her hand, and took a seat at the end of the row.

'We're still gathering evidence.' Milla's voice was soft, but Posy could hear steel underneath her words all the same. 'We feel that there were lines of investigation that weren't pursued by the police, once they'd arrested Scott. By our reckoning, there are four possible alternative suspects to pursue – six if you include Sarah and myself.'

'Why now?' Rosalind asked. 'Why pursue this now? It's been, what, four years?'

'Five since the murder. Four since the trial finished,' Milla replied. 'And we're doing it now because Scott just lost his last appeal. In fact . . .' She pressed a button on the remote control in her hand. 'I'll let him explain himself.'

The screen flickered for a moment, then settled, as Scott Baker's lips began to move.

'I . . . Sarah asked me to make this video but, uh, I don't really know what to say.' Posy didn't know what she'd expected from Scott Baker's voice, but it wasn't this. He sounded diffident, gentle. Not like a murderer at all.

Although, murderers didn't always sound – or look, or seem – like murderers. She'd learned that over the past couple of years.

'I'm Scott and, well, five years ago I was arrested for a crime I didn't commit. I . . . I know why they thought it was me. I get it. And I can't prove that I didn't *do it. I mean, it's like Dahlia always says, right?* It's far easier to prove than disprove. *But I guess that's what I'm asking you to do. Because you're my only hope now, I think. And I don't want . . .'* His voice broke, and they could all see his Adam's apple bobbing as he swallowed, larger than life up on the big screen. *'I don't want to spend the rest of my life in this place for something I didn't do. I did other things wrong, I know that. But I've paid for them with years of my life. And I've learned to do better. But I never, ever killed anyone. And I never would.'*

The camera didn't move, and neither did he, but suddenly Posy felt like he was staring straight into her eyes. It felt intimate and immediate, in a way the film they'd actually gone to watch that evening never could.

'Help me. Please.'

The screen went black and, for a long moment, they all sat in the semi-darkness in silence. Milla pressed another button on the remote, and the informational film that had been playing before whirred back into life again.

'I still don't see where we fit into this,' Posy said, staring somewhere between the screen and the podcast hosts. 'Why ask for us?'

'I know,' Rosalind said. 'We're the public interest. Right?'

'But what's the link?' Posy carefully didn't look at Caro as she asked. There was a fine line here somewhere, and she suspected they were already a long way to the wrong side of it. But whatever was upsetting Caro . . . they couldn't help her unless they knew what it was.

'Victoria was found with a paper flower beside her, made from the pages of a Dahlia Lively novel,' Sarah explained. 'Just like in the Lettice Davenport mystery, *D is for Dahlia.*'

'The Paper Dahlia Case,' Rosalind whispered, and Posy started with surprise.

Five years ago, she'd still been in LA, struggling with everything that had almost ended her. Around the time the case must have gone to trial, she'd have been moving to London – alone and lonely, and ignoring the outside world. But even she'd heard of the case, in passing.

'Not to mention the fact that you three have been making something of a name for yourselves solving crimes over the last couple of years. You're *good* at it, by all accounts. And yes, also newsworthy. If you're involved that gives us an added edge.' Eleanor didn't seem at all bothered to admit the commercialisation of their notoriety.

Rosalind was staring at Caro. 'Are those the only reasons?'

'Of course not,' Caro snapped. 'They don't *just* want us for the lurid publicity of it all, or because they think we might actually solve the case. Or even because of that bloody paper flower. No. They want me to stand up in public and say that he's innocent, because I'm the one who put him behind bars in the first place.'

Caro

She'd known, Caro realised. From the instant she'd seen Sarah Baker in the crowd outside the premiere, she'd known this moment was coming. She couldn't even really blame her. Wouldn't she do the same if Posy or Rosalind or, God forbid, Annie were accused of something she knew in her heart they couldn't have done?

Because Sarah had never believed her brother was guilty – had said so loudly and often to anyone who would listen at the time. And now she was here again, asking to reopen a period of Caro's life she'd hoped was behind her for good.

Seeing him up there on the screen . . . it made her insides feel cold.

'You . . . you testified at his trial?' Posy asked, tentatively, and Caro sighed.

Of course she would have to explain it all to her sister-Dahlias now. They weren't the sort of women who let something like this pass without asking a lot of questions. Fat lot of good they'd be as detectives if they were.

She just wished the questions they were asking each other were still about their love lives, rather than their past associations with murderers. Which, between them, they really had too many of already.

'I did,' she admitted. 'I'll explain after. But honestly, I only came in at the end of the whole thing.' And she really didn't want to talk about why in front of his sister.

'But yours was the face next to his in all the papers.' Sarah sounded almost apologetic about that, as if it was her fault her brother had dragged Caro into the whole mess. 'Which is why your involvement in freeing him would make such an impact.'

'So you want us to prove he didn't do it? Or catch the person who did?' Posy sounded doubtful of them achieving either, which Caro thought was fair. The trail was long since cold.

And she wasn't remotely convinced that the right person wasn't already behind bars, anyway.

'Ideally both,' Eleanor admitted. 'It would make incredible listening. Maybe even a TV show, I don't know. But first, we just want you to poke around, ask a few questions. See if you think there's a story to uncover here.'

'People will talk to you,' Milla added. 'In a way they won't talk to Sarah or even me about the case. We were both there, we were part of it. But you . . . you're coming from outside, you're famous, and you've solved murders before. They'll talk to you.'

'Who is they?' Rosalind asked. 'Who, exactly, do you want us to speak to?'

Caro suspected she knew. She remembered them, all lined up in the court room that day for the sentencing.

'There were seven people who attended the Market Foxleigh Crime Writing Festival committee meeting at Victoria's house on the day of the murder, besides Victoria herself,' Sarah explained. 'Scott and I, Milla, and the other four committee members. And every member of that committee had issues with Victoria, not just Scott. All we're asking is that you talk to the others – and to us, of course – to see if there's anything that stands out to you. Something that doesn't make sense. A clue, I suppose, to what really happened.'

It didn't sound like much, when she put it that way.

Caro glanced between the other two Dahlias, and knew they were already wavering.

'Obviously you'd be credited on the podcast,' Eleanor said. 'You could be as involved as you like, once we start recording. If we end up going ahead with it, I'll get my people in touch with your people to draw up contracts.'

'Contracts?' Those shivers inside her were being replaced by an angry warmth at least. 'We haven't said yes yet.'

Rosalind shot her a look, and she realised what she'd said. *Yet.*

From Eleanor's slow smile, she'd noticed it too. She held out her file to Posy over the back of the cinema seats. 'Just take a look through this. That's all I'm asking. Then, when you're done reading, maybe we can talk.' She got to her feet, smoothing down her dress. 'Come on, Sarah, Milla. We're done here for now.'

They inched their way out of the row of chairs, the flip-up seats crashing against the back rests as they moved. Caro flinched at the noise.

'I'll see you next weekend, Caro,' Milla said, throwing the words back over her shoulder as she followed Eleanor out of the room.

Caro looked away. And for a moment, the only noise was the faint sounds of the party below, and the whirring of the projector playing the detective documentary that still flickered on the screen.

Then Rosalind turned to Caro and said, 'Well. I think you'd better tell us your side of this story. Don't you?'

She felt slow, like the air in the little cinema room had thickened, holding her still. Her memories of that horrible time felt like that, too. Stuck, so she could never get rid of them.

Caro swallowed, and forced herself to speak. 'How well do you remember the case?'

'Only a little,' Rosalind said. 'And only because of the paper flower, really.'

Caro nodded. That was the detail that had drawn her in, too, before she even realised she had any connection at all to the case.

'I heard about it, I think,' Posy said. 'But I was still in the States when it happened and, well, it wasn't a good time.'

Right. Five years ago Posy wasn't close to being the woman she was today. Caro gave her friend a reassuring smile. She wasn't the only one with memories she could never fully outrun.

'I'm sure that Eleanor's file will tell you anything you want to know about the actual murder,' she said. 'But the TL;DR version—'

'TL;DR?' Rosalind asked.

'Too long, didn't read,' Posy murmured.

'Right. Okay. Sorry. Carry on.'

'Basically, aspiring author and festival organiser, Victoria Denby, daughter of Charles Denby, was murdered less than a week before the fifth Market Foxleigh Crime Writing Festival, after what was described by several people as a 'contentious' festival committee meeting. There was no sign of a break-in at her house, but people in Market Foxleigh didn't tend to lock their doors until they went to bed, apparently.' Which sounded like tempting fate to Caro, but she didn't live in a bucolic little market town, so what did she know? She'd never even visited Market Foxleigh. That wasn't her part of the story. 'She was hit over the head with a blunt object – later determined to be a trophy from the awards due to be given out at the festival – and a paper flower was left at her side.'

'Made from the pages of a Dahlia Lively novel,' Posy said. 'Is that how you got involved?'

'Sort of. I'm getting to that.'

'Sorry.' Posy looked chastened, and Caro realised she *must* be on edge if they were *both* apologising to her unnecessarily.

Caro ordered her thoughts to get through the rest of the story quickly.

'Like I said, there'd been some meeting that afternoon that had everyone worked up. But Scott Baker was the prime suspect more or less from the start. He was crime-obsessed, in serious debt from an online auction habit, and the bank had just contacted Victoria to say that someone had been taking money from the festival accounts – and Scott was the treasurer. Added to that, a neighbour came forward pretty quickly to say that they'd seen him fleeing the scene. He was missing for a couple of days, but when they tracked him down he was sitting outside my house, another paper dahlia in his pocket, and *that's* how I got involved.'

The police told her the last thing Scott had bid on was a charity auction for afternoon tea with Caro, as Dahlia Lively.

Annie had been terrified. It wasn't that long after they'd got married, and suddenly she'd been drawn into this world of celebrity Caro had never wanted her to see. The idea that a man so obsessive could get close to them, and they'd never even known, only made it scarier. Because that meant there could be other fanatics like him out there and next time they might not know until it was too late.

'The papers at the time kept talking about a possible serial killer,' Rosalind said, softly. 'Because of the flowers, I suppose.'

Caro nodded. 'That was the worry. Because of what the flowers meant in the book, too.'

'In the book?' Posy's forehead furrowed. 'Is this in one of the later ones I haven't read yet?'

Posy was making good progress working her way through the works of Lettice Davenport, but in fairness there *were* a lot of books, and she had been busy filming. Not to mention solving murders. Caro could forgive her for not having read all seventy plus novels and short stories yet.

'One of the very late ones,' Caro confirmed. '1975, I think. *D is for Dahlia.* Dahlia solves a case where a murderer leaves paper flowers by the bodies of his victims. It was one of the last of my episodes to air, before the show was cancelled that year, and they think that's what gave Scott the idea. They found . . .' She swallowed, then forced the words out. 'They found something of a shrine to me in his bedroom, it seems.'

Under other circumstances, Annie would have found that hilarious. As it was, she'd clung to Caro all night long, instead.

Caro really wanted to stop talking about this and go home to her wife. But from the looks on Rosalind and Posy's faces, that wasn't about to happen any time soon.

'So they got me to stand up in court and confirm that I'd seen the car outside our house. That I was the woman in the photos and things he'd pasted up on his wall, but that I'd never met him or had any other communication with him. That sort of thing. It wasn't so much a testimony as . . . confirming the police evidence.'

But the prosecution had used it to paint a picture of a man obsessed. One who had stalked and threatened a well-known actress, and perhaps had killed Victoria Denby as practice for the real thing – as well as to cover his obvious embezzlement of festival funds.

Annie hadn't slept for a week. And if she knew Caro was even *considering* getting involved in the case again, especially with a view to getting Scott Baker out of jail . . . well. That would go down like a lead balloon.

Except, she wasn't considering it. She knew she wanted to stay as far away from Sarah, Milla, Eleanor and their podcast as possible.

She just wasn't sure that her fellow Dahlias were on quite the same page.

Chapter Three

A few days later, they bumped along the private road from the village of Little Chumpingford in Susie, Dahlia's motorbike and sidecar, heading for Chumpingford Hall. Johnnie had objected to being relegated to the sidecar, bags stashed around him on all sides, but Dahlia expected he was enjoying the ride, really. Whatever his grimace under his driving goggles said.

Dahlia Lively *in* Sapphires for Supper
***By* Lettice Davenport, 1949**

Rosalind

Rosalind didn't think she'd ever seen Caro scared before, not like this. Oh, she'd seen her terrified in the moment – when someone's life was at risk right then, that second. But not when they were sitting safe and sound somewhere like this tiny cinema room, the after-show party still going on outside, just talking about a case.

If Caro was still so afraid of Scott Baker when he was safely behind bars, maybe they shouldn't be considering getting involved in this podcast at all.

Except Posy was already flipping through the file Eleanor Grey had handed her.

And the podcast was going to happen with or without them.

And . . .

'What if the police really did get it wrong?'

'They didn't.' Caro's reply was swift and sharp. But Rosalind wasn't sure she didn't hear just a tiny bit of doubt behind it.

She glanced up at Posy and knew she'd heard it too. That sliver would be their way in.

If they wanted to investigate this case.

'Sarah sounded pretty determined to get Eleanor to do this podcast and this investigation whatever we say,' Posy said, slowly. 'At least if we were involved we could control it more. Protect you and Annie from whatever it digs up.'

'We don't need protecting from a podcast,' Caro scoffed. But she still sounded scared. And Rosalind knew that what she was really saying was, *We just need protecting from a killer.*

Which raised another point. 'What if the real killer is still out there, though?'

'Then there's no evidence they had any interest in me,' Caro replied. 'Or killing anyone else, since there hasn't been another paper dahlia murder in the last five years.'

'That's a good point.' Posy tapped a pen against the file, and Rosalind had no idea where she'd found it. There couldn't possibly be enough room for her usual investigating notebook in the tiny clutch bag that went with her silver gown.

Look at them. All dressed up in evening wear and discussing murder again. Honestly. What would Jack say?

She didn't dwell on that thought, mostly because she already knew the answer.

He'd hate it. And not just because they'd be starting from an assumption that the police had screwed up. He wouldn't want them putting themselves in danger if they were right.

Jack had never liked the idea of her being involved in murder, even if that was how they'd met again after years of drifting apart. But she got the impression he thought that the events at Aldermere, and in Wales, were freak occurrences. That the possibility of her getting caught up in a murder a *third* time was just against the law of averages. Maybe he even believed that if the opportunity presented itself again, she'd walk away this time, being even older and presumably wiser.

Because that was what she'd let him believe. Because it was easier than trying to explain the strange pull in her chest, the need to know, to find out. To prove something.

If Sarah and Milla were wrong . . . if the police had been right all along . . . wasn't that worth proving, too?

'Yes, it *is* a good point,' Caro said, suddenly, and Rosalind had to cast back to remember what they'd been talking about. The lack of subsequent murders. Right. 'The papers at the time were certain that it had to be a new serial killer, because of the flowers. For two days before they caught him the whole country was waiting for another murder. And if it *wasn't* Scott, there would have been more murders by now. So Eleanor and Sarah are wrong, and the right man is behind bars.'

'Or the papers got it wrong,' Rosalind said softly. They all knew how often they'd done that before – even in stories about the three of them. Sometimes it was little details – more often, huge inaccuracies. Maybe the killer hadn't planned any further deaths at all – not even Caro's. Maybe they'd got exactly what they wanted – Victoria Denby dead, and someone else to blame.

Caro's shoulders slumped, just a little, the green silk of her gown sighing with the movement. 'You two want to take the case, then, I suppose.'

Rosalind shared a quick look with Posy before answering. 'We don't even know if there is a case to take, yet.'

'But . . . if there is,' Posy went on. 'If I see something in this file when I read through it that makes us think that maybe the police *did* miss something . . . wouldn't you want to know? I mean, if they got it wrong, an innocent man is behind bars—'

'Innocent?' Caro interrupted. 'You do remember the part where he was apparently stalking me, right?'

'Innocent of *murder,* anyway,' Posy corrected. 'Wouldn't you want to put that right?'

And that was the million-dollar question, wasn't it? Rosalind could see Caro wrestling with it in the way her mouth twisted, how her jaw tensed.

Because Caro would want an innocent man to go free, of course she would. She just also wanted Scott Baker behind bars.

Rosalind wasn't entirely sure how Caro was going to reconcile those two things inside her head, but one way or another she would have to.

'Look, maybe we could prove that the police got it *right,*' Rosalind said. 'If we stay on the sidelines, Sarah and Milla could twist any evidence they find to fit their own theories. They already know where they want this investigation to end up – with Scott freed. They *said* they had four other people they were concentrating on – you can't tell me you don't think they've already mentally accused one of them. We can't let them frame someone else publicly, even if it *doesn't* get Scott released. I mean, that person's life would be ruined, even if they were completely innocent.'

Caro gave her a surprised look, and Rosalind suspected she'd let that get a little too personal. But after the online conspiracy theory that claimed *she* was behind the deaths at Aldermere two years ago took hold enough for even the mainstream media to pick it up, she had some experience of being falsely accused. Even if she hadn't spent five years in jail as a result. If Eleanor and Sarah were right, Scott had.

'There's something else in here.' With a frown, Posy pulled out a sealed envelope from inside the file and held it out towards Caro. 'It's addressed to you.'

Caro didn't take it. 'What is it?'

'I don't know.' Posy reached out a little further, eyebrows raised, until Caro finally took the envelope. But instead of opening it, she tucked it into her bag, which made Posy pull a face.

'Look. Let Posy read through the file, then she can get us up to speed. We can see where we stand then and decide what to do,' Rosalind suggested. 'Does that sound okay?'

'I suppose. You'll have to read fast, though,' Caro said.

Posy frowned. 'That's right. Milla said she'd see you at the weekend, didn't she? Why, exactly?'

'Because I'm one of the headline guests at this year's tenth anniversary Market Foxleigh Crime Writing Festival,' Caro replied, with a wry smile. 'And I think we can safely assume all their suspects are going to be there too.'

Posy

In the end, they convinced Caro that it was easier if they just *all* went to the festival together.

'That way, I can fill you both in on what Eleanor, Sarah and Milla have been up to on the drive,' Posy said, probably with more pep than was strictly necessary. Caro glowered at her, but agreed.

'But I'm driving,' she added. 'I'll pick you up.'

Which was how Posy found herself, two days later, racing around her flat cursing the alarm function on her phone, shoving things into her suitcase, as Caro pressed the buzzer on the outside door. Repeatedly.

'Are you sure this is the right address?' Caro obviously didn't realise the intercom automatically transmitted every word she said. 'Do you think she's all right up there?'

Posy heard a car door slam, and then the buzzer was pressed again, short and sharp, before Rosalind's voice echoed tinnily through it. 'Posy, darling, let us up before Caro calls the police out for you.'

Posy detoured from packing her washbag to press the button to let them in.

'I'm nearly ready,' she told them, as she swerved into the bedroom to grab the last of her things. 'The coffee machine is in the kitchen though, if you want.'

But Rosalind stayed standing by the doorway, coolly assessing Posy's new home, while Caro darted straight to the window, peering out at her car parked below. 'Still there so far,' she said. 'I thought this area was supposed to be the next big thing in London?'

'There's a vegan deli just opened down the road,' Posy replied. 'That's the first sign.'

Rosalind didn't look convinced. Her eyes had narrowed and her lips were doing that sour lemon thing. 'When did you move in again?'

'Before Christmas.' Posy took a moment to view the flat through their eyes. She'd forgotten they hadn't been here before. They'd spent Christmas together at Caro and Annie's, and since then they'd mostly got together at restaurants and events. Until now . . .

It looked a little sparse, she supposed. That large blank wall she kept meaning to get some art for. The fact that the only mugs she had in the kitchen were plain white ones that had come with the place.

She'd bought the flat for the glorious summer light pouring in through large windows, and high ceilings that gave a feeling of space despite the city-centre footprint. For the window seat nook between the living area and the kitchen that she kept meaning to buy cushions for.

It was just a lot, trying to make a place a home, all on her own. Especially when she wasn't really sure what one looked like, for her.

'I haven't been here much.'

'We can tell,' Caro murmured. 'Come on, we'd better get going. Unless you've both changed your mind . . .?'

'Not a chance.' Posy zipped the last pocket on her suitcase, and slung her handbag over her shoulder. 'Come on. Let's go.'

Minutes later, she was crammed into the petite back seat of Caro's red sports car, along with two overnight bags that wouldn't fit in the equally tiny boot space. The car might look fancy, and was probably very expensive, but Posy was pretty sure it wasn't intended for three people to take an extended road trip in.

She looked to Rosalind for support, but the eldest Dahlia sat coolly elegant in the spacious front seat, her eyes shaded by dark glasses as she stared up at the building housing Posy's new flat with obvious dissatisfaction.

'Just be grateful I didn't decide to bring Susie,' Caro told Posy, as she shoved another bag in beside her. Posy had to admit, even the close quarters of the back seat of the sports car was better than riding pillion in the motorcycle and sidecar Caro had acquired somehow from the *Dahlia Lively Mysteries* set, once the show was cancelled. 'The fans will be disappointed not to see her.'

'They might not,' Posy said. 'You're not going to talk to Dahlia Lively fans, remember. You're there to speak to Caro Hooper fans.'

Caro brightened a little at that. 'I suppose that's true.'

'Heaven only knows what they'll make of all three of us being there together. Just like in your book, Caro.' Rosalind settled herself in. 'Posy, can I move this seat back a little?'

'Not if you want me to be able to breathe well enough to read from this file for you, no.' Posy twisted a little so her legs were at a better angle to fit in. Rosalind left her seat where it was.

They waited until Caro had navigated her way out of London, and they were on the open motorway through the English countryside, before they talked about the case.

'Go on, then.' Caro turned down the music that had been blaring through the car. 'You might as well start.'

Posy crunched through the sherbet lemon Rosalind had given her – apparently the eldest Dahlia was a firm believer in sweets for the journey – and flipped open the file. Caro still hadn't shared the contents of the letter she'd found, but maybe if Posy told her what else was in there she'd be more likely to talk.

'Okay. I won't go over the basics again, you both know those.' She thumbed through the sheets of copied police reports, newspaper articles and eyewitness statements. 'Although I would like to know who their contact in the police is, because they've got a lot of official info here.'

'Could just have submitted a *lot* of freedom of information requests,' Caro mused. 'You'd be amazed how much you can find out that way.' Something she'd learned working as a private investigator with Ashok over the last eighteen months, Posy assumed. She sometimes forgot that Caro knew more about this world now than she did.

'Means they're taking this seriously, either way,' Rosalind said, words slightly muffled as she spoke around her own sherbet lemon. 'Eleanor probably wants to make sure that if they do go ahead they're doing it properly.'

'Looks like,' Posy agreed. 'Their main theory seems to be that the police were too quick to act against Scott, and it meant they ignored other possibilities.'

'The case against him looked pretty strong, in fairness,' Rosalind said. 'They had an eyewitness placing him at the scene, for a start.'

'And forensic evidence, too,' Posy added. 'There's no doubt that he was there. But I guess they're talking about the other people on the committee.'

'The six others at the meeting?' Caro asked. 'They're people with motives? I know Milla said they all had "issues" with Victoria, but that's not the same as a motive to kill.'

Posy flicked through to the last sheet of the file. 'I'm guessing that's what they're hoping to find out. All I've got here is a list of names of the seven members of the festival committee at the time of the murder, including Scott, and a few notes about where they are now.'

'I know we're still considering Scott a possible suspect,' Caro said, 'but what about Sarah and Milla?'

Posy considered. 'I think we have to. I mean, yes, Sarah is the one who wants the case reopening, which makes her unlikely to have done it – same for Milla I suppose – but that doesn't mean we rule them out entirely.'

'Not to mention that they might hold evidence they don't even realise they have,' Rosalind added. 'We need to talk to everyone who was at that meeting, and not jump to any conclusions before we've gathered all the evidence.'

Caro shot her a side eye that made Posy wince. 'I assume you mean me?'

'I mean all of us,' Rosalind insisted. 'We don't know these people, and they've had five years to come up with their versions of events.'

'So trust no one, then?' Posy guessed.

'Exactly,' Rosalind said. 'Right. We know Sarah and Milla, and Scott I suppose. Tell us about the other four suspects. They're not all still in Market Foxleigh?' Rosalind asked, twisting around in her seat to offer the bag of sherbet lemons again.

Posy shook her head, to both the question and the sweets. Her teeth were starting to ache. 'Looks like they scattered after the murder, apart from Sarah and Milla.'

'Suspicious,' Caro admitted, around a sherbet lemon.

Posy scanned the page again. Seven names, four of them unfamiliar to her now, but she suspected they'd become very familiar very quickly if they took on this investigation. It wouldn't hurt to get a handle on them all before they met them.

'Okay, so, the festival started as a writing group,' she explained, reading from the file. 'Victoria set it up, I guess, and the others all joined. Then it morphed into the committee for the festival when they decided to go big. Victoria was the chair, Scott was the treasurer, Sarah was the secretary.'

'The victim and our first two suspects,' Caro said. 'Who else?'

'Milla, obviously. Her mum was Victoria's cleaner and Milla helped out too, it looks like, before she took over the festival. Not sure how *that* happened, but it's something to ask. Then there's Danny Whitlock, journalist on the local paper.' There was a photo of a dark-haired man in his thirties. 'He left to work for a bigger paper in Bristol a while after the murder.' She handed the piece of paper with Danny's details forward to Rosalind.

'Iain Hardy, who was retired already, I think, and then seems to have moved away to . . .' She checked the file again. 'Scotland, apparently.'

'Suspicious.' Rosalind reached out for Iain's file.

'Or he moved to be closer to his grandkids,' Caro said.

'Also possible,' Posy agreed. 'Next is Rachel Cassidy, who worked at the cafe in Market Foxleigh before she moved to London, where she now works as a tour guide. And finally, Hakim Malik, who now teaches English and creative writing at a school in Bath.'

'All scattered to the winds, then,' Rosalind said.

Posy nodded. 'It looks like most of them are expected to be back in town for the festival, though. There are emails here – I think Milla invited them all.'

'Which explains why they approached us this week.' Caro sighed, as the car sped up a little more, past the speed limit, and overtook the car they'd been behind for the last ten miles. 'They know this weekend, the festival, is their best chance to find out everything they need to know to make a case.'

'Seems like,' Posy agreed. 'As long as they'll speak to us. I'm not sure why they think we'll have more luck than they would, publicity notwithstanding.'

'Which is exactly what I've been saying all along,' Caro said.

It wasn't, but Posy and Rosalind both silently agreed to ignore that. Getting Caro this far was achievement enough, and Posy knew that neither of them wanted to risk her going back on it now.

'I've been thinking about that,' Rosalind said. Posy had a suspicion it was mostly to prove she'd been working on the case too, while Posy read the files and Caro stewed over the past. 'And the fact that most of them moved away fits in with my theory.'

'Which is?' Caro reached over and Posy heard the sherbet lemon bag rustle.

'They were all trying to put distance between themselves and what happened,' Rosalind said. 'Which means they might not take kindly to Sarah digging around the case again.'

'In fact, since it was her brother who they believe killed their friend, they might not want to speak to her at all,' Posy agreed. 'But what about Milla? Or even Eleanor? She's the professional. Why would they be more likely to talk to us? Three actresses who sometimes solve crime?'

'We have a track record of *actually* solving crime, not just coming up with unsubstantiated theories that make compelling telly watching or podcast listening,' Caro corrected her.

'And one of us—' Rosalind shook the sherbet lemon packet in Caro's direction. 'One of us has actually written a book about how we did it. One that's destined to be a bestseller.'

'That's a good point,' Posy acknowledged. Maybe it was just her who had trouble believing that they were really good at this. That they – or rather, she – could be taken seriously, after everything that had come before.

Maybe she just wasn't used to thinking of herself as a real adult, even at the age of just turned thirty.

As if Caro could read her thoughts, she said, 'Believe it or not kiddo, compared to them, we're the real deal. Yeah, I can see them wanting us to do the dirty work for them, and get them their evidence for the podcast.'

'And are we going to?' Posy asked, her voice tentative. 'Do the investigation, I mean?'

Caro sighed, but stayed silent, even as she flicked her indicator on to come off the motorway. The sign they sped past read Market Foxleigh, Posy realised. They were nearly there.

And she still didn't know what they were really there to do.

Until, a few minutes later, as the main roads gave way to smaller country lanes, and then brown temporary road signs directing them towards the Crime Writing Festival Car Parking, Caro said, 'Just for this long weekend. Three days, that's all. After that, I never want to hear anything about this case again. Agreed?'

Rosalind looked back around the seat and met Posy's gaze. She shrugged, and Rosalind nodded.

'If we don't have any leads by the time the festival ends, we'll drop the whole thing,' she said.

That wasn't *quite* what Caro had insisted, Posy realised. But if Caro wasn't going to question it, neither was she.

Chapter Four

The village green remained festooned with brightly coloured bunting, the cake stalls and the tombola still set up in the shadow of the ancient, flint-walled church. It looked every inch the perfect English village fair.

'Hard to believe a woman was murdered here just yesterday, isn't it?' Dahlia said.

Dahlia Lively *in* May Day for Dahlia
***By* Lettice Davenport, 1938**

Caro

Market Foxleigh was everything Caro had expected it to be.

Only a couple of hours' drive outside London, it managed to give the appearance of being in a different realm all together – or maybe a different time. From the cheerful bunting that lined the cobbled side streets, to the friendly smiles and waves from the people who directed them to the parking site for the festival, Caro felt like she'd slipped through time into a 1950s Sunday night cosy drama.

But for all its quaint English market-town nature, it certainly knew how to organise a festival. Or, at least, someone there did – presumably Milla.

As soon as they drove past the Welcome to Market Foxleigh sign, they were flagged down by a distracted volunteer in a yellow vest, who explained to them that large parts of the town were pedestrianised for the period of the festival, so it was best to park in the assigned festival parking, which they would happily direct them to. When Caro explained she was there as a speaker, the volunteer's eyes widened in recognition, and she was instantly on her radio calling ahead so there'd be someone to meet them.

'This festival certainly seems like a highlight in the town's calendar,' Rosalind observed, as they drove under what appeared to be a handstitched banner that read 'In memory of Victoria Denby', and then a second that read 'Welcome to' and finally a third with the words, 'the tenth annual Market Foxleigh Crime Writing Festival!'

With the car parked in the preferential parking zone, they were met by a smiling young man with a trolley who wrestled their bags from where they were wedged into the tiny boot – and around Posy – and headed off towards what they hoped was their hotel.

'Do we follow him?' Rosalind asked, but before they had to decide another voice was welcoming them.

'Caro! How wonderful to see you!' Petra, Caro's sleek and smooth literary agent, dressed all in black as usual, approached with her arms and her smile wide. Behind her, a bemused-looking boy in a festival vest, who looked only just old enough to drive, moved a black mini with the personalised number plate PE7R4 into a parking space. It appeared Petra had just abandoned it in the middle of the road.

Caro found it impossible to tell exactly how old Petra was, even after meeting her multiple times, except to say that she was clearly older than her, but probably younger than Rosalind – mid-fifties, or so, at best guess. She was also either highly successful, or came from family money, if the discreet labels on her handbags told the truth of it.

Petra took hold of Caro's shoulders and kissed her cheeks, then turned to Milla, who seemed to have appeared from nowhere, and did the same to her. Given the rain that had fallen the night before, Caro couldn't help but be impressed at the commitment to style they both showed in their decision to wear heels.

'Caro, this is Milla Kowalski. I suspect you've both been emailing about the event?'

'We've met actually,' Milla said with a smile. 'I'm so thrilled the three of you were able to make it. It's quite a coup for our little festival, having all three Dahlias here!' She didn't mention the investigation, which Caro took as a sign they were keeping it quiet for now.

'Hardly little.' Caro gestured towards the banners and the military-level parking operation. 'Seems to me you're putting on quite a show here.'

'We do our best,' Milla said, with a pleased smile. 'I actually work for the town council directly now, organising all sorts of different events around the area. The crime fiction festival is still the jewel in our crown, though.'

'And all in memory of Victoria, of course,' Rosalind added, as she stepped forward to greet Milla. 'I hope we haven't put you out by tagging along with Caro?'

'Not at all! Although I'm afraid I only got Caro's email late this morning, and the festival hotel is rather full, and guests have already checked in. I've managed to arrange a twin room for the two of you, or two single rooms at a different hotel if you'd prefer?'

'A twin room is fine,' Posy said, even if Rosalind's face didn't look convinced of that. Caro hid a smirk. This time, *she* was the star, which, unwanted murder investigation notwithstanding, felt good. At least she got her own room, anyway.

'If you'd all like to follow me, I'll take you up to the hotel. It's really very close.' She laughed lightly. 'But then, nothing is very far apart in Market Foxleigh!'

The hotel *was* close, Caro was pleased to note. They followed Milla back up the road, under the banners and the bunting, and past the high street. Now she wasn't driving, Caro was able to take in a lot more of the details – the independent shops all with posters about the festival in the windows, including one or two with her face on them, the converted horse-box coffee shop situated on the small square by the town hall, with bistro tables around it.

It seemed like such a gentle, gentile little town. If this had been a murder mystery – especially one of Lettice Davenport's – then Caro would have said it was inevitable that it be the setting for a gruesome, senseless murder. But in the real world, it was hard to imagine such a thing happening here.

But it had. And someone here this weekend might be hiding the truth about what really happened to Victoria Denby.

As much as she'd resisted taking part in the investigation – and she still thought it was probably a terrible idea – Caro had to admit, she was intrigued by it. Posy's words had niggled at the back of her brain the whole drive down. *If they got it wrong, an innocent man is behind bars . . .* They were countered, always, by Rosalind's: *Maybe we can prove the police* right.

Either way, if they solved this case, there would be a definitive answer to the question of who killed Victoria Denby. And Caro couldn't deny her investigative tendencies were itching to get started on that.

They turned down the next cobbled street and followed it a little way from the high street, through grand wrought-iron gates into a garden in full bloom. Up ahead, secure in its own grounds, was a beautiful building bearing a sign that read The Red Fox Hotel.

It was built in pale Cotswold stone, with lush green ivy climbing the walls, circling some of the windows and forming an arch over the entranceway.

Inside, the foyer was done in a tastefully classic interpretation of English country-house style. The wallpaper featured tangled, trailing vines and branches in muted green and gold, with the occasional red fox or squirrel peeking out, and cream and olive chairs were placed strategically around the area for arriving or departing guests to take the weight off. A large fireplace – unlit, given the summer warmth – dominated one wall, with an oversized, gold-framed mirror resting above and reflecting the whole space in a way that made it feel twice as big.

'All our special guests of the festival are staying here at The Red Fox.' Milla smiled at the receptionist and was instantly handed three large envelopes, and three keys, which she handed to each of them in turn. 'The other speakers and attendees are scattered around the other hotels, B&Bs and even some local homes belonging to supporters of the festival.'

'Where do the panels and events themselves take place?' Rosalind asked. 'It doesn't seem like there'd be space here!'

'Well, some of the smaller talks do happen in the conference rooms here at The Red Fox, and there are other fringe events in other venues around town,' Milla explained. 'But the main programme takes place in the marquee out in the hotel grounds – which is also where the festival bar is set up, so just follow the noise and I'm sure you'll find it!'

'It certainly seems like a huge event for the town,' Caro observed. 'Surely you can't be organising all this on your own?'

Milla laughed. 'Oh, no. There's always been a committee behind the festival, even when it was just starting out. Trust me, I have a lot of help.'

Posy had already dived into her envelope. 'I don't suppose there's an attendee list in here, is there?'

'I'm afraid not. Data protection, you know.' Milla dropped her voice, as Petra checked her phone a little way away. 'But I'm sure I can arrange for you to meet all the attendees I think you'll want to speak to.' She gave them a knowing smile.

Voices sounded above, and two familiar figures appeared on the sweeping staircase that led up to the bedrooms.

'Caro! You're here!' Caro's editor, Charlotte, skipped down the stairs with a smile. She, at least, Caro had been able to put an age on – mostly by stalking her LinkedIn profile and working backwards from her school and university dates. It hadn't made her feel any better to know that the woman in charge of her publishing future was a full twelve years younger than her, though.

Following her down the stairs was Caro's publicist, Jemima, who was, if anything, even younger. Still, they were both full of enthusiasm, ideas and, if she was honest, had considerably more knowledge of the publishing business than she possessed.

Caro performed the usual introductions and managed to smooth over the moment where it became clear that Jemima was now staying at the budget hotel on the outskirts of the town thanks to the late addition of Rosalind and Posy to events.

'So, what's the plan after we get all settled in here?' Caro asked.

'Well, there's the informal kick-off event this evening.' Milla glanced down at her clipboard, even though Caro was certain she knew all the details by heart. 'We've got Eleanor Grey hosting, which is lovely! I hope all three of you will be able to be there?' She didn't quite give them a secret wink, but Caro got the impression that she might as well have done.

'Of course,' Caro promised, with rather more excitement than she felt. She wasn't overly eager to come face to face with Eleanor again so soon, but she supposed it was inevitable. And besides, she *was* the star guest. It would be rude not to show up for the opening event.

'And before that we've got a little dinner arranged,' Charlotte said. 'Just for some of our authors. If that appeals?'

'Dinner *always* appeals,' Caro assured her.

Far more than murder did this week, anyway. Or opening that still sealed letter from Eleanor's file.

Rosalind

The twin room Rosalind and Posy had been assigned was spacious and bright, with a picture window complete with window seat that looked out over the gardens that surrounded the hotel. Leaving her handbag on the bed, Rosalind noted absently that their suitcases had already been brought up, and were each leaning against one of the two small double beds on either side of the room.

Posy set about unpacking straight away, but Rosalind found herself drawn to the window. She was tired after the journey – not that she'd admit that to her companion – and she'd been hoping for a little space and privacy to rest, and perhaps call Jack and see how things were in Llangollen. Instead, it seemed Posy wanted to talk about the case.

And Caro.

'I think she's coming round to the idea, don't you?' Posy pulled out a black and white polka dot dress, and hung it on the door of the large, wooden wardrobe that dominated one corner of their room.

Rosalind settled onto the window seat, easing her shoes from her feet, and looked out over the grounds. Outside, a bright white marquee shone in the late afternoon sun, while people bustled around preparing for the first event of the festival.

It reminded her of another window, another summer, she realised. If she didn't look back at the room, at Posy, she could be in the Library at Aldermere, watching the preparations for the Dahlia Lively festival where she'd met Posy for the first time. Where they'd become the three Dahlias.

Where they'd solved their first murder and seen their first body.

She turned her back to the window, and watched Posy unpack, instead.

Rosalind had no interest in going backwards. She just hoped that this case wouldn't raise the sorts of ghosts for Caro that Aldermere, and even their adventures in Wales, had for her.

'Don't you think?' Posy paused in hanging some sort of kimono-style dressing gown by the bathroom door and looked over at Rosalind for an answer.

What had they been talking about? Someone coming around to something . . .

'Caro? I think she can't resist an investigation, however much she protests,' Rosalind said. 'But we still need to be careful with this one. She might not like what we uncover very much.'

Rosalind knew how that felt, too.

'That's true.' Posy zipped up her now empty suitcase, and shoved it into the corner by the wardrobe. Then, apparently full of restless energy Rosalind couldn't help but envy, she made her way across to the window and took in the view. 'Looks busy out there. I might get changed now and go down and get the lie of the land before this opening event. See if I can find anyone worth talking to – maybe even some food, since Caro's out at this publishing dinner. Want to come with?'

Rosalind felt a surge of relief at her words. 'Ah, actually, I've got one or two things to take care of here. You go ahead, though.' She peeked out of the window again. 'I'd recommend sunglasses and a hat if you don't want to be mobbed.'

Posy flashed her a smile. 'Nah. I want to get the lie of the land – unfiltered by Sarah and Milla. If Milla's setting up official interviews for us, this is probably my best chance at chit-chatting about the case unofficially – I reckon people knowing who I am can only help with that.'

She had a point, Rosalind decided, as Posy swept off towards the bathroom, grabbing the dress from the wardrobe door on her way. People often talked to celebrities as if they were old friends – a consequence of appearing in their living rooms regularly, even if it *was* only on screen, she supposed.

A mere fifteen minutes later, Posy was out the door again, a red jacket thrown over her polka dot dress, white trainers on her feet, and a splash of bright red lipstick that made her look more awake and alert than Rosalind had felt in months.

She stood just inside the door and watched her go, smiling to herself as an older gentleman – probably not quite her own age, with clipped-close grey hair, wearing jeans and trainers – did a double take at Posy gliding past.

'The energy of youth, eh?' he said to Rosalind, in a warm, Scottish brogue, as they both watched her go. Then he looked back and obviously recognised her, because he added, 'Not that you've aged a day these last twenty years or more, Ms King.' He sketched a small bow, with a twinkle in his eye.

'You're too kind,' she replied. He nodded to her once more before going into his own room opposite, pulling the door shut only for it to spring open again. She smiled sympathetically as she watched him close it again, and heard the lock turn inside. The problem with old buildings, she supposed. However nicely refurbished this one had been, little things like uneven doorways often got missed.

Rosalind closed her own door with care, waiting to check it stayed shut, then reached for her phone.

Jack answered on the fourth ring, sounding slightly breathless. 'Everything okay?' she asked, hoping that something new hadn't collapsed or started leaking at the cottage. Old houses were much the same as old hotels. Jack's house was very picturesque, and the views were hard to beat, but there was a lot to be said for serviced flats that had been built within the last century . . .

'Just chatting with the postie,' Jack replied. 'He was late today. How are things there? Did you make it to the festival, or did Caro turn you around halfway and take you home instead?'

It had been a concern. Caro was their link to this case. If she changed her mind about investigating, Rosalind knew she and Posy wouldn't carry on alone.

Was she imagining the hopeful tone in Jack's voice, though? He hadn't been particularly impressed when she'd filled him in on their meeting with Eleanor, Sarah and Milla at the premiere.

'We made it.' Rosalind reclined on the bed, propped up by the fluffy pillows at the headboard. From here, she had a glorious view out of the window, over all the hustle and bustle below, and out to the gently rolling hills beyond. It was almost like being at Jack's, except for the gently rolling part. The Welsh countryside was rather more striking and dramatic. Jack said that was what he liked about it. Said it reminded him of her.

'And how is it?' She knew what he was really asking. *Are you sure this is a good idea? Why don't you just come home instead? Why go digging up bodies that have already been properly buried?*

Those weren't the questions she answered though. 'It's fine. I'm sharing a room with Posy though, so it's just as well you didn't come.'

'Hopefully she snores less than Caro.' Jack didn't press her for the answers to his unasked questions. That was what she liked about *him.* He gave her space. Whole mountains' worth, if that was what she needed.

But he was never far away if she called.

Still, as the months went on, she couldn't help but wonder. Was space just another word for avoiding the issues that divided them? Like her penchant for investigating murders, among other things.

'Hopefully.' She paused, trying to find the right way to frame her next question. 'I know you think this is a bad idea . . .'

There was a heavy sigh down the phone line, followed by the familiar creaking of Jack's leather wingback chair in his study. 'But you want to know if I've been able to find out anything about the Paper Dahlia case. Right?'

She hadn't told the others she'd asked him to look. Not with Caro still so uncertain about everything. But if they *were* going to do this, they'd do it with all the information at their disposal.

Posy seemed wedded to the file that Eleanor had handed her at the premiere, but Rosalind wasn't willing to trust the podcast host, or Sarah and Milla for that matter, to give them everything. They had an agenda. What if they'd held back any of the less favourable evidence they'd uncovered?

This case had already been thoroughly investigated once. It made sense to start there, and the police case notes in Eleanor's file were nowhere near complete – not to mention that she hadn't told them how she'd got her hands on them in the first place.

Posy might be impressed at the stack of papers, and Caro might talk about probable FOI requests, but Rosalind couldn't trust information she didn't know the source of.

She trusted Jack, though. Which, after the last few years of having her faith in humanity systematically undermined, was saying something.

'Have you?' she asked.

Another sigh. 'I've spoken to a few people, yes. Honestly though, Rosa, I'm not sure there's much to find that you don't already know. Nobody doubts they got the right guy on this one.'

'Well, they wouldn't would they?'

'They would if there had been more paper dahlia murders,' Jack said.

That was the sticking point, wasn't it?

'The papers thought there would be, didn't they?' Rosalind recalled the tabloid clippings in Eleanor's file. 'Because of the paper flower. They thought it was a calling card.'

'I think the guys on the case were worried there might be, too,' Jack admitted. 'And even if they weren't, the fact that the media had the *public* worrying about it meant there was some pressure to solve the case fast, and stop any sort of hysteria building about it.'

'Hmmm.' She knew what he wasn't saying. Pressure to find a murderer fast meant more chances a mistake could be made. 'You think they cut corners?'

'I doubt it.' Jack frowned. 'Back when I started policing? Yeah, that might have been the case. But not so much these days.' From the hesitation in his voice she could tell he wasn't sure about that.

'Did they figure out where he got it from? The flower, I mean. Did he make it himself?'

Jack huffed a laugh. 'No. Ordered it from some online craft site. Book flower bouquets are all the rage for weddings among a certain bookworm set, apparently. It was traced in practically no time by the team.'

'Not exactly a master criminal, then.' Had Scott not known how easily such things could be traced? Or had someone else ordered them in his name, with his email, to frame him? She knew which one Sarah and Milla would opt for – and which Caro would choose.

'Rosa. No one ever thought anyone but Scott Baker was responsible for Victoria Denby's murder,' Jack said, firmly. 'There are witnesses putting him at the scene, and he had a clear motive – Victoria was about to call the police and accuse him of embezzlement of festival funds. Plus he was clearly unstable – you *know* all the stuff about Caro, right?'

'Then perhaps we can help prove the police right,' Rosalind said, remembering she'd said the same to Caro the night of the premiere.

She'd meant it then.

So why was she starting to doubt now?

The silence on the phone line stretched out awkwardly. She didn't want to end the call this way, but she didn't know what else to say, either. Not without stepping into conversational minefields neither of them wanted to address.

Finally, Jack broke the impasse. 'I just want to know . . . why do you feel you need to do this? Investigate this case, I mean. Why not just let it lie?'

The answer sprung, fully formed, to her lips. 'Because it's Caro. Because I know that if she doubts herself, for a moment, if she thinks she helped to put the wrong man away for murder . . . the guilt will consume her. Because even just putting the possibility out there has her on edge, and she needs us here to support her through whatever happens next. Like she came to Wales for me last year.' She took a breath. 'Because it's Caro, Jack.'

'And if I asked you *not* to do it?' Jack asked.

Rosalind swallowed, her throat suddenly dry. 'You'd never ask that.'

Because they both knew who she'd choose.

Chapter Five

Posy pulled the sheets of paper from her voluminous handbag and laid them out on the table. I honestly had no idea what else she was stashing in that thing, but it seemed larger than was strictly necessary for day-to-day life. Dahlia would never have carried something so unwieldy. But then, all Dahlia needed was her lipstick, her cigarettes, and someone to pay for the cocktails.

Caro Hooper *in* The Three Dahlias
***By* Caro Hooper**

Posy

The Market Foxleigh Crime Writing Festival didn't officially start until the following day, but that night's informal kick-off event was clearly a can't miss for those in the know, because the festival bar was already packed.

Situated on the lawn behind the hotel, the bar took full advantage of the warm summer evening, being set underneath a large sail marquee with open sides, and strung with more fairy lights than Posy thought she'd ever seen in one place before. The tables and chairs underneath were rustic, wood and metal types, suitable for outdoor use, and the bar itself was a veritable garden of green plants growing up and out of railway sleeper planters, topped by a rough, live-edged wooden surface. Behind the bar hung rows of brightly coloured bottles, forming an optics wall, and a large chalkboard detailed an extensive cocktail menu that Posy didn't linger over.

The queue at the bar was already several people deep. Posy didn't actually want a drink, but she knew that joining the waiting throng was the best way to get talking to people – and that's what she was there to do.

It didn't take long for someone to recognise her. More than one someone, in fact.

She knew from long experience when people were looking at her, talking about her, even sneakily taking photos of her by pretending to be taking a selfie or a shot of a friend. It just made a change to feel that the talk and the looks were fuelled by pleased excitement, rather than gossip and stories she never wanted to hear again.

Still, she smiled at people who acknowledged her – some, she knew, trying to figure out how they knew her, others well aware – and even posed for a couple of selfies before signalling that she needed to move on. Most people were fairly respectful about giving her space at events like this, in her experience – after all, the authors and other celebrities they were there to see expected the same.

She turned towards the bar, and almost immediately pulled back to avoid crashing into someone.

'Sorry!' A young woman with stark, straight black hair blinked up at her from cheerful blue eyes as she juggled two glasses and her phone in the hope of not spilling wine or Coke all over herself, or Posy. Then her eyes widened. 'Wait, aren't you—'

'Posy Starling,' the man beside her, who'd just handed over his card to the bar staff, said. 'Our very own Dahlia Lively. What an honour.'

'You must be here with Caro Hooper!' The woman bounced a little on her toes, and Posy took a step back to avoid getting sticky soft drink on her shoes. 'I saw that she was the big name guest for tomorrow, and *everyone* knows about the three of you all being best celeb pals now and everything.'

'It's kind of you to come to support your friend,' the man said, rather more sedately. 'And a big boost for our little festival to have you here. May I buy you a drink?'

'Oh, I—'

'Hakim! We mustn't bother her. I'm sure she has plenty of other people to meet and drink with.' The woman's smile turned a little mischievous. 'But it *is* lovely to meet you, Miss Starling. I'm Raven, and this is Hakim. And, well, if this is your first time at the festival, Hakim and I could definitely give you the expert's guide. We've been here from the start, you see . . .'

Hakim. Posy recognised that name from Eleanor's file, even if Raven was a mystery. Hakim Malik was one of the early members of the writing group that started the festival with Victoria. What were the chances this was a different Hakim, if he'd been here from the start?

'Oh, well, a tonic water would be lovely, if you're sure?'

Hakim turned back to the bar.

Drinks in hand a moment later – Raven had given the Coke to Hakim, and things were looking less precarious there now – they made their way to one of the tables on the outskirts of the bar area, and took a seat. She couldn't quite get a read on the two of them. They didn't act like a couple, but they obviously knew each other well. Old friends then, she assumed, sharing a common interest in crime fiction. And if they'd *both* been involved from the start, chances were they could give her some good background before she and her fellow Dahlias started interviewing the other suspects on Milla's timetable.

'This is quite the set-up the festival has going here,' Posy observed, as she sat back to admire the growing crowds of people. There was already a queue snaking up the hill towards another large marquee she could see peeking through the trees, presumably in advance of the 'unofficial' kick-off event, and the summer evening air was filled with the hum of conversation, laughter, and the clink of glasses. 'Are you two involved in the organisation, then?'

Raven took a sip of her wine. 'Not anymore. We used to be, back when it was more of a casual, throw-it-together local event. These days it's much more corporate, you see.'

'And better organised,' Hakim added, drily. 'Milla runs the thing like a military operation. But, as you can see, it works. The festival just keeps getting bigger and better, every year.'

'And you both keep attending, so it must be good! I guess you both still live locally?' She knew from the file that Hakim didn't, but a little feigned ignorance sometimes went a long way in an investigation, she'd learned. Dahlia used that trick all the time.

Hakim shook his head. 'I'm over in Bath now, most of the time, teaching there. But I always come back for the festival.'

'Me too,' Raven said. 'Although I'm in London the rest of the year. In fact . . .' Her cheeks turned pink in a way that had nothing to do with the fading sunlight. 'I write murder mysteries, as it happens, so being here is sort of a professional obligation as well as a personal one. And Hakim teaches creative writing evening classes, with a special focus on crime fiction, so it is for him, too.'

'That's brilliant,' Posy said, her mind already whirring. 'What sort of stories do you write?'

It was clearly the question Raven had been waiting for. 'Actually, that's why it's kind of fortuitous that I met you here today! I write mysteries where the detective is actually Lettice Davenport herself! I mean, a fictionalised version of her, of course, but I've done my research, and it's all based on her letters and diaries and such as far as possible. They're set in London, between the wars, mostly, just like the Dahlia Lively mysteries, with a few in surrounding small country towns and villages.'

Were people allowed to just . . . make up stories about real live people? Posy had no idea. She supposed Caro's book was sort of the same, except that it was based on things that really happened. Posy had read it, so she knew Caro had taken liberties with strict facts now and then, to make it a better story, but she'd cleared the final draft with both her and Rosalind before it went to print, to make sure they were happy with how she portrayed them. 'Wow. That sounds . . . how many have you written?'

'Twelve, so far.' Raven reached into her phone case and pulled out a business card with a book cover on the front. It showed a dark blue background, and a woman in 1930s dress holding a magnifying glass, with Big Ben in the background. *The Marble Arch Mystery*, by Raven Cassidy, the cover read. Posy peered at the picture again. Definitely no sign of Marble Arch.

Raven must have guessed what she was looking for, because she said, 'Most of my audience is overseas – especially in America – so I need the covers to scream London, even if they're not exactly representative of where the mystery takes place. Although I can usually manage to have Lettice wander past a few traditional London landmarks in each book.'

'Twelve books is a lot.' Posy made to hand the card back, but Raven signalled for her to keep it, so she tucked it into her phone case. 'How long have you been writing?'

'Four years. When you indie publish, you have to meet the market where it is,' Raven explained. 'And cosy mystery readers read a *lot.* So the faster you can publish, the more readers get hooked into the series. Three books a year is nothing compared to what some other authors are putting out, but I've got my day job to consider, too.'

'Rachel – sorry, Raven,' Hakim corrected himself, off Raven's glare. 'Raven runs Dahlia Lively tours of London, visiting all the places that feature in the original Dahlia books, and telling stories about them. They're incredibly popular.'

'The aforementioned day job. They've been featured in all sorts of London guides.' Raven pulled out her phone case to find another card – this one emblazoned with a logo for The Official Dahlia Lively London Tour, although as far as Posy could tell there was nothing actually official about it. She'd have to ask Libby if she knew any of this was even happening. 'You should come take a tour! You could do it incognito.'

'Hat and dark glasses,' Hakim agreed, with a serious nod. 'But really, the tours are great fun.'

Posy added this business card to the first, and smiled. 'I'll check them out when I'm back in town.'

Hakim looked up, over her shoulder, staring at something, or someone at the far side of the bar. Then he nudged Raven, who followed his look. Posy resisted the urge to turn around and stare, too.

'I can't believe she'd come here,' Raven murmured. 'After everything.'

'It's a free festival,' Hakim replied, but the same shock was clear in his voice, too. 'And it's been five years. She does still live in town, you realise.'

Posy gave up resisting, and turned to find – as she'd expected – Sarah and Eleanor standing by the growing green bar.

'A friend of yours?' she asked, mildly.

'Not exactly,' Hakim hedged.

'Not anymore.' A frown line had settled between Raven's eyes, and suddenly she looked five, even ten years older. 'What's she doing with Eleanor Grey?'

Raven was obviously a pen name, wasn't it? Hakim had slipped and called her Rachel – and there was a Rachel Cassidy on the original list of the writing group members who'd formed the festival committee, the year of the murder. Posy would take odds that this was the same woman. She'd been right then – old friends.

'Her name is Sarah Baker,' Hakim explained. 'We used to belong to the same writing group until, well. Something terrible happened . . .'

Maybe it was time for Posy to stop playing ignorant. Hakim and Raven could talk around the subject forever otherwise.

'I actually met Sarah recently, along with Eleanor and Milla, at the premiere for *The Lady Detective*. I believe they're working together on the next series of Eleanor's podcast.'

Hakim and Raven both looked at her sharply. 'A podcast? About what?' Raven asked.

'*Writing a Wrong*. It's a true crime podcast,' Posy explained. 'This one's going to be about a murder that happened here five years ago. The daughter of Charles Denby, I think. Victoria Denby?'

Hakim and Raven didn't look at each other now. Or at Posy. Or even at Sarah. They both seemed lost in their own reactions and emotions. Posy took the opportunity to study their faces. Hakim's was frozen, perhaps in shock, or fear, or something else entirely, she wasn't sure. Raven, on the other hand, looked simply furious.

'Of course,' she muttered, almost too low for Posy to hear, but not quite. 'It's still all about her.'

'Surely there's nothing else to say about that horrible time,' Hakim said, quickly, and Posy got the impression he might be trying to cover up Raven's initial response. 'After the police investigation, all the coverage in the papers, then the trial . . .' He shook his head. 'It is better to just put it behind us, I feel. For the sake of the community.'

Not 'the family', Posy realised. There wasn't much about Victoria's family in the file, either. Her father was already dead, and Posy thought the mother might be, too. But was there anyone else? Something else to look into.

Suddenly, Raven looked up at Posy, her blue eyes wide and blazing. 'Oh my God. They're going to try and get him off, aren't they? Like that podcast in the States did. They're going to try and find a way to make people believe that Scott's innocent, so the police have to apologise and they let a killer out of prison.'

Posy shrugged helplessly, unsure how much she was allowed to say about it yet. 'I take it you'd . . . object? If they did? If you were friends with Sarah . . . were you friends with the victim, too?'

'Nobody was really *friends* with Victoria,' Raven said, shortly. 'Not around here, anyway. But she ran the writing group, and then the committee, and enjoyed bossing us all around. We were . . . I don't know. What's a word for someone who should be a friend but isn't, somehow. Hakim? Is there one?'

'*I* was friends with Victoria,' Hakim said, ignoring Raven's hunt for clarity of language. 'And yes, I would object. Scott killed her, and no amount of media buy-in from a famous presenter or a distraught sister is going to change that. They shouldn't try to . . . rehabilitate his reputation, or whatever it is that's going on here.'

Across the bar, Posy saw Caro appearing around the side of the hotel with a gaggle of other people, presumably done with her early dinner. With her trademark perfect timing, Rosalind stepped out of the back door of the hotel at the exact same moment.

'I'm sorry that I've upset you both,' Posy said. 'I honestly don't know how far they're going with their podcast plans. But I hope it doesn't cause either of you too much distress.'

She got to her feet, stepping away from the table with an apologetic smile. 'Thank you for the drink. It was lovely to meet you both. I'm sure I'll see you again before the festival is over.'

Because if they were going to take on this investigation, she had a lot more questions to ask both of them.

Caro

Dinner was much as Caro had expected – a group of authors all talking about the ups and downs of writing, creative and financial. The food was good, the wine better, and the only slightly sour note was that she wasn't sure one or two of the others actually believed she'd written *The Three Dahlias* herself.

'Why would I hire someone else to write a book I'd already lived through once?' she muttered to herself after saying her goodbyes, and making her way over to where Rosalind had emerged from the hotel.

'Everything okay?' Rosalind asked, which Caro took to mean she was glowering.

'People think I hired a ghost-writer to write my book.'

Rosalind shrugged. 'Of course they do. You're a celebrity. In their minds, you have a staff for everything, even your actual job. They probably don't believe we actually solved the murder, either.'

'Hmph.' Well, maybe that was something she could put right in her panel tomorrow. What was the *point* of writing *The Three Dahlias* to tell their side of the story if no one believed it was based on fact – or that she'd even written it at all?

Posy joined them from the bar, where she'd apparently been having more success at making friends. The small group of women standing to one side trying to pretend they weren't watching them stopped trying to be surreptitious about taking their photos at that point. Rosalind ignored them, so Caro did the same. The three of them together were always more of a draw than individually.

'I met two of the original writing group,' Posy told them, breathlessly. 'And they are *not* happy that Sarah is here with Eleanor. Or about the podcast.'

'That makes three of us then,' Caro said, darkly. And it didn't bode well for their investigation either.

Milla appeared after that, and ushered them all up the slight rise towards the main marquee, where the opening event was taking place. They bypassed the queues, and Caro tried to cheer herself up by reminding herself that *this* was the other side of fame.

Yes, people would think they knew her better than herself, and would assume that everything she said or did was a performance rather than the truth. They'd believe that the world as a whole was free to gossip and say anything they liked about her, and take her photo when she was just trying to spend time with her friends.

But sometimes she got to go to film premieres, and skip queues. Things could be worse.

There were solar-powered torches stuck into the ground alongside the path to guide the way. The sun was still sinking slowly, as it did in early August, but under the trees and the foliage that lined the path it was already darkening. Posy had skipped ahead with Milla, and already seemed to be peppering her with questions. Caro expected she'd have her notebook out in a moment, too.

Rosalind slipped a hand through Caro's arm, and Caro patted it, unsure if her friend was acting out of support for her, or because she needed support herself on the uneven ground. Her back had been bothering her more lately, but Rosalind was determined it could be healed by yoga rather than a doctor's visit, and neither Caro nor Jack had been able to persuade her otherwise.

She was probably right. And she'd accused Caro of clucking like a mother hen, which was definitely someone else's job, so Caro hadn't mentioned it again.

A team of people in festival waistcoats and wearing lanyards with passes were checking tickets at the front of the marquee, but Milla led them around the side and past another, smaller tent marked with a sign reading 'Green Room'.

'That's where you'll need to be tomorrow, before your event,' Milla called back to Caro over her shoulder. 'I'll take you in and show you around properly later, if you like.'

Caro figured that writing-festival green rooms probably weren't hugely unlike every other green room she'd been in over the course of her career; filled with coffee and slightly stale pastries, and other actors – or writers – nervously checking over the details of whatever they were about to do next. Or gossiping, obviously.

Milla held open a rope barrier so they could enter the marquee by the stage. 'The first two rows are reserved for our special guests, so please, sit anywhere in those.' She dropped her voice. 'And I was just telling Posy, I've set things up for you to talk to the suspects at the hotel tomorrow.'

She whirled away and was gone, dealing with another festival issue, before Caro could point out they still hadn't *actually* agreed to take the case.

Apparently just showing up had been enough to do that.

'Have you opened that letter, yet?' Posy asked, as they made their way through.

'Not yet.' Caro wasn't entirely sure what was stopping her – fear, perhaps, or maybe just stubbornness. After all, she was pretty sure she knew who it was from.

Posy glanced back at Milla's retreating form, her expression unhappy. 'I really think you should.'

Ah. So Milla knew, too – or suspected. And she'd told Posy.

'Later,' she promised, without saying exactly how much later.

The front rows were already filling up, although Caro didn't recognise very many of the faces. Still, they found three seats together at the very front, on the far side, and settled in just as Eleanor Grey took to the stage.

'Good evening! And welcome.' Arms spread wide, Eleanor beamed out at the crowd as they quietened. 'It is *such* an honour to be here with you all at the Market Foxleigh Crime Writing Festival this year!'

She waited for a small cheer and a smatter of clapping, before continuing.

'The programme that the festival committee have put together for this special year is *astounding*, I know you'll all agree. Not to mention the surprise special guest we're told to expect tomorrow . . .' She held up the programme with its bright red circle on the cover reading *Surprise Special Guest.* Caro wondered who it was. And, more importantly, if they were more famous than her. She'd been enjoying being the headline guest.

'There really is something for everyone, and I know that I'm going to be torn between a few of the panels taking place at the same time.' Eleanor stepped closer to the edge of the stage and put one hand to her mouth. 'This is where I'm supposed to remind you that recordings of all the panels are available to purchase from the festival online shop after the event is over, so let's pretend I did that, yeah?'

Laughter, as the audience realised that she *had* done that, but in a way that didn't feel like they were being sold to. She was good at this.

Caro folded her arms over her chest, and started paying a little more attention to Eleanor Grey.

'Anyway, I'd like to start by asking you all to give a big hand to our festival committee. Stand up you lot, and take some praise!' She gestured to the front row on the other side of the marquee, and eight men and women stood up – some awkwardly, some with showmanship – and turned to face the cheering crowd.

None of them, according to Eleanor's file, were the same people who'd been on the festival committee five years ago, at the time of the murder.

The committee sat again, and the crowd quietened down. Eleanor dropped her voice as she continued, bringing the tone down to more serious matters.

'This year's festival is a particularly poignant one,' she said, her gaze moving slowly around the audience, as if she could make eye contact with everyone there. 'This year, we mark not just the tenth anniversary of the festival, but also five years since its founder, Victoria Denby, was taken from us in a shocking murder that stunned the nation. I think everyone old enough remembers the front pages at that time – the speculation, those photos of the paper dahlia left beside her body, the hunt for a possible serial killer.'

There was a confused hum in the crowd now, the audience uncertain where this was going. It wasn't the hyped-up, get-everyone-excited event they'd been led to expect.

'Nobody remembers better than those who were affected by the tragedy. Friends and colleagues of Victoria. And the family of the man accused of her murder.' She gestured down to the seats below again, and Caro realised that Sarah sat, looking at her hands, just behind the festival committee.

The crowd might be confused, but Caro had a solid idea what Eleanor was doing. 'We should leave,' she whispered to Posy beside her.

'We can't,' Posy murmured back. 'Everyone is watching.'

'We're just going to have to go along with it,' Rosalind said, without moving her gaze from the stage.

'This year, as part of the festival, we'll rightly be remembering Victoria Denby, and everything she contributed to Market Foxleigh and the crime-writing community. But I also want to announce a new project that I'm undertaking in her memory, to ensure that her death does not go unpunished.'

The buzz in the crowd grew louder with every word, and Caro sank down deeper into her plastic chair, desperately hoping she was wrong about what was about to happen next.

'You all know that Scott Baker was tried and convicted for Victoria's murder. But his sister, Sarah, has long fought to prove his innocence – and recently, new evidence has come to light which suggests she might have known better than the police all along.'

Caro scoffed, her chin pressed to her chest. New evidence. New publicity opportunities for Eleanor, more likely. Nothing in Posy's file was new, as far as she could see. It was the fact that the three of them had shown up at Market Foxleigh that had Eleanor making this announcement. She hadn't been nearly so certain of it happening when they first spoke.

'To that end, I'm hoping to reopen the investigation into the paper dahlia murder for the latest series of my true crime podcast, *Writing A Wrong.* And I am thrilled to announce exclusively here tonight, the team of investigative masterminds that will be helping us to uncover the real truth of what happened to Victoria Denby five years ago: Caro Hooper, Posy Starling and Rosalind King – or, as we all now know them, the three Dahlias!'

There was a moment of confused silence before the applause started, but once it was going it caught on like wildfire, even though the three Dahlias stayed firmly in their seats.

'Well, there goes the element of surprise,' Posy muttered.

And with it, Caro suspected, any chance of them backing out of this investigation.

Chapter Six

A murder always starts with a victim, not a murderer.

Dahlia Lively *in* Death by Moonlight
***By* Lettice Davenport, 1937**

Rosalind

Posy, thankfully, didn't snore, and Rosalind felt much brighter the following day for a good night's sleep. The beds at The Red Fox Hotel were wide and comfortable, and the breakfast provided in the hotel restaurant was more than adequate.

'So,' Caro asked, after draining her second cup of coffee. 'What's the plan for today?'

'I want to explore the rest of the town, the wider festival site,' Posy said, promptly. Rosalind wasn't surprised; the youngest Dahlia had been bouncing on her toes waiting to come down to breakfast, and tapping her nails against her teacup ever since she finished eating. Rosalind had been about to send her out to run off some energy anyway. 'I managed to find two of our suspects just by visiting the bar yesterday. Who knows what – or who – I'll bump into further afield.'

'I thought Milla had already set up interviews with the suspects?' Caro reached for the coffee pot and poured herself another cup. Either she hadn't slept well, or she was nervous about her panel later. Rosalind wished Caro hadn't told Annie to stay at home this weekend – even though she understood why she had. Caro would be far less nervous with her wife there to see her perform.

'She has.' Posy pulled the ever-present file from her capacious bag and flipped back to her list. 'But I was thinking, there must be other people to talk to. People who can tell us what Victoria was like without being defensive because they're a murder suspect. What about Victoria's family? Or other friends? Surely this investigation is wider than just seven people?'

'Six, if they get their way and we discount Scott from the start,' Caro said, drily. 'Which, of course, we won't be doing.'

'I think the point is that the *podcast* has seven suspects,' Rosalind said, thinking it through. 'If they open it up, the investigation could go on forever. No, I think they've set those parameters for artistic reasons, rather than investigative ones.'

Posy was nodding, even as she looked down at the list of suspects in her file. 'Okay, but do we have to take the same limits?'

'Yes,' Caro said, bluntly. 'Because that's the only way we can clear this up for good and draw a line under it. We clear or convict each of these seven people – Scott included – and then we're done. Forever, this time, please.'

Her tone was sharp, but her hand shook slightly as she reached again for her coffee cup. Caffeine or fear? A bit of both, Rosalind suspected.

She leaned back in her chair. 'I think we're getting ahead of ourselves. Have we considered calling Ashok in on this one?' The private detective Caro worked with as another part of her portfolio career had been useful to their investigations before. It wouldn't hurt to have another pair of eyes looking over this one.

But Caro shook her head. 'He's away in the States right now at some sort of official gumshoe gathering or another. I don't know. We had a lull in cases, and I was busy with the book launch, so he decided to take advantage and tack on a road trip to the end of the conference. Anyway, he won't be back for weeks.'

They couldn't wait that long. Looked like they were on their own for this one.

Rosalind watched Caro drain another cup of coffee, then reached for her bag. 'Come on. Let's take a walk while we plan.' Otherwise Caro might vibrate off the stage later from a caffeine overdose.

Milla was in the hotel foyer, looking fresh and polished as she straightened one of the large signs with the festival logo on.

'Good morning, ladies!' Her heels clicked and clacked on the polished floor as she hurried over to them. 'Now, I've set you up in the library over here this afternoon, to speak to our . . . friends. All four of them have arrived, and been contacted and asked to attend – after Caro's panel and signing of course, but before the awards this evening.'

Rosalind looked behind her and saw the door marked 'Library'. At least it had a door they could close. Holding questioning sessions in the foyer would have been awkward.

'Did you tell them what it was for?' Caro asked.

Milla shook her head. 'I might have framed it as a pre-awards get-together. Just to avoid suspicion.'

'Wait. So it'll be all of them at the same time?' That wasn't ideal. Rosalind would have far preferred to talk to them one by one.

'It was the best I could do,' Milla said. 'Sorry. It was hard enough to find a reason to get them all here in the first place.'

'Will you be around then too?' Rosalind asked. 'Obviously we'd like to get your account of things as well.'

'Of course,' Milla replied, slightly more faintly. 'I'll be rather busy with the preparations for the awards dinner over at the Queen's Head Hotel, but I'll be here whenever you'd like to speak to me.'

'That's great,' Posy said. 'Thank you.'

'Oh, and, Rosalind . . .' Milla's voice had turned strangely hesitant, which immediately rang alarm bells with Rosalind. She was about to be asked for something, she'd bet on it. 'I was wondering if, since you're here, you might like to co-host tonight's awards with Caro?'

'What happened to the surprise guest?' Caro asked, sharply.

Milla's fixed smile looked uncomfortable. 'Sadly they won't be able to join us now until tomorrow.'

'Why doesn't Posy do it?' Rosalind said. 'She's the Dahlia of the moment – alongside Caro, of course.' She also didn't have a hip that ached if she stood for too long in heels.

'Are you sure?' Posy asked.

'Very,' Rosalind assured her.

Milla clapped her hands together. 'Well, that would be lovely! Thank you. And don't let me keep you from exploring our festival!'

Outside, the day had dawned bright, sunny and with blue skies that spoke of picnics in summer meadows. Rosalind put on her sunglasses.

If she'd been in Wales with Jack this weekend, as they'd originally planned, they'd probably have wandered down to the pub-restaurant on the river, and sat out watching the water skipping and skimming over the rocks. They'd have shared a bottle of something cold and white, ordered the specials, and listened to the birdsong or the hoot of the vintage steam train whistle as it left the station.

Instead, she was hunting for suspects at a crime festival.

The worst part was, she honestly couldn't say which one she'd prefer.

The town of Market Foxleigh looked more ready for a jubilee street party rather than a celebration of murder, in Rosalind's opinion. The festival atmosphere was clearly contagious, however, as clumps of excited visitors gathered outside bookshops and cafes, chatting about the weekend ahead.

Some furtive looks and whispered conversations made it obvious that they'd been spotted, though. Rosalind wondered if they were talking about their acting histories, or their latest investigation.

'So, we've already found Hakim Malik and Rachel – or Raven – Cassidy.' Posy had her notebook in her hand, barely watching where she was walking as she studied her list. It was just as well the streets had been pedestrianised for the festival. 'That just leaves Danny Whitlock and Iain Hardy from Eleanor's list, and we'll speak to them, and Milla, this afternoon – as well as being able to question the other two properly.'

Five suspects. Add Scott Baker, who had actually been convicted for the murder, and that was six people who might have committed the crime.

No, it was seven, wasn't it?

'I think we've been looking at this wrong,' Rosalind said, as they passed another cafe table of people wearing festival badges and staring at them. 'We need to start with Sarah. She's the seventh suspect, after all.'

'And she's the one who's convinced her brother is innocent.' Posy tapped her notebook against her thigh. 'I'd like to hear more about why.'

'Exactly.' Rosalind signalled for them to leave the high street to continue the discussion, and they turned down a cobbled side street, the path narrowing until they couldn't walk three abreast. But at least there were fewer people staring at them here.

They huddled beside the window of a shop selling local prints and artwork, pretending to admire the watercolours of the local scenery, and a bold block print of the Market Foxleigh high street that took up much of the available space.

'I don't know exactly what Eleanor is looking to get out of this, but we *do* know what Sarah wants – her brother free,' Rosalind explained. 'And, like I said before, I realise that having seven concrete suspects is useful for a podcast – they've probably got an episode planned around each of them, depending on what we find out from them. But in real life, an investigation is seldom so neat. There *are* going to be other people we need to speak to – like the neighbour who saw Scott running away from Victoria's house that night.'

Posy nodded. 'We've got a transcript of his interview in the file, I think.'

This wasn't a closed-circle mystery, the likes of which Lettice Davenport had been so accomplished at writing. Nobody was snowed in for Christmas in a secluded Scottish castle. They didn't have a locked room to contend with. They had a whole market town, and a victim they barely knew.

Maybe that was where they needed to start.

'We need to understand this murder better,' Rosalind said. 'We need to know who Victoria was and why she was killed. And why people were so ready to believe that Scott was the killer.'

Posy nodded again, her reflection bobbing in the glass. 'That makes sense. So, that's where we start? We talk to Sarah about her brother and Victoria. Then we'll move onto the other people on Eleanor's list. Which is probably just as well since, after her announcement last night, I'm not sure how keen any of them are going to be to talk to us.'

They continued down the cobbled side street, past an antique shop crammed with relics from recent history, a florist and a window filled with knick-knacks for the home, and emerged at the far end onto a wide pathway beside a river.

'It certainly is a pretty little town,' Rosalind observed, as they followed the river as it curved around, back towards the high street.

'Perfect for Eleanor's purposes,' Caro said, darkly. 'Quintessential quaint English town hides dark secrets. It's the classic true crime podcast hook.'

'I suppose.' Posy stared out across the river, towards a small smattering of houses on the other side. 'But I guess every place – and every person – has secrets, don't they?'

'And we're here to dig them all out,' Rosalind agreed. 'Then we can figure out which ones matter, and which ones don't.'

They walked in silence, turning away from the river as it wended away from the town centre, and making their way back towards the town square. But even though none of them said it, Rosalind was sure they were all thinking the same thing.

Nobody here would want to give up their secrets. Especially now Eleanor had told them that they'd be exposed for the world to listen to in her podcast.

They'd been brought in to investigate a murder – but getting to the heart of this case was going to be harder than any investigation they'd undertaken so far if nobody was willing to speak to them.

Posy

They'd barely made it back to the high street, with its bunting and cafe tables and staring eyes, before Caro checked the vintage watch on her wrist and declared she had to go and meet Petra, her agent, ahead of her event that afternoon.

Posy and Rosalind stood and watched her hurry away up the slight slope of the street towards where The Red Fox Hotel stood in all its grandeur, Cotswolds stone glowing in the sunshine as it looked down over the town.

'Do you get the feeling she's regretting letting us come here this weekend?' Posy asked.

Rosalind didn't answer. Posy took that as a yes.

She scanned the high street and spotted a familiar blonde figure sitting at one of the tables outside the horse box parked on the town square that seemed to have been turned into a coffee shop. She wondered if Caro had seen her too; it would explain her sudden departure.

She nudged Rosalind. 'You wanted to talk to Sarah? There she is.'

They didn't give Sarah much choice over accepting their company, but then it didn't look like anyone else was planning to join her, either. While Posy queued for coffees, Rosalind took one of the empty seats at Sarah's table, and began to talk. From the queue, Posy could see the eldest Dahlia smiling politely, and examining Sarah's festival programme. Getting all the small talk out of the way, Posy hoped.

Sure enough, by the time Posy had got their drinks and was able to join them, Rosalind had already steered the conversation in the direction they wanted.

'Posy has spent a lot of time studying the file Eleanor gave us,' she was saying, as Posy took her seat. 'And it's full of useful facts and information.'

'The thing is, facts only get us so far.' Posy handed Rosalind her coffee, then placed the three cookies she'd bought in the centre of the table, gesturing for Sarah to help herself. 'They only tell us what people at the time thought was important, what questions *they* asked.'

'With our investigations, we find it's so often the little things behind the facts that lead us to the truth,' Rosalind went on. 'The interplay between people, the almost unnoticed gesture or comment, that would never get recorded in an official file.'

'You want to ask me questions about Scott?' Sarah perked up instantly at the idea, as if she'd just been waiting for someone to actually *listen* to why she knew he couldn't be a murderer. Probably she had.

Posy gave her a gentle smile. 'No. We want to ask you about Victoria.'

'*A murder always starts with a victim, not a murderer,*' Sarah quoted, softly. 'Dahlia Lively said that, didn't she? Well, Lettice Davenport, I suppose.' She nibbled at the edge of her biscuit, then nodded. 'Okay. If that's what you need, I'll talk about her, of course. But . . . not here.'

Her gaze darted around the busy town centre, and the full tables that surrounded them.

Rosalind and Posy exchanged a look. What did Sarah want to tell them about the victim that couldn't be overheard? Or was it just that she didn't want to be seen to be taking Victoria's name in vain, so near the banner proclaiming that this whole weekend was in her memory?

'Let's finish our drinks, then,' Rosalind suggested. 'And we can take a walk.'

Their table was grabbed by waiting customers the moment they stood, none of whom seemed in the least bit interested in who the three women departing were, which was refreshing, if unusual. From the snatches Posy heard of their conversation, she suspected they were just more absorbed in their own dilemmas – which panel to watch and which to miss – than the people around them. Certainly, the festival-goers seemed to be taking the whole planning of the programme very seriously.

'Caro Hooper is on this panel, though,' one of them said. 'She's written that book about the murders that happened at Lettice Davenport's house.'

Her companion scoffed. 'I doubt she wrote it herself, Shelley. Still, could be interesting.'

Posy decided not to report that part of the conversation to Caro.

They headed back down towards the river, following its curve away from the town centre. After crossing a sturdy-looking stone bridge of indeterminate age, Sarah led them to a small park on the other side, where the river slowed and ducks paddled. Further along, Posy spotted a houseboat moored to the side that looked like it had been transformed into a bookshop.

'So,' Sarah said, once they were all settled on a wooden bench that held a brass plaque in memory of another dearly departed local citizen. 'I can tell you that's Victoria's cottage over there. What else do you want to know?'

Posy looked where Sarah pointed, to a perfectly maintained, chocolate-box cottage on the end of a row of three similar dwellings. There were more modern houses behind, but from the right angle, all a visitor would see was that perfect, bucolic vision of a thatched cottage by a river, with no indication of the blood that had been shed within.

Rosalind glanced at Posy's bag where it sat by her feet and, understanding the look, Posy pulled out her notepad. Their investigation was properly under way now, and that meant taking notes. Lots of them.

Caro liked to pretend she could hold all the information pertaining to a case in her head, and Rosalind acted as if she sifted through and only retained what really mattered. But Posy knew that if she didn't write it down, the information she gathered would be lost forever.

It was how she'd learned her lines for films when she was younger and just starting out, and everything felt overwhelming – from the sets to the lights to the costumes and the adult co-stars. Writing them out, over and over, helped them stick in her head, to the point that, when she tried to remember the words she was looking for after the director called 'action', she often *saw* them written out in her own, rounded handwriting before she said the line.

Now, seeing the words a suspect spoke on the page, after she'd had time to think about what had been said, often showed her the links and connections between people's observations. *That* was where she found the secrets, the hidden messages. The things that people didn't say, but hinted at all the same.

'Victoria organised the first ever crime-writing festival here, right? Ten years ago. And it was linked to your writing group?' Rosalind folded her hands in her lap as she waited for Sarah's answer.

'That's right,' Sarah said, as she looked out over the river. 'Victoria was . . . she liked to organise things. And people. She liked to be in charge.'

'And not everybody liked that?' Posy guessed.

Sarah shrugged one shoulder. 'With groups and events you need *someone* to take control, I suppose. But . . .' She sighed, and looked up to meet Posy's gaze as she started again, more confidently this time. 'Scott met Victoria at this writing retreat on the south coast. He always wanted to be a writer when he was a kid – we both spent hours coming up with stories together. But it's not exactly the easiest profession to get into. Dad told him he needed to study a proper subject, so he did geography. But after university he, well, he didn't know what he wanted to do next. He just kind of . . . drifted.'

Posy nodded as she scribbled the information down. It seemed that Sarah would be talking about Scott, after all.

'But then he met Victoria. There were three of them from the area on the course, and they sort of bonded together, even though Scott was only twenty-two and Victoria must have been in her early thirties. She'd just got divorced and I think she was searching for something new to focus on and, well, she picked Scott almost as a project.'

'You were worried about him,' Rosalind said.

Sarah raised her eyebrows. 'Wouldn't you have been?'

'Yes,' Posy admitted.

With a sigh, Sarah looked away. 'It was just the two of us by then, you see. Dad . . . he died when Scott was nineteen and I was twenty-one and Scott . . . He didn't deal well with that.'

'How do you mean?' Rosalind asked, but Posy already knew. It was all in the file.

'Your father died by suicide, didn't he?' she said, so Sarah didn't have to.

Sarah nodded. 'He did. But for the longest time . . . Scott was convinced it was murder. He had his own investigation going, complete with a pinboard up in his bedroom with suspects and red string linking clues, and he was pestering the local police . . . It was a difficult time for everyone.'

'What happened?' Eleanor's file had been sparse on details for Scott, but Posy suspected this incident was vital to understanding why the people of Market Foxleigh were so ready to accept Scott as a murderer.

'He got therapy, and anti-depressants, and eventually accepted that it was suicide,' Sarah said with a shrug. 'He moved on.'

'That was when he got into writing again?' Rosalind asked.

'And crime fiction in particular,' Sarah confirmed. 'And when he met Victoria. When they got back, Victoria decided that they should start a writing group, to keep the vibe from the retreat going. So I told Scott I wanted to join too. Writing had always been *our* thing – I would have been at the retreat too, but something came up at work, and I sold my place to a colleague instead. And if it was going to be a Market Foxleigh Writing Group, well, I lived in Market Foxleigh too.'

'How did Victoria feel about you joining?' Rosalind asked.

Sarah's lips twisted into an ironic smile. 'She didn't like me, and I knew it, but she hid it, mostly, when we were with the others. She got a handful of people to join, through her contacts, or notices at the library and in the paper, that sort of thing. Her father was a famous writer, you see, and part of a sort of clique of other writers at the time.'

'You think she was trying to recreate that sort of thing for herself?' Posy had seen that before, among the nepo-babies of Hollywood.

'Maybe. She wanted to *be* someone, I know that. To be known. But . . . I think she was afraid of failure, too. She never shared much of her writing with the group – claimed it ruined her process, but I think she worried we'd laugh at it. She couldn't bear to be laughed at.' Sarah seemed to be on a roll, now, sharing all her reminiscences of Victoria. 'And she was also the sort of person who wanted everyone to think the best of her, or at least that she really was a good person, giving back to the community. She was always all smiles promising the festival in public. But behind closed doors . . .' Sarah shook her head. 'She was demanding. Impatient. Intolerant, even.'

'How did Scott feel about her?' Rosalind asked. 'And be assured, we're not going to take anything you say as evidence against him. We know it's possible to dislike a person and not kill them.'

Sarah gave them a thankful smile. 'I wish more people around here did. Except . . . I don't think he *did* dislike her. Their relationship was . . . complicated, I guess. He admired her, I think – how easily she got along with people, even if in reality she was manipulating them. He saw her bad sides, I know that for sure – so many nights he'd come home from working with her on the festival just fuming about how unreasonable she'd been, or how she didn't understand what she was asking him to do. She made him treasurer, our second year, when we actually had some money to spend on the festival – but then she'd constantly be second-guessing him, doubting his records, accusing him of not doing things she'd never asked him to do in the first place!'

'Why didn't he quit?' Posy liked to think she would have done, in that situation.

'The same reason I didn't,' Sarah replied. 'We believed in the festival and what we were doing. And the thrill of being part of it was something neither of us had ever had before. We weren't the cool kids at school, we never really mattered to people. But with the festival, we mattered. We were important. And I think for Scott, especially, that kind of acceptance, after everything he'd been through, made a real difference to his life. That's just *one* of the reasons I know he couldn't have done what they say he'd done. He'd never have jeopardised the festival that way.'

'Except he was embezzling the funds, wasn't he?' Rosalind said, calmly. 'And Victoria was about to call the police on him.'

Sarah shook her head violently, her blonde hair fluffing around her shoulders. 'That . . . that was a misunderstanding, I'm sure of it. It wasn't that much money. He'd have paid it back as soon as his wages came through. He didn't mean . . . he needed help, if he really had the sort of problem they say he did. Not the police. If she'd been a real friend, she'd have wanted to help him.'

None of which really dismissed that motive. Which meant they couldn't yet, either.

'Was there anything . . . romantic between Scott and Victoria?' It hadn't come up in the file, but the way Sarah talked about them made Posy wonder.

The question seemed to take some of the heat out of Sarah's answers, though. 'No, I don't think so. In fact, I'm sure of it. They just didn't have that sort of relationship. I think . . . Scott loved writing. Loved stories and creating – or at least inhabiting – fictional worlds. It was his escape. He didn't really care about getting published or doing it professionally at that point, he just wanted to write. But Victoria, she always said she wanted to be an author like her father, though I don't think she ever finished anything, let alone submitted it. Maybe it was that fear of failure again. But actually . . . I think that what she really loved was the community, the events, the people – being part of the world where the famous authors lived. She'd write reviews, and do interviews, and Scott would post them all to the website, or run the tech for online events. She needed him, but that was all it was.'

And she didn't like Sarah stepping in, standing up for her brother. Posy could see that.

Sarah was painting a picture of a woman who could have put backs up and made enemies, even while charming the people who could give her what she wanted. But the way she told the story, it still seemed that Scott was the most likely to have wanted done with her.

Rosalind changed track. 'How did the others see Victoria? Were they as frustrated with her as you and Scott?'

Sarah considered carefully before answering. 'I don't know. Actually, it was really only as the group grew that Victoria got . . . obsessed with the festival being perfect, getting bigger and better every year. By the time we were a couple of years in, Iain had recruited Danny and Hakim to the group, then Rachel joined, then Milla last. When we were all there together, it wasn't so bad. Iain in particular used to hold Victoria to account. But . . . they all had their own issues with her, too, I think – and, well, one of them must have most of all, mustn't they?' The early August sun pounded down on them, and Posy wished she'd remembered to bring her hat. But despite the warmth, Sarah shivered. 'Have you ever been part of something, a group or a project, where everything just got so . . . insular? Like everyone was connected and there was no way out?'

Only on every film set she'd ever stepped on. And most especially the original shoot for *The Lady Detective* in Wales.

Of course, that had ended in murder, too. 'Yeah, I know that feeling.'

'That's how it felt, that last year. Like . . . everyone wanted out but nobody could see a way. Until Victoria was killed and everyone just . . . scattered.'

This would be the point in a movie where a cloud passed in front of the sun, or a loud noise broke the silence and made them all jump. But neither happened. Posy almost wished they would.

'That last day . . . there was a committee meeting that went badly?'

Sarah nodded. 'You know how it gets close to an event. Tempers get . . . frayed.'

'Can you tell us what happened?' Rosalind asked. 'That way, when we talk to the others this afternoon, we can compare accounts.'

Sarah checked her phone for the time, then nodded. 'Of course. It'll have to be quick, though. I'm meeting my husband for lunch. And you two need to get back, too, if you want to watch Caro's panel.'

She was right, Posy realised. 'Just the basics, then.'

'Well, Victoria was mad with everyone about things that weren't quite perfect or hadn't been done – even though most of them were her fault, that was par for the course. She was in a bad mood before it all even started – I heard her yelling at someone on the phone before I went in, but I don't know who. From the stuff she was saying . . . Um . . . well, I assumed it was someone she was in a relationship with.'

'Did you know she was dating someone?' *That* hadn't come up in Eleanor's file.

Sarah shook her head. 'I might have been wrong, I don't know. That was kind of it, really. Nobody could do anything right for her that day, so it sort of descended into bickering.'

'And she got the message from the bank during the meeting?' Rosalind pressed. 'About the embezzlement?'

Sarah's cheeks were pink, and Posy didn't think it was just due to the sun. 'The bank called, but she didn't answer it then. She told us who it was, though. She just wanted to show that, even though Scott was the treasurer, she was the one who was really in charge.'

'And after the meeting?' Posy asked

Sarah looked frustrated. 'I left with Scott, straight away, so I don't know. Hopefully one of the others might. Because I've been over and over it in my head, and I think that something must have happened after the meeting, something that never came out. Something that caused someone to resort to murder.'

Well, at least they knew what questions they needed to ask this afternoon, now.

'I'm sorry,' Sarah said, as she got to her feet. 'I really do have to go. But I'll be around the festival all weekend if there's anything else I can help you with.'

'I'm sure there will be,' Rosalind replied.

'Just before you go . . .' Sarah stopped, half turned away, at Posy's words. 'You said the others all scattered. Didn't you think about leaving, too? It can't have been easy staying here, with everyone thinking your brother was a murderer.'

Sarah's smile was sad. 'Of course I did. But I've lived in Market Foxleigh my entire life, and I wasn't about to be driven out of my home by malicious gossips who were always ready to think the worst about people. Besides . . . if I left, it would almost be like I was admitting they were right. Wouldn't it?'

Chapter Seven

Dahlia pulled the felt cloche hat further down over her forehead. 'It's very hard to go incognito when everyone knows what you look like.'

Dahlia Lively *in* Diamonds for Dahlia
***By* Lettice Davenport, 1958**

Caro

The green room, as Caro had expected, wasn't anything particularly luxurious. But it *did* have more comfortable chairs than the marquee, and a top of the range coffee machine that she was taking full advantage of.

Caro wasn't the only one. Alongside a couple of other authors she'd never have recognised by sight, but whose names on their badges were familiar from the festival programme if nowhere else, and a very glamorous-looking young woman, there was one person she'd known instantly on arrival.

'Caro Hooper, as I live and breathe!' Will Pollinger, large as life and twice as loud, strode across the green room with his arms outstretched to welcome her.

Caro smiled as she stepped forward to embrace her friend. 'Will! I didn't know you were going to be here.' Clearly, she hadn't read the programme well enough.

Possibly she hadn't read much past the point where she was the headline guest for tonight's award ceremony. In fact, she'd barely registered her appearance on today's panel until Milla had reminded her about it that morning.

'Oh yes. Got to talk up the book, apparently.' He flashed her a cheeky smile, famous across Britain to everyone who'd ever watched a certain sitcom. 'Should probably read it as well, I suppose.'

'I didn't think you were likely to have taken up scribing, I have to admit.' Having worked with Will on *The Dahlia Lively Mysteries* for a stretch in series ten, when he took on the role of a visiting, bumbling detective, Caro knew Will could never sit still long enough to type the damn thing. *I suppose he could have dictated it . . .*

Will led her over to his corner of the green room, where he'd assembled a stash of snacks, a large travel mug of coffee, and a stack of books with his name on the cover that he seemed to be working his way through signing.

'For some charity auction, or something,' he explained. 'And some of the bookshops around here, I think. Having lived around here years ago for about six months, apparently I count as a local author or something. I don't really know, I just sign what I'm given!'

'You want to watch that,' Caro joked. 'Not checking what you're signing is what got you into trouble with that production company that time.'

It was good to joke about old times with Will as he signed his stack of books, and it took the edge off her nerves about the panel ahead. Caro had never been one for stage fright, but this was a very different stage, and a very different audience. And, most of all, she wasn't stepping up there as Dahlia, but as herself. That made all the difference.

'So, what made you decide to take up the role of author?' Caro flipped idly through one of the signed copies, and found herself instantly engaged. Whoever had ghost-written it, they were good, she had to admit that.

Will shrugged, and moved the book he'd just signed onto the pile beside him before reaching for the next one. 'Diversification, I suppose,' he said. 'I'm lucky, I know – there are always roles for middle-aged white men like me. But all the same, you have to plan for the day the jobs stop coming, don't you?'

'I hear you there,' Caro murmured.

'Given my last few big roles were all detectives, my agent thought crime fiction could be a good fit,' Will went on. 'We spoke to a couple of publishers, got their thoughts, and before I knew it one of them was offering money and introducing me to this fantastic ghost-writer and . . . well. Here we are.'

'Did you have anything to do with the book at all?' Caro knew this was how it worked, for a lot of people. The bigger the name, the bigger the advance, and they were basically being paid to put their name on the front cover to draw readers' attention.

Will nodded. 'Oh, yeah. I mean, I sat down with Jeff – that's the writer – and we came up with the ideas and characters and stuff together. The first one was set on a TV show, so I was able to give him all the information about how that stuff worked, and come up with some of the twists for the plot based on my behind-the-scenes knowledge. But he's the one who actually wrote it all down – I mean, he's the writer, after all. It worked great – book two is out later this month. You should come to the launch!'

'I'd love to.'

'I'll get my publicist to put you on the list.' Will pulled over the next stack of books, his name prominent on all of them. No mention of Jeff.

'Is Jeff here this weekend?' Caro asked.

'God, no. As far as everyone here is concerned, this book is all my own work. Which is what I'll tell them out there when they ask about my writing process and so on. Jeff, bless his heart, is probably already onto his next project. Do you know, he writes something like four or five books a year?'

Caro blinked. 'It took me the better part of a year just to write my one,' she admitted. 'But then, it was my first book.' And she had been solving the odd murder, and working with Ashok at the detective agency, in between.

'You wrote it yourself?' Will looked half impressed, half pitying, as if wondering why she'd bother putting in the work when someone else could do it for her.

'Well, it was my story to tell,' she said. 'I lived it. Me and Rosalind and Posy.'

'Ah, yes! I heard about your sudden interest in true crime,' Will said. 'Work dried up on the acting front, I take it? You're not the only one, believe me.'

As if the fact that other women of her age were also struggling to get cast as anything, having apparently turned invisible at the same time as they turned forty, made anything any better.

'That's one of the reasons I wanted to come, actually,' Will said. 'Julia's been a bit down lately, since that last pilot of hers didn't get picked up. I'd heard a rumour that her favourite author – Dexter Rush – was going to be the secret surprise guest, and I'd hoped to nab her a signed copy, maybe even invite him down to lunch to meet Julia next time he was in town. But sounds like the bugger isn't coming down until tomorrow, and I've got to get back to town tonight.'

'Dexter Rush?' The name was familiar to anyone who'd been in a bookshop, or a supermarket, or seen a train-station poster in the last few years, but the man himself was famously reclusive, never attending festivals or giving signings. He'd be quite a coup for Milla if he actually showed up. 'Actually, we share an agent.' When Caro had started sending out query letters to agents, the fact that Petra represented one of the UK's biggest crime and thriller writers had put her top of her wish list. 'I could ask her to get in touch, see if we can sort Julia a signed book at least, if you like?'

Will's smile lit up the tent. One of the things she'd always liked most about him was his devotion to his wife. And Julia really was a sweetheart.

'That would be wonderful. And you and Annie must come for a dinner or something soon! It's been an age.'

The conversation devolved into a more personal than professional catch-up, and before Caro knew it, Milla was corralling the next panel towards the door, ready to be micced up to go on stage.

'Break a leg,' Will said, as his microphone was attached, and blew her a kiss. 'And if I miss you in the scrum later, don't forget about Dexter Rush, will you?'

Beside her, Milla started suddenly at the name, knocking into the technician who was fitting Caro's microphone around her ear.

'I won't,' Caro promised Will, then lowered her voice to explain to Milla. 'Sorry, I think the secret's out. His wife's a fan, and we share an agent.'

'Um, well,' Milla hedged, unfailingly appropriate and polite.

'He cancelled, didn't he?' The tech attached the microphone pack to the belt at Caro's waist, while she kept her arms out of the way. 'On tonight? That's why you asked Posy to stand in?' Well, she'd asked Rosalind, but she'd got Posy, and that was almost the same thing.

Milla's smile was fixed and awkward. She obviously didn't want to say anything that could be construed as badmouthing festival authors, which Caro could understand.

'He had planned to be here tonight, but there was a change of plans. He'll still be here for the twilight reading in the square tomorrow, though, I'm sure.'

'Right,' Caro said. 'Still . . . maybe make sure you've got a backup, too, yeah?'

'That's you ready,' the technician said, and moved on to the next author.

'Then let's get this show on the road.' Caro straightened her shoulders, and marched into the marquee, ready to do battle with interviewers, panellists and crime fiction fans.

They couldn't be worse than facing down murderers, right?

Rosalind

They almost didn't make it back in time for Caro's panel.

'Think we can sneak in the VIP entrance again?' Rosalind asked, as they joined the queue that snaked back almost all the way to the bar.

'We're not VIPs here this weekend,' Posy replied. 'Just hangers-on.'

'Hmm. I don't think I like it.'

But when they finally reached the entrance to the marquee, Milla was waiting for them, anxiously tapping her pen against her festival programme. '*There* you are. I just saw Danny now – he's chairing this panel but was late getting here and Caro was already up on the stage. He says he can't make this afternoon!'

'This afternoon?' Rosalind felt suddenly very slow beside the mile-a-minute Milla.

'The *suspect interrogation.*' The words came out in a sharp whisper that drew more attention from the passing queue than just talking normally would have done.

'Danny Whitlock,' Posy said. 'Right. Why can't he make it?'

'Something about promising he'd pop home and help his wife with the kids. Except he's supposed to be back here for the awards this evening anyway, and it's at least an hour and a half round trip back to Bristol,' Milla said. 'Longer if he hits traffic.'

'So he's trying to avoid us,' Rosalind surmised.

'Looks that way.' Milla hit her pen against her programme again with frustration. 'I'm sorry. I thought I'd managed to get them all together in a way that wouldn't make them suspicious. But after Eleanor's announcement last night . . .'

'Well, yes. That wasn't entirely helpful for any of us.' Rosalind sighed. 'Don't worry. We'll see if we can grab him after this panel.'

'After the signing,' Milla corrected. 'Festival business first.'

'Naturally.' Posy took Rosalind's arm. 'Come on, it's about to start.'

The marquee was filled almost to overflowing, but Rosalind spotted a figure waving madly at them from the front row. 'Is that Eleanor?' she asked, squinting to be sure.

Posy didn't need to squint. 'It is! I think she's saved us seats.'

From the way Eleanor was pointing violently to the chairs beside her, Rosalind suspected Posy was right.

'Looks like we're still VIPs to somebody,' Rosalind muttered.

They pushed their way through the gathered throng in the aisle, all the way to the front row where, as Posy had guessed, there were two empty seats awaiting them.

'Cutting it fine, ladies,' Eleanor said, grinning. 'Good job I got here early.'

Up on the stage, four wingback chairs, of the sort that might be found in a gentleman's library in a Lettice Davenport novel, had been set out incongruously against the black backdrop of the stage. There was also a standard lamp with a tasselled shade, and a low, antique coffee table with a cut-glass water jug and matching glasses.

Given that they were in a tent in a field, sitting in the world's most uncomfortable plastic chairs, it seemed a little over the top to Rosalind – like they were trying to pretend the panel had gathered in the sitting room of some old house, ready for a *J'Accuse* moment. But she supposed they were setting a scene, just like a play would.

The panel Caro was speaking on was all about celebrities turned authors. Up there with her sat Will Pollinger – big and blonde and enthusiastic – and a fine-boned, dark-haired young woman called Melody who had apparently appeared on a reality TV show before turning to crime fiction.

The moderator, however, was something different.

'Danny Whitlock,' Posy muttered, as she flipped through the festival programme they'd been given at the hotel. She'd be running through everything in Eleanor's file in her head, Rosalind was sure.

'There are bios at the back,' Rosalind said absently, as she watched Danny greet each of the guests with a handshake. Melody, last in line, got a kiss on the cheek. 'See if it tells us anything new about him.'

'Found it!' Posy held up the programme triumphantly. A headshot of Danny, with perfectly styled dark hair and a knowing grin, looked back at her. 'Listen to this: *Danny Whitlock is the author of—*'

She broke off as the marquee fell silent and Danny began to speak.

'Welcome, everyone, to this star-studded panel! I'm fairly sure everyone up here will be familiar to you from their past celebrity lives, but today we're going to be hearing about their reinvention as crime writers.' He reached out to pick up three books from the coffee table. 'First, we have Will Pollinger with his crime debut, *Second Blood,* about a jaded, divorced detective who is drawn back in after quitting the force when his TV actress daughter is kidnapped by the serial killer he failed to catch five years ago. And the sequel is out later this month. Welcome Will!'

There was a smattering of applause at that, and Rosalind expected there'd be plenty of female readers of a certain age queuing for autographs later – and probably a good few men, too. Will Pollinger had that everyman quality that made everyone feel like his best friend, even if they'd never met him.

'At the far end, we have Melody Kane,' Danny went on. 'While she might be most famous for appearing on our screens in that very tiny white bikini, she's taken the experience of being a contestant on *Tropical Trysts* and turned it into what *Glitz* magazine calls an "edge-of-your-seat thriller about being young and beautiful".'

Well, Rosalind had to agree that Melody could probably talk very honestly about those two things.

'Finally, in the middle, is a writer best known to us all as a detective herself – in her iconic role of Dahlia Lively, the Lady Detective, who she first starred as over fifteen years ago now, can you believe?'

Even from down in the front row, Rosalind could see Caro's eyes narrow at that.

'Uh-oh,' Posy murmured.

'But more recently, we've all watched Caro Hooper turn into an amateur detective in her own right, first solving a murder at the home of Lettice Davenport herself, before turning her hand to the terrible events that happened on the set of the new movie version of *The Lady Detective.*' Danny gestured down to the front row of seats, and Rosalind heard the rustle of movement behind her as the crowd tried to see who he was pointing at. 'Along with her fellow stars, Rosalind King and Posy Starling, she is now one of the three Dahlias, and she's written a fictionalised version of their first adventure in crime solving in a book of the same name.'

Danny placed the books back on the table, and sat back in his chair. 'So, that's our panel today!' He paused for the inevitable applause, then continued. 'I'll be your chair – and I know I'm not nearly as recognisable as my guests! So, briefly, I'm Danny Whitlock, and I've been a friend of the festival since the beginning, when I was plying my trade as a journalist here in Market Foxleigh. These days, I'm working further afield, but I've also just published my first – non-fiction – book.' Here, he held up a copy of a hardback with a stylised dahlia flower on the front. '*The Paper Dahlia Cases* is a study of the three different murders all connected by a paper flower left at the scene, one of which sadly took place in this very town, as I'm sure you all know. And if you'd like to know any more – about any of these books – we'll all be signing copies in the festival bookshop after this panel. Now! To business. My first question is for Melody—'

Rosalind frowned, tuning out whatever the reality TV star had to say as she ran back over Danny's words in her mind. Something there had snagged, and she couldn't quite—

Three. He'd said there were three paper dahlia cases. But she only knew of two – Victoria Denby's, and the fictional Dahlia Lively mystery in *D is for Dahlia.*

'Do you want to talk to him, or shall I?' Posy murmured, pointing to the same line in his bio.

Up on the stage, Danny Whitlock had yet another question for young Melody Kane.

'I rather think you'll have better luck than I will,' Rosalind said.

Posy glanced up at the stage, then pulled a face. 'The things I do for murder.'

Posy

Posy couldn't leave the marquee before the end of Caro's panel, knowing that if her friend looked down and realised she'd gone she'd assume the worst – that Posy had been bored. Which, given the way the host, Danny, focused on Melody, and Will Pollinger fought for equal airtime by interrupting all the time, she was, a little. At least until the end, when the audience questions focused in on the panel's inspirations and writing routines, and suddenly the other two were far happier to let Caro speak.

There didn't seem much point in rushing, either, since Danny wouldn't be signing books until he was offstage and the panel finished. But then he and Caro and the others were led out the side of the marquee, and Posy had to battle her way through the crowds, and by the time she'd made it down the hill to the festival bookshop – set up in a lovely gate house on the edge of the hotel grounds – the queue for Danny Whitlock's signing table was already significant.

Not as long as Caro's, though, Posy noted with a smirk in her friend's direction.

Caro looked up from the book she was signing and raised her eyebrows at Posy as she joined the end of the snaking queue. Posy jerked her head towards Danny's table then, when Caro looked confused, picked up a copy of his book from the nearest sales table and pointed to the paper flower on the front.

Caro mouthed, 'Ah!' and nodded, so Posy assumed she'd got it, and left her to get back to her own signing queue.

While she waited, Posy took the opportunity to observe all four authors with their fans. Melody's line definitely skewed younger, but was equally split gender-wise, and she posed for a selfie with every person who asked. Will, on the other hand, had cornered the older, mostly female market, and his smile was already starting to look a little forced as his fans recounted their reminiscences of his past glories.

Caro was having the time of her life, as far as Posy could tell. She'd lapsed into her best Dahlia voice, calling everyone kiddo regardless of their age, but was also answering questions about their investigations as the three Dahlias – and whether she'd be writing a sequel about what had happened in Wales.

Mercifully few people seemed to bring up the podcast, which probably contributed to her good mood.

Danny's queue was mostly made up of true crime fans and historians, and as such the questions he was answering as he signed seemed deeper and more technical. But he appeared genuinely engaged and fascinated by his subject. Posy wondered if that was because of his personal involvement in one of the cases – and just how far that involvement went.

As ever on an investigation like this, the trick was to get the suspect to answer her questions without necessarily realising they were a suspect. By the time she reached the front of the line, Posy had settled on her approach. She wasn't sure Kit would approve of it but then, Kit wasn't there, was he? He was already off filming his next project, staring lovingly into another leading lady's eyes. Just as he should be. That was his job. And, right now, this was hers.

'Posy Starling.' Danny looked up at her from his seat behind the signing table, his smile warm and welcoming. 'This is a treat. You know you could have asked Caro to get you a signed copy in the green room, and save yourself the queueing?'

'Ah, but then I wouldn't have got to talk to you myself, would I?' Posy placed the book she'd picked up in front of him, and he eased it open, smoothing over the title page. She clocked the ring on his left hand and relaxed a little. Of course. Milla had said his excuse was that his wife needed him home. That meant she could smile and charm, but never need to worry he thought she planned to take it any further, because he was married. And if he did, well, that just told her everything she needed to know about him.

'And what were you hoping to talk to me about?' There was still warmth in his voice, but he focused on the creamy paper in front of him rather than Posy. 'Not this podcast, I hope? I've already told Sarah I have no interest in getting involved.'

'You don't think that writing a book about the case means you're already involved?'

'It's not *just* about that particular case,' Danny said, uncomfortably.

'That's right. You said there were two other cases, is that correct?' She knew it was, but she got the feeling Danny was the sort of man who liked to explain things to people. 'Do you think they were linked?'

'Yes. The fictional one in Lettice Davenport's novel, where two women are killed, and the real-life serial killer case from over forty years earlier that she based the mystery on.' Danny uncapped his pen, and swept the felt tip over the page in sharp, jagged movements.

Lettice had based *D is for Dahlia* on a real-life case? Well, that made everything a little more interesting.

'Given the timescales, I find it highly unlikely there's any connection beyond the obvious copycat nature of the crimes, don't you?' Danny said, capping his pen. 'Besides, as far as I'm concerned, this case has been tried and solved – I say as much in my book. Scott Baker was a disturbed man who took inspiration from both a true crime, and a fictional one, when committing a murder of his own to save his skin. It's an interesting *literary* link, but not an investigative one.'

He slapped the book closed, and held it up to her, clearly meaning his to be the final word on the subject.

Posy leaned closer in as she took the book from him. 'Honestly, I agree with you,' she said, softly. 'And I'm far more interested in the historical case and its links to the Dahlia story than the more modern interpretation.'

'Then why get involved in this blasted podcast?' Danny asked, eyebrows raised, but his expression softening.

'We weren't actually given a lot of choice in that,' Posy said, wryly. 'But now that we are involved . . . if it turns out, as we suspect, that the police had the right guy all along, we're going to need a new angle to sell to the listeners. And I think your book probably has the best one.'

'What exactly are you suggesting?' She could see the calculating look behind Danny's eyes, trying to figure out what this could mean for his book sales, and how to ensure he didn't get screwed over.

Posy gave a light shrug. 'Perhaps we could talk about it, when you're finished here? See if there's any mileage in us working together on this? Unless you have somewhere else you need to be . . .'

He sat back in his seat and surveyed her for a moment, clearly still weighing his options, then nodded. 'Meet me in the bar in about twenty minutes?'

Posy beamed and nodded. 'I'll see you there.' It would be better to talk to him alone than in a group, anyway.

She stepped out of the way of the next person in the line, passing behind Caro's table to whisper the plan to her. She nodded her understanding without ever looking away from the fan who was telling her about the time Caro had filmed near her grandparents' farm for *The Dahlia Lively Mysteries.*

It was only once she was back outside in the warm August sunshine that Posy opened Danny's book, and looked at the title page, the ivory paper almost glowing in the sun, making his scrawled black inscription all the clearer.

To Dahlia, from one investigator to another. Danny Whitlock.

Chapter Eight

'What's that frown for?' Dahlia asked, as she climbed into the car. 'I got the information we needed, didn't I?'

'I suppose,' Johnnie replied. 'But did you really have to flirt with him quite so much to get it?'

Dahlia gave him a wicked grin. 'Oh, yes. That's half the fun.'

Dahlia Lively *in* Midnight in London
***By* Lettice Davenport, 1962**

Caro

It was closer to another half an hour after Posy left before Caro was able to finish up at her signing. She hadn't realised there were that many Dahlia fans at the festival, let alone ones willing to queue for so long to talk to her. Most gratifying of all was the fact that some of them weren't Dahlia fans at all.

They were Caro Hooper fans. Or, at least, fans of the *three* Dahlias. People who'd followed their investigations in the press and now wanted to read the real, behind-the-scenes story.

Yes, even if it had meant getting coerced into investigating an already solved murder, Caro couldn't regret coming to the Market Foxleigh Crime Writing Festival this weekend. Not when readers seemed so pleased to see her.

By the time she reached the bar, Posy and Danny were already sat on opposite sides of one of the wooden tables, with Rosalind perched beside Posy like a Victorian chaperone. Caro grinned at the sight; Danny didn't seem nearly so amused, though. If Caro had to guess, he'd been hoping to get some alone time with their Posy, despite the wedding ring on his left hand.

'Caro! You made it.' Posy beamed at her as Caro slipped onto the bench seat next to Danny. 'Danny was just about to tell us all about the background and the links between the paper dahlia cases. Did you know there were actually three of them?'

'I did not,' Caro admitted. 'Please, Danny, go on.'

He looked a little disgruntled as he took a sip of his pint, but clearly his desire to lecture people on his pet subject outweighed his disappointment at not being allowed to flirt with Posy in peace.

'The theme I took as my starting place, when I began working on the book, was the one thing that really linked all three cases,' Danny said. 'Obsession.'

Caro blamed the cloud passing over the sun for the shiver that ran up her spine at the word.

'The first documented case where a paper flower was placed beside a murdered body was in June 1930,' he went on. 'A woman was found strangled in her bed, in the Finchley area of London. The flower wasn't formally identified as a dahlia – at least, not at the time.' Danny took another gulp from his pint, leaving them in suspense until he continued. 'Over the next two months, another three bodies were found – two more women, and a man – all with a paper flower next to them. By this time, the police had brought in a gardening expert who'd officially declared them dahlias, and so that's what the headlines all went with. The newspapers had an absolute field day

– not least because the police were stumped. There was just no obvious connection between the victims, nothing to make it clear why the murderer had targeted them.'

'Was there a link to Lettice Davenport, or Dahlia Lively?' Caro asked. 'It would have been only a year or so after the first novel, *The Lady Detective,* was published.'

Danny shook his head. 'Not as far as I can tell.'

'Did they catch the killer in the end?' Posy leaned across the table, her juice forgotten, clearly engrossed in the story.

Danny nodded. 'They did. Although he proclaimed his innocence all the way to the gallows.' He reached for the copy of his book that Posy had in front of her, and flipped through to the photographs in the centre pages. 'That was him. Wilhelm Underwood.'

Caro stared at the black and white photo of the condemned man, taking in not much more than the dark, lost eyes and the huge moustache the man was sporting.

'You said the thing all the cases had in common was obsession,' she said, looking away. 'In *D is for Dahlia* it turns out that the secret obsession is the love of a man for his step-daughter, I believe.' And a gruesome case that had turned out to be. She hadn't much enjoyed filming it. Some of Lettice's later books really did get quite dark.

She nodded towards the book again. 'What was his obsession?'

'Purity,' Danny said, succinctly. 'Not bloodline or heritage, but *sexual* purity. He believed that all of his victims had sinned, committing not just adultery but vile acts, too. *That's* why he killed them.'

'Except he said he didn't.' Rosalind reached out and lifted the book, studying it closely. 'Right up until the end, it says here.'

'Well, he would, wouldn't he?' Danny said.

'Just like Scott Baker,' Caro murmured, and his head jerked around as his gaze met hers.

'Scott Baker killed Victoria Denby,' he said, shortly. 'I have no doubt on that matter. And I'm surprised you do.'

'Why?' Posy leaned her chin on her hand, her eyes innocently wide as she asked the question, and Caro hid a smile. Her friend had clearly already established that Danny was the sort of guy who couldn't help but mansplain. 'What makes you so sure? You knew him, right? So what was it about him that makes you so certain he was a murderer?'

Danny tapped the side of his glass slowly as he considered his answer. Around them, the buzz and hum of the bar continued, laughter and chatter and birds overhead, and the warm breeze rustling through the trees around them. It was a perfect British summer day – which Caro supposed Lettice Davenport would have said was just right for a murder.

'When I first met him, I wouldn't have said that,' Danny said, eventually. 'To be honest, I just thought he was one of those guys – you know, quiet, geeky, happy to be bossed around by a woman who showed the slightest interest in him, even if she was fifteen years older than he was. Victoria said "jump" and he—'

'Asked how high?' Caro guessed.

'Made a graph showing all the possible variables of height, and a website for everyone to vote on their choices,' Danny finished. 'He couldn't make a decision on his own, as far as I could tell – always looking to Victoria for guidance before agreeing to anything. Or his sister. His writing was the same. We'd workshop ideas and scenes in our meetings sometimes, and he'd always want to hear everyone's opinions before going away and trying to write something that satisfied everybody. Except that's not how good writing works, is it?'

He looked to Caro at that, as the other author at the table, and she shook her head. 'Just as well, really. I've never been any good at pleasing many people besides myself.'

'So what changed?' Rosalind asked. 'With Scott, I mean?'

'I'm not sure anything did, really,' Danny replied. 'More that I . . . saw him more clearly, perhaps, the longer I spent in his company. I'd assumed he was weak but harmless. But weakness can be dangerous, too.'

'Especially if someone else tries to exploit it,' Rosalind murmured.

'He was an obsessive, that much I can say for sure.' Danny glanced up at Caro before he continued. 'I mean, you saw the stuff in the papers. And I'm sure the police told *you* at the time. He was obsessed with Dahlia Lively. And with the woman who portrayed her.' He lifted his glass to Caro.

'The murder happened just after our version of *D is for Dahlia* aired,' Caro explained to the others. 'And not long after it was announced the series would be finishing.'

She hated thinking back over that time. How it felt like her professional life was crumbling as fast as her personal one.

'He let the obsession take him over,' Danny went on. 'That's what led to all the stuff with the online auctions, and embezzling the funds from the festival to pay for it.'

'Nobody noticed?' Rosalind asked.

'Apparently not.' From Danny's dry tone, he didn't believe that either. 'His sister, Sarah, spent most of her time covering for him. All the stuff he'd promised to do for the festival and hadn't, that sort of thing. Victoria made her life miserable, I have to admit that much. Vic liked being the queen bee, and it didn't suit her to have another woman around. But, I mean, it was a writing circle – it needed actual people. I just think Vic would have preferred it if they were all guys like Scott, ready and willing to do her bidding.'

Instead, she'd ended up with Sarah, and the gorgeous Milla and young, enthusiastic Rachel. Caro suspected Victoria might not have liked that at all, if Danny's representation of her character was accurate.

'Why did Sarah stick it out, then?' Caro asked. 'If Victoria was so awful to her.' They'd heard Sarah's explanation, but she was interested to hear Danny's take on it.

He shrugged. 'Maybe because of Scott. But mostly . . . I think she really wanted to write. She was good, too. Better than her brother, anyway. I don't know if she's still writing . . .'

'What about you?' Posy asked, turning the conversation back onto Danny's home turf again. Clever girl. 'You're obviously doing non-fiction now, but what about then?'

Danny gave a self-deprecating laugh, and stretched out his legs under the table, leaning his torso backwards. 'Back then, I was working for the local paper – the Market Foxleigh Meteor – and my brain felt like it was shrivelling up. So I tried my hand at some fiction – sci-fi crime, mostly, inspired by the classic American hardboiled detectives, but transposed into space, yeah? But in my heart, I'm a reporter, so non-fiction suits me much better.'

'You moved away not long after the murder, is that right?' Rosalind asked.

'Mmm. The wife had been desperate to move back to the city, and then this job came up on the paper in Bristol and, well, it just all came together.' He glanced around him at the pleasant, English market town atmosphere of Market Foxleigh. 'Getting away from all this – and everything that had happened – was just a bonus. That group, even before the murder, it was toxic. I didn't realise how much so until I left.'

He tipped his glass up to his mouth, swallowing the last inch or so of his pint, then slammed it down on the table. 'Right. I'd better get going.'

'Need to get home to the wife, hmm?' Rosalind said.

'Uh, no, actually.' Danny looked confused. 'I'm up for an award at the dinner tonight, and I need to get changed. There's a drinks thing beforehand I said I'd stop in to if I had time.'

'Oh good. I think we're expected there too, so we'll have more time to chat.' Rosalind's smile was wide and innocent as Danny froze, obviously realising that in his hurry to get away from them he'd caught himself in the lie he'd told Milla earlier – and now had no excuse not to attend the drinks Milla had arranged.

'Great,' he said, unconvincingly. 'I'll look forward to that.'

He stood up, and Caro exchanged a quick glance with the other two Dahlias before saying, 'Actually, there was just one more thing . . .'

Danny smirked. 'That one's not a Dahlia catchphrase.'

'Still. You might prefer to answer this question here, rather than in front of everyone else.'

'Sounds ominous,' he said.

'Perhaps.' Caro held his gaze, wanting to see his every reaction. 'We heard about the meeting the afternoon before Victoria was killed.'

His smile fell away. 'Yeah. That wasn't a lot of fun. But if you've heard all about it from Sarah or the others, I'm not sure how much I can add. Honestly, I was just sitting there wishing I was anywhere else.'

'I'm sure,' Caro said, soothingly. 'But it *is* always useful to get different perspectives of the same event.'

'Fine. Um, I was late getting there, I can't remember why, but Victoria was already laying into Milla about something by the time I arrived. Iain was working double time trying to smooth everything over – he was always the peacemaker, you see. Then there was that thing about a message from the bank – she made a big deal about having to sort it out, even though it was Scott's job as treasurer, but I don't think we actually knew what was going on just then.' Danny shrugged. 'That was it. A few more festival details and I hightailed it out of there as fast as I could.'

'Sarah said that before the meeting, she heard Victoria arguing with someone on the phone, and it put her in a bad mood before the meeting even started,' Posy said.

'Sounds about right for Vic,' Danny agreed. 'So?'

'Apparently it sounded like . . . whoever it was, they had an intimate relationship with Victoria.' Caro left it hanging there and waited for Danny to grasp her meaning.

His eyes bulged as he did. 'And you think it was me? God, no. Even if I wasn't happily married . . . No, sorry. You're barking up the wrong tree there. Anyway, if you're interested in an argument, I'd find out which one of them was arguing with her *after* that meeting. I went back to grab a notebook I'd left behind and heard Victoria giving one of them hell. Don't know who, though – I abandoned the notebook and left them to it. And on that note, ladies . . . it's been, well . . . Maybe not a pleasure. But lovely to meet you all. I'll see you at the awards later.'

He turned and walked away, his leather jacket slung over his shoulder.

He sounded convincing, Caro had to admit, denying any affair with Victoria.

But she couldn't ignore the way he was turning his wedding ring on his finger as he said it.

Rosalind

The library back at The Red Fox looked more like it was set up for a drinks party than an interrogation, but Rosalind supposed that was Milla's forte. And it suited their outfits too; she and the other two Dahlias were already dressed and ready for the awards dinner, like this really was just a pre-event drinks. She suspected the element of surprise had pretty much gone out of the window by this point, but putting their suspects at ease before bombarding them with questions couldn't hurt. Even if it meant standing around in high heels that her bad back really didn't appreciate.

'I'll send a waiter in with some canapés once everyone is here,' Milla explained as she showed them the set-up. 'But I thought you'd probably want to serve the drinks yourself, rather than have a staff member in here manning the bar?'

Rosalind nodded, and smoothed down her teal and black embroidered dress. 'You're right. They're more likely to talk if it's just us.'

Or if they'd been able to speak to them each individually. Rosalind still wasn't happy with this set-up, given that all four suspects could just corroborate each other's stories and there was no chance to catch anyone out in a lie. Milla obviously didn't watch enough crime dramas on telly, or she'd have realised that when she was setting things up.

Still, they'd already caught Danny alone, and Posy had spoken to Hakim and Rachel – or Raven, as she now preferred to be known, professionally and personally – before they even knew about the investigation, or their involvement. If they could just catch Iain alone for a few moments, they wouldn't be doing too badly.

'I'm sorry I can't stay,' Milla said, as she backed towards the door. 'There's so much to do before the awards tonight. But I'll be around if you need anything.'

She almost crashed into Sarah, coming in, as she left. Sarah steadied her with a hand on her arm and an amused smile. 'You're going to have to slow down one day and realise you can't actually organise the whole world, Mil.'

Milla flashed a grin in return. 'But not today!' She bounced out into the foyer, leaving Rosalind with the usual simmering sense of envy for her vitality. She really had to stop resenting people for being young and energetic.

'Eleanor sends her apologies, too.' Sarah made her way across the room to the table where the drinks were set up, and helped herself to a glass of Prosecco. 'She's back in London for some meetings today. I don't think she was supposed to announce the new series quite so soon, so now she's trying to smooth things over with her bosses.'

'Why did she, then?' Posy asked. 'Announce it, I mean.'

Sarah shrugged. 'She said she didn't want to miss the moment. I guess having all three of you here gave things momentum?'

The library door opened again, and three people with wary expressions entered. Posy crossed over to them with a friendly smile.

'Hakim, Raven, it's lovely to see you both again.' She shook their hands, then turned to the third person. 'I'm sorry, I don't think we've met?'

It was the older gentleman Rosalind had seen going into the room opposite theirs, but there was none of the gentle charm and pleasantries they'd exchanged the day before. In fact, *his* expression looked more than wary. He looked as recalcitrant as Jack did when dealing with the ongoing neighbourhood bin feud.

'Iain Hardy.' His voice was low, his accent Scottish, and his tone dismissive. 'And don't worry, you don't need to remember it. I won't be staying.'

Rosalind glided forward to take over. Maybe a more generationally equal approach would help.

'We're so glad you were able to come,' she said, ignoring his comment about leaving. 'We just had a very few questions we wanted to ask you.'

Beside him, Raven was frowning. 'I thought this was supposed to be a drinks reception for the awards dinner? What's *she* doing here?' The glare she sent Sarah's way made it very clear who the 'she' in question was.

Sarah managed a tentative smile. 'Milla invited me too,' she said, which was only slightly disingenuous, given that the whole investigation was her idea. 'I think she hoped we'd all be able to get along, and discuss things like adults.'

Iain snorted a humourless laugh. 'Because you were all so good at that before? No, I'm done with all of this. I moved hundreds of miles just to be done with this, and there's none of you going to pull me back in now. Victoria is dead and buried. And you should just let her rest.' That last was directed at Sarah, too, with a pointed glare.

With a final glower around the room at each of them, Iain turned and stalked out, heading for the stairs that led up to the first-floor bedrooms, brushing past Danny as he approached the library.

'He does have a point.' Raven stood sideways, one foot pointing at the door, the other towards the drinks, obviously uncertain whether to stay or go. 'We've all moved on. Do we really want to rake all this back up again?'

'Scott hasn't moved on, Rachel,' Sarah said, softly. 'He's right where you all left him – in jail.'

'Because he was convicted of murder.' Danny had changed into evening dress, his hair slicked back, and looked rather more dapper than he had earlier. Rosalind approved.

'And I'm telling you, he's innocent. In fact . . .' Sarah dug into her bag and pulled out four envelopes that looked a lot like the one Posy had found addressed to Caro in Eleanor's file. 'He asked me to give you these.'

She handed one each to Danny, Hakim and Raven, checking the names on the envelopes first, leaving one in her hand.

'That's for Iain, I take it?' Danny held out a hand. 'I can take it up for him after.'

With a nod, Sarah gave him the letter.

None of them opened the envelopes, though, which made Rosalind wonder if Caro had read hers yet. From the way Posy was carefully watching Caro from the corner of her eye, she wasn't the only one wondering.

It was easy to get caught up in the intrigue of the case – the what had happened when and the who was where. But they needed to remember that Caro's connection to the case was rather more personal. She'd ask her about the letter later.

'You just want to talk to us about what happened, the day Victoria was killed?' Hakim looked to Posy for an answer, but it was Caro who stepped forward.

'That's right. We . . .' She paused, and gave them all a disarming smile. 'I'll be honest, because you were all in court that day and you all saw me there testifying against Scott. When Sarah and Eleanor asked us to be a part of this investigation, my first answer was a flat no, too.'

'What made you change your mind?' Raven asked, softly.

Caro cast a glance back towards Sarah. 'To be frank, I'm still not completely sure I have. But . . . what made me willing to consider it was something my friends said. They pointed out that if I was wrong, an innocent man was sitting in jail. And even if I was *right,* there was enough doubt swirling around that the matter wasn't fully settled. Either way, if I could do something to get some closure – for myself, for Sarah, for the police, for all of you . . . it felt like the right thing to do.'

Well. It looked like Caro did listen to them sometimes, after all. Who knew?

Raven, Hakim and Danny all exchanged glances.

'Do you want me to go see if I can get Iain back down?' Danny asked.

'No,' Rosalind replied, before the others could answer. She knew Iain's sort. He wasn't going to come back with his tail between his legs now he'd made his stand. 'We'll talk to him separately, later.'

Danny looked relieved. 'That'll probably work best.'

'He's a peaceable man, Iain,' Hakim said. 'But everything that happened . . . it affected him deeply. It affected all of us, of course. But Iain had spent so long being our peacemaker, I think he took it more as a personal failure.'

'He was very close to Victoria,' Sarah added, moving closer in to the circle of conversation at last. 'He was one of the first members of the writing group, after Scott and me. I think she shared more about her writing and her ambitions with him than with the rest of us.'

'And of course on that day—' Raven broke off. 'No, I'm getting ahead of myself.'

Rosalind shared a quick look with Caro and Posy. It seemed they had their suspects on board at last – four of them, anyway, if they included Sarah.

Time to start asking the real questions.

'Why don't we all have a drink,' Rosalind suggested. 'And then we can start at the beginning.'

Chapter Nine

Obsession is a very dangerous thing. Through the centuries it has led to heartbreak, war, revolution – and murder.

The Paper Dahlia Cases
***By* Danny Whitlock**

Posy

The most difficult part about questioning four suspects at once, it turned out, was keeping them from all talking over each other. Not to mention the challenges of keeping them from wandering off topic. Or the distraction of the canapés that arrived shortly after they started. They got the waiter to put them on the desk and leave them to it, but focus was still sorely lacking.

'This isn't working,' Caro muttered in her ear, as Rosalind once again tried to wrangle the conversation back to what they actually needed to know.

'I've got an idea.' Posy stepped forward and clapped her hands, feeling for all the world like one of her old drama teachers, about to instigate an ice breaker, or a trust exercise, with a new class.

Rosalind raised an eyebrow at her, Dahlia style, but gave her the floor.

'What we really want to understand right now is exactly what happened the day Victoria died,' Posy said. 'So maybe it would help for us to recreate the day from your recollections?'

'Like a re-enactment?' Raven asked, dubiously.

'Exactly!' Posy tried to smile encouragingly. 'We'll have to use our imaginations a bit, but . . .' She pulled out a couple of chairs from under a nearby desk. 'Let's start with the committee meeting that day. Who arrived first? And who sat where?'

'I was first.' Sarah, at least, was happy to jump into things. 'No, not quite – Milla was already there, because she was covering for her mum who was sick. Her mum was Victoria's cleaner,' she explained.

'Okay, so where was Victoria?' Caro pulled over an extra two chairs. 'How was the room set up?'

It took only minor rearranging to get the library in order. The small table that held the drinks became Victoria's desk – 'Where she sat the whole time because it gave her more power,' according to Raven – and seven other chairs were set out in a horseshoe around it, for their seven suspects.

'Do you remember who was sitting where?' Rosalind asked.

Brow furrowed, Hakim walked around the back of the chairs, tapping them each in turn. 'I was here by the door, like always, then Milla came and sat next to me. Then it was Iain, then Scott, then Danny, then Raven, then Sarah next to Victoria at the desk.'

'You remember all that?' Danny asked, looking impressed. 'I barely remembered that there was a meeting.'

He was exaggerating, Posy was sure. He had a journalist's eye for detail. But perhaps he was just hoping to be able to manage their expectations for his recollections. If he had something he wanted to hide about that day, that would make sense.

'So, Sarah, you and Milla were here first. What did you see or hear?' Caro asked.

Posy watched the faces of the others. They already knew that Sarah had heard Victoria arguing with someone on the phone; was it someone here now?

'I heard Victoria on the phone at her desk,' Sarah said. 'So I waited outside the door until she'd finished. Milla was dusting in the hallway too, so she probably heard as well.'

'Do you remember what she was saying?' Posy asked.

Sarah closed her eyes in concentration. 'Something about . . . things being over when she said so, otherwise she'd tell someone everything.'

'You don't remember who?' Caro pressed, but Sarah shook her head.

'Sorry, no.'

Posy had been watching Danny through Sarah's account, but he hadn't reacted at all. When she looked away, though, she saw Hakim watching him too. Maybe he knew something.

'What happened next?' Rosalind asked.

Danny shrugged. 'The meeting was pretty much like all our committee meetings. Victoria demanded to know who had done what, and then picked fault with everyone's work. I think we had the list of winners for that year's awards in from the panel. Other than that . . . it's hard to separate the memory of one meeting from another, to be honest. I remember we didn't even get to doing any of our writing group stuff that day because it was so close to the festival. She was yelling at Milla for something or other when I arrived, but I don't know what.'

Posy glanced around the others, but nobody seemed able to elaborate. 'Sarah – you must have been there then. Do you remember what that was about?'

'Oh, I . . . um.' Sarah seemed flustered to be questioned about her friend. 'I think it was about something that had been misplaced when she was cleaning. Nothing important.'

'Sounds about right,' Danny said. 'Other than that . . .'

'Victoria got a call from the bank,' Hakim said, suddenly. 'About halfway through. She let it go to voicemail, but . . .'

'But she made a big deal about it being the bank, and how she was sure it was about the festival,' Sarah finished for him. 'I asked why the bank was calling her not Scott, when he was the treasurer. She just ignored me.'

'They were calling about the embezzlement, I assume?' Rosalind said. 'They left a message?'

Posy nodded. 'According to the police files, yes. She called back and spoke to the bank after the meeting and they told her that a payment had bounced because of insufficient funds.'

'Is there anything else that happened at the meeting we need to know about?' Caro asked.

'Or immediately after it,' Posy added, looking pointedly at Danny. He'd told them he heard someone arguing with Victoria after the meeting, but now he wasn't saying anything at all.

The suspects all glanced between each other, then, as one, shook their heads.

Posy was almost certain they were all lying. Covering for each other out of friendship, or because they knew they had their own secrets they didn't want to come out? Posy would put her money on the latter. But maybe that was the sort of information they needed to get them alone for. At least the day of the murder was starting to take shape in her head. And it *was* possible that it had been Milla, Iain or even Scott arguing with Victoria after the meeting.

She checked the clock above the library fireplace. Milla would be back to fetch them for the awards soon; time to move it along.

'So, after the meeting, Victoria called the bank.' Posy pulled out the relevant reports from Eleanor's file to double check the timings. 'Then it looks like she did some investigating of her own, before sending a text message to—' She frowned. 'To Sarah's phone? Why did she text you and not Scott?'

Sarah's mouth tightened into a thin line before she answered. 'Because that was the sort of woman she was. She knew that Scott would probably have a perfectly good explanation, but she wanted to cause trouble with it. Frighten me. So she sent me that text, telling me that she'd made a very upsetting discovery about Scott and needed to see me urgently. But I didn't get it.'

'Why not?' Rosalind asked. 'Actually, this is a good time to ask, where were you all that evening?'

They knew what each of the suspects had told the police, of course – they had their statements. But they'd been made five years ago, and it was always possible that if one of them had lied they might have forgotten the details of the lie they had told. A long shot, but worth a try.

But everything they told them tallied up, even if it didn't clear any of them from the running.

Raven had been online, chatting with friends, but she could have done that from anywhere. Danny had been at the pub with his friends, but he'd left early enough and taken long enough to get home that there was opportunity. Hakim had been working alone in his garden office – but his garden had a back gate, so there was no one to say he hadn't slipped out for a while. At the time, both Danny and Hakim lived within easy walking distance of Victoria's house, and Danny had actually had to pass it to get home, but had seen nothing, as far as he was willing to say.

Milla, too, had actually passed the scene of the crime, according to her statement, on her way home from an exercise class. And Iain had been home alone with only a bottle of whisky for company. Not a solid alibi between them.

Sarah's was a little better, but only a little. Everyone knew that the word of a partner or spouse was practically worthless in this sort of situation.

'I was at my then-boyfriend, now-husband Eric's house, watching a movie,' she told them earnestly. 'I'd forgotten my phone at home; that's why I didn't see the text.'

'But Scott did,' Posy said. 'According to his statement, he came down the stairs at your house to pick up his post and saw your phone on the table, and the message from Victoria flashed up on the lock screen. He realised that this meant she knew about the missing money, and so he headed over to her house to talk to her.'

Sarah's face was pinched as she nodded. Scott had told the police all this; she couldn't disagree.

It was what happened next that was in doubt.

Caro reached behind her and picked up a statue of some sort from the mantlepiece. 'From here, we have to go on the crime scene and the medical examiner's report. Someone – presumably someone she knew, because the door wasn't forced – visited Victoria that evening and, in the same room where you'd had the committee meeting earlier that afternoon, bashed her over the head with one of the festival trophies that were waiting to be awarded that weekend.' She brought the statue down in slow motion from over her shoulder onto the desk, rattling the remaining glasses.

Sarah looked away. Raven stared at the statue. Hakim and Danny just looked uncomfortable.

Posy moved them on again. 'Scott's statement says that he arrived at the house and found the back door already open. He went inside and found the body, realised she was dead, and ran – knowing he'd be the prime suspect because of the embezzlement.'

'How does he explain the paper dahlia?' Rosalind asked.

'He said it must have fallen from his pocket,' Posy replied. 'It had just arrived in the post that he'd opened when he saw the message on Sarah's phone.'

'Convenient,' Caro muttered.

'He ran, and we know he ran because one of Victoria's neighbours saw him leaving. And that's the whole account.'

'Not quite.' Hakim crossed to the desk and ran a finger down the edge of the trophy. 'What does he say happened to the murder weapon? The police found it in his car, didn't they?'

Posy checked the statement again. 'He said that the car was an old clunker and the boot never locked properly. Anyone could have hidden it there.'

It would have taken a huge coincidence of timing for the killer to be leaving Victoria's house, be able to hide so Scott didn't see them, then stash the murder weapon in his car before he left.

Sarah was nodding sagely, though. 'That's right. Our car was ancient, and everyone knew it didn't lock properly – or start properly half the time. It would have been easy for someone else to hide it there.'

Before Posy could challenge that, Milla appeared in the doorway. 'Sorry to interrupt everyone, but it's time for us to head over for the awards dinner now. Especially you two,' she added, to Caro and Posy.

That's right. They were presenting, weren't they? Posy had almost forgotten about that, she'd been so wrapped up in the investigation.

'Milla, the day of Victoria's murder, do you remember what she was mad at you for?' Rosalind asked.

Milla blinked at them. 'Oh, gosh, um . . . not specifically. Probably not dusting something properly. Or moving something she didn't want moved so I could dust it. That was usually the problem.'

That sounded like another lie to Posy, but there wasn't time to call her on it now.

Everyone put down their glasses and headed for the door. As she trailed behind, Posy saw Sarah take Caro's arm, and murmur something to her.

'Come on,' Rosalind said, reaching out to take her arm. 'You've got to go and be fabulous now.'

'Remind me why *you're* not doing this again?' Posy asked.

Rosalind flashed her a wicked smile. 'One of the best things about growing older. You get an awful lot better about saying no to things.'

Caro

The outfit Caro had chosen for the awards dinner was a lightweight, wide-legged jumpsuit that swished around her legs as she walked. The top half was a more structured affair, giving her curves some extra shape where there was supposed to be, but still with a hint of vintage in a modern styling that she thought was suitable to the occasion.

She wasn't there as Dahlia, so she wouldn't go in costume, but Caro knew she'd always be synonymous with the detective – and that Dahlia was why people would buy her book – so it made sense to give a nod to Lettice Davenport's creation.

The fact that Annie had honest-to-God whistled when she'd seen Caro in it for the first time hadn't hurt, either.

She felt good in it, and it gave her confidence as the whole group of them strolled into the venue for the evening. But in her head, Sarah's words were still swirling around, unanswered.

Have you read Scott's letter to you yet? You really should.

Of course she should – if only to stop it hanging over her head all weekend. Reading it and getting it out of the way was the sensible thing to do.

But Caro Hooper had never really been known for doing the sensible thing.

Milla, in deference to the occasion, had switched out her usual black suit for a black shift dress with a shorter jacket, similar to the one she'd worn for the premiere. Her clipboard remained her most prominent accessory, though, as she led them into the venue for the evening.

The awards dinner was being held in another of Market Foxleigh's fancier hotels. For a small market town it did well for accommodation thanks to the picturesque Englishness of its appearance, and its reasonably easy road and rail links back to the capital.

The Queen's Head Hotel had a rather unfortunate painting of Anne Boleyn losing hers in the entranceway, but apart from that it was quite lovely, in Caro's opinion.

Milla caught her looking at the incongruous painting and grinned. 'Apparently keeping that up was part of the condition of sale of the place by the old owners,' she explained. 'Which is why everything else is . . .' She opened her arms to indicate the sleek, modern interior, with its calming robin's egg blue trim and creamy walls and furnishings. 'And that painting is relegated to that rather dark corner over there.'

'You know everything there is to know about this town, don't you?' They really needed to spend more time interrogating Milla. It was entirely possible she had a time log of the day of Victoria's murder somewhere in the stack of papers on her clipboard.

Caro made a mental note to suggest it to Rosalind and Posy.

The awards were taking place in a well-proportioned private dining room at one end of the hotel, looking out over more picturesque gardens, lit by tiny lights strung through the trees and around wooden posts. The wide glass doors were open so guests could wander freely between the dining room and the gardens, and there was also a small, private bar and cloakroom just next door.

'Where's Petra? Wasn't she supposed to be meeting us here too?' Her agent had been adamant about being at her side for this – Caro suspected because she was afraid of what she'd say when she got up there. She did okay with a script, but when left to ad lib . . . well, there had been one or two occasions when it hadn't been ideal.

'She had to cancel,' Milla explained, with an apologetic smile. 'Something about another client needing her urgently. She sent her apologies.'

'Right.' Another, more famous, important and lucrative client, Caro assumed. Well, it was always good to know where she sat in the pecking order.

While the others went to find their tables, Milla led Caro and a rather reluctant Posy into another anteroom to run through the arrangements for the event.

'There are more drinks and canapés first, plus the obligatory mingling,' she explained. 'Then we'll all sit down for dinner. Starters and main, then you two will present the awards while dessert and coffees are being served, if that's okay?'

Caro gave her a look.

'Obviously we'll ensure there's a pudding saved for you,' Milla added, having correctly interpreted the look. Posy had her hand to her mouth as if stifling a laugh.

'All sounds fine, then,' Caro said. 'Do we have envelopes to open, or . . .?'

'There's a screen with a mini film that will show for each category, detailing the nominees, then when that finishes you just announce the final winner and hand them one of these.'

She turned to gesture to the shelf behind her, and Caro noticed for the first time the row of gleaming gold and glass awards, each with a small plaque at the bottom engraved with the winner.

She picked one up and felt the heft of the thing. Sharp edges, too. Yes, a definite weapon, if someone wanted it to be.

Victoria Denby had been killed by one of these. Irrationally, Caro wondered which category, and whether they'd changed the design since the murder.

Milla detached a few stapled pieces of paper from her clipboard, and passed them to Caro and Posy. 'These are your scripts for the evening. You can take a look now, then I'll pop them into the folder up on the stage for you, so no one can peek at the winners over dinner. Almost all of the winners are here tonight, so will be able to come up and collect their award in person. I've noted the only two who aren't on the script – there'll be a representative for them.' Milla frowned. 'Or there should be. Will you be okay here for a moment? I just need to go sort something out . . .'

Caro waved a hand towards the door. 'Go, go. I'll be fine.'

Alone, Caro glanced through the carefully written script, already knowing she'd probably ignore all of it except the names. Presentations like this always sounded so stilted when they were written down and read out. She might be an author now, but she was still an entertainer at heart. She'd give the audience a good show.

She wanted to be reading something else, anyway.

Posy read through hers a little more carefully, before placing it on the nearest table. 'I'm going to go freshen up before we start,' she said.

Caro nodded absently, pretending to be engrossed in the script still. Then, once Posy shut the door behind her, she put the pages Milla had given her aside, and pulled a long envelope with her name scrawled on it from her bag.

She'd assumed, when Posy had first found the letter in Eleanor's file, that it would be from Scott. That wasn't a surprise. The fact that he'd written to the other suspects, and that Sarah had delivered the letters, was a little less expected, though.

She'd put off reading it because she wasn't sure she wanted to know what it said. But if the others weren't going to share the contents of their letters, she at least owed it to the investigation to read hers.

With a deep breath, she ripped open the envelope.

Dear Ms Hooper,

I'm sorry for writing to you like this, but you and your friends are my last chance at proving my innocence. And if you're going to work with Sarah, Milla and Eleanor like they hope, you deserve the full story – the whole truth.

Well, now. This could be interesting. Especially if Scott was about to say something that contradicted the contents of his police statement.

But to her surprise, the rest of the letter focused on the parts of the case that concerned her.

It's true that I had a lot of photos of you in my room. And that I'd become unhealthily obsessed with your TV show – speaking to my counsellor here has made that much clear to me. Borrowing money from the festival (I really had always intended to pay it back) to bid on memorabilia from the show and even afternoon tea with you was a clear symptom of this obsession.

But you have to believe that I never meant you any harm. I'd driven past your house before, it's true, but never spied on you. And the day the police found me there . . . I wasn't there to hurt you like they said.

I was there to beg for your help.

When I found Victoria's body, it was as if my world stopped. I knew that I'd be the prime suspect if anyone knew I'd been there, and I didn't know what to do. I was so scared, so confused . . . I didn't know who could have wanted to kill Victoria or why. I still don't. She wasn't always kind, or easy. But she was my friend.

Anyway. I freaked out – I'm not ashamed to admit it. And I knew that I was going to need help if I was going to get out of this mess without being arrested for murder.

It sounds crazy, I know, but in that moment, in my confused brain, I just knew I needed Dahlia Lively to solve the case for me – to find out who really did it and help me clear my name. And to me, you will always be Dahlia Lively, so that's why I drove to your house.

Caro's heart gave a double beat. Could that be true? Could he really have been there seeking her help, not to stalk or attack her? Even when Scott was safely behind bars, just knowing that he might be released one day and blame her for his imprisonment had kept the fear hanging over her, and Annie. But now she wondered. Had she been scared for years for nothing?

Of course, later, when that confused fog cleared, I realised how ridiculous that was. You were an actress, not a detective. By then, I was in jail anyway, and I knew nobody was going to help me.

Except then I read about you solving a murder at Lettice Davenport's house. And then on that film set in Wales. And suddenly I began to hope again.

When Sarah talked to me about the podcast, I knew that you were the only one who could help me. That I hadn't been wrong to go to you after I found the body – I'd just been a few years too early.

I know it's a lot to ask. And I know you have no reason to believe me. I told the police everything I knew; I don't have any new evidence or revelations to share.

I just hope that you'll ask yourself, what would Dahlia do?

Because I think Dahlia would want to help.

Yours sincerely,

Scott Baker

Caro stared at the letter for a moment, then read it again. Then, when Posy reappeared, she pressed it into her hands and said, 'Read this.'

She watched Posy's eyebrows jump higher and higher as she read.

'Huh.' She put the letter down. 'Do you believe him?'

'I don't know.' She wasn't even sure if she wanted to. Was it better to have been scared for no reason, or to have been right?

It didn't read like a letter from a killer. But how much did that mean, really?

Posy nodded. 'I guess we'll have to solve this case and figure it out then, won't we?'

Chapter Ten

Dahlia looked Johnnie up and down in his dinner jacket and bow tie. 'Well, Detective Inspector. I must say you scrub up pretty nicely – for a policeman.'

'And you, Miss Lively, solve crime surprisingly well for a lady,' Johnnie replied.

Dahlia Lively *in* A Lady's Place
***By* Lettice Davenport, 1934**

Rosalind

Milla had obviously made some last-minute rearrangements to the table plan to avoid too many empty spaces. Their table – which Rosalind was mentally calling the suspects table – had only eight seats rather than everyone else's ten, presumably because Eleanor was still in London, and Iain was nowhere to be seen.

'I dropped his letter off,' Danny told her, when she asked. 'He took it, but I don't know if he'll read it. He said he was done with this whole thing. I don't think he'll be joining us for dinner.'

'Unfortunately not,' Milla confirmed, swinging by. 'Oh well. At least it means I get a seat for dinner after all; I'll join you all once everything's settled.' Then she was gone again, turning around a waiter who had the wrong wine, then moving on into the foyer to keep the guests moving.

Caro and Posy joined them just as the wine was being poured, Posy placing her hand over her glass before she even sat down. They'd taken two of the three empty seats on the opposite side of the table, leaving the last for Milla. It left them not badly spread out for eavesdropping on what their suspects had to say when they *weren't* officially being questioned.

To Rosalind's left, she heard Hakim talking in soft tones to Sarah beside him.

'I'm just saying that you can't let this take over your life,' Hakim said, with feeling. 'Bad enough that Scott has lost his freedom over his actions, that he wasted his life that way. But for you to give up on yours too? That is more than a waste, Sarah. That is a tragedy.'

'I haven't given up,' Sarah replied. There was a core of steel in her words that belied the softness of her voice. 'I'm still living my life, Hakim. I'm married now, you know? I'm working. I have friends. And I have a mission – to find out the truth of what happened that day.'

'Even if the truth is that Scott really did commit murder?' He sounded almost apologetic as he said it, Rosalind thought.

She was interested to find out if Sarah's answer would be the same to Hakim as it had been to them.

'He didn't,' she said, firmly. 'If there's one thing I'm sure of, it's that.'

Hakim didn't look convinced, Rosalind thought, but he moved the conversation on, all the same.

'What about your writing? Are you still writing?'

Sarah shook her head with a small smile. 'That was always Scott's thing, more than mine. And without him . . .'

'You had talent, Sarah. You shouldn't just give up because of everything that happened that summer.'

'Perhaps not,' she replied, with a noncommittal shrug and an ironic smile. 'Maybe when we get Scott freed I'll celebrate by writing another short story all about it.'

'When he's freed?' Across the table from Sarah, Raven scoffed, tossing her dark hair back over her shoulder as she looked at her with disdain. 'Do you really believe you're going to overturn a conviction with a *podcast*?'

'Why not?' Sarah asked. 'Others have.'

'Because the others were innocent,' Raven said, sharply. 'Trust me, I'm not doubting the power of new media or new methods – that was Victoria's bag, not mine. But I *am* doubting your case. Nothing any of us said today pointed to any other motives or clues, did it?'

'Rachel – sorry, Raven,' Milla corrected herself with a wince as she slipped into her chair. 'I don't think this is really the time or the place . . .'

Raven turned her glare on Milla. 'If you didn't want us talking about this, you really shouldn't have sat us all on the same table, should you? The one thing we all have in common is Victoria, and an interest in her murder. What else are we going to talk about?' Her gaze moved slowly around the table, settling on Rosalind, in the end. 'But I imagine that was the point, wasn't it? To capture all our more private conversations after your little re-enactment. All ready for you to use in episode one.'

Rosalind opened her mouth to reply, but Raven didn't wait to hear it.

'Well, if you want my thoughts, you can have them for free,' she said. 'I think Sarah knows as well as anyone that her brother murdered Victoria, and she's just trying to find another scapegoat she can pin it on, because of their sibling bond or something. That's what I think.'

'You're wrong,' Milla said, jumping to Sarah's defence. 'Sarah—'

'Sarah can speak for herself.' Sarah's voice cut across whatever anyone else had been about to say, silencing the table. 'You want to know what *I* think? If we're sharing opinions, I mean. *I* think that you all know there was more going on with Victoria than the police or the papers reported, but none of you want to talk about it. None of you want to even *consider* the fact that Scott is innocent, because it means that one of you is probably guilty. That's what I think.'

'Oh, I really wish I'd been able to persuade Iain to come down to dinner,' Danny said, half under his breath and seemingly to nobody. Iain, Rosalind remembered, had been the peacemaker. No wonder he'd opted for room service instead tonight. Keeping this lot civil was a job of work.

'What do you mean by "more going on",' Rosalind asked, banking on everyone being riled up enough to talk without really considering whether they wanted to say such things in front of them. 'You all said there was nothing else notable at that meeting the day of her death.'

'Maybe not that day,' Sarah admitted. 'But everyone on that committee had clashed with Victoria over something, hadn't they? And she was worked up about something else *before* that day's meeting. Even you have to admit that much, right?'

She turned to Raven, who shrugged. 'When *wasn't* Victoria freaking out about something? It was right before the festival, and she was pretty stressed.'

'Stressed about what, though, exactly?' Caro asked.

Raven sighed dramatically and rolled her eyes, but it was Danny, sitting beside her, who answered the question.

'Victoria had got it into her head that someone was plagiarising her stories,' he said. 'She accused Rachel in the meeting the previous week. But none of us took it very seriously.'

'Sounds like the sort of thing a writing group should take very seriously to me,' Caro observed, one eyebrow raised in Rosalind's direction. That was new information.

But Rosalind was trying to remember something one of them had told them before. *Ah! There it is.*

'Sarah told us that Victoria seldom read out much of her own work in the group, though. So how could someone have stolen it?'

'Most of it was saved on the cloud account for the festival committee and writing group,' Milla explained now. 'Any one of us could have accessed it. But it doesn't matter, because there was no evidence that anyone did.'

'All that had happened was that Victoria had seen a book for sale on Amazon with a synopsis that sounded quite like hers,' Danny went on. 'None of us recognised the name of the author. It didn't mean anything.'

'That happens all the time,' Hakim added. 'There are no truly original ideas in the world, after all. And besides . . .'

'Victoria never finished writing anything she started, anyway,' Milla finished.

Hakim nodded. 'Precisely.'

'It was only because it was a self-published book,' Raven went on. 'That was why she was mad. She had an irrational thing about people skipping the gatekeepers and publishing their own work – probably because of her Daddy issues. Because, like, why should writers trust *readers* to choose what they want to read, instead of publishers?'

Raven's books, Rosalind remembered, were independently published.

'That was just one of *many* reasons why I'd already decided I needed to get away from here, leave the group, even before Victoria died,' Raven said.

Caro looked up suddenly. 'Did Victoria know that?'

'Yeah,' Raven said, looking puzzled as to why it mattered. 'I told her just before the meeting where she started accusing me of stuff, the week before her death. Obviously she lost it and ranted at me, like she always did when someone wanted to do something *she* hadn't planned.'

'She did like to be in control,' Danny said, with a wry smile. 'Do you remember the year with the sheep?'

The mood lightened as he told an anecdote about an earlier, less murderous festival, which had unfortunately coincided with a nearby country show and, due to some ill-placed roadworks, ended up with an entire flock of sheep interrupting an open-air author reading in the town square.

'Which was why we moved almost all the events to the marquee the following year,' Hakim added.

Once the main meals were finished, Caro and Posy were called up onto the stage to present the awards. Rosalind saw Milla speak with the waiter, and a dessert be put aside for Caro, so that was one disaster averted, anyway.

They did a good job, although from Posy's expression Rosalind suspected Caro might have been completely ignoring the script they'd been given. But the crowd were entertained, and the right awards went to the right people as far as she could tell, so that was good. And best of all, she didn't have to stand up there in her highest heels and do it.

The screen behind the stage lit up with a rolling film of each of the nominees for each category, something Rosalind only paid vague attention to – more concerned with her lemon posset with crème fraiche, to be honest – until Danny's name was announced, and the rest of the table moved to congratulate him.

'Well, I haven't won it yet,' he said, modestly – just as the nominees film came to a close, and Caro said, 'And the winner of this year's Non-Fiction Crime Prize is . . . Danny Whitlock, for *The Paper Dahlia Murders*!'

There was much applause and cheering as he headed up to claim his prize, but Rosalind kept her gaze on Sarah.

She wasn't clapping. She wasn't smiling.

In fact, the glare she shot at Danny's back looked much like daggers.

Posy

The next morning, Posy perched on the edge of the display table holding very serious, literary hardback titles, and tapped a pen against her old, bulging notebook, as she tried to make sense of everything they'd heard and learned so far.

The next page remained stubbornly empty.

She'd taken notes on yesterday's interrogations before bed, and was reasonably sure she hadn't missed anything. Even if she had, breakfast had been filled with the rehashing of events anyway. She had all of the facts and the information, but still none of it seemed to be coming together in Posy's head. Between the re-enactment in the library and Scott's letter to Caro, she could run through the day of the murder down to the minute now, but she still couldn't place all the pieces – or the players – on the board.

Then Petra had arrived at the breakfast table at The Red Fox to take Caro off for a signing at Market Foxleigh's premier bookshop, and Posy and Rosalind had followed along behind once they'd finished their tea.

'Don't forget that Victoria was cross with *two* people before the meeting – Milla, and whoever she was on the phone to before that,'

Caro said, turning around in between signing books for people in the queue. Posy wished she'd focus on what she was supposed to be doing, rather than trying to do Posy's job for her too.

Rosalind wasn't much better. She'd ensconced herself on the comfortable sofa the bookshop provided for browsers, and was flipping through the file Eleanor had given them the night of the premiere. Every few moments she'd look up and call out something else for Posy to add to her notebook, oblivious to the fact that she'd already made all the necessary notes.

Add in the shoppers who wanted photos or autographs from all three of them, not just Caro, or even just the ones loitering nearby pretending to take selfies clearly framed just to get her or Rosalind in the background, and Posy's focus was shot to hell.

This wasn't working. She needed to get away and clear her head, blow away the cobwebs with some fresh air, and maybe a fresh perspective.

'I think I need a break from this,' she said, making both Caro and Rosalind look at her with surprise. 'I'm going to take a walk.'

Rosalind instantly put the file down beside her on the sofa, closed of course, so no one else could see the contents, even though she'd been calling them across the bookshop.

'Do you want me to come with you?'

Posy shook her head. 'No, no, really, I'm fine. I just need a bit of a break.'

She couldn't tell her she needed a break from them, but they were intelligent women. She was pretty sure they got it.

Without really thinking about it, she swept up the file from the sofa and shoved it in her bag before she left, giving Caro a small wave as she headed to the door. The line of people wanting a signature on their copies of *The Three Dahlias* was snaking out onto the pavement, which Posy supposed had to be a good thing. This weekend was Caro's time to shine, and Posy intended to let her have it.

Outside, the streets were filled with festival-goers, weekend passes hanging from lanyards around their necks, and tote bags filled with crime novels slung over their shoulders. Despite Eleanor's announcement on the opening night, nobody else there seemed to be very concerned about the possibility that there was an actual murder mystery going on underneath their noses.

She was glad that she'd chosen a casual outfit for the day. In jeans, a loose T-shirt and a light jacket, with a baseball cap pulled down over her hair and her sunglasses in place, she could almost pass unnoticed. One or two people did a double take as she passed, but as long as she kept walking most of them probably convinced themselves they were mistaken as to her identity. Which was just what she needed today.

The fresh air felt so freeing, and the sunlight so safe, that Posy walked further than she'd intended. Before long, she found herself on the riverside again, but continued further than they had with Sarah, passing the bridge rather than crossing it.

Up ahead, she spotted the same houseboat bookshop she'd noticed before, moored on the river. Curious, she moved closer, and saw the sign on its roof, brightly painted in red and blue, that read '*The Floating Bookshop – second-hand books*'.

She could hear jazz music emerging from the boat, and a fluffy black and white cat wound itself around a flower pot on the roof. Best of all, there was the smell of strong coffee swirling in the air.

This looked like a bookshop where she could think.

She stepped up from the bank onto the boat, and called out a greeting in the hope of locating the cat's owner. As she entered the boat's interior, she found tables and racks of books filling almost every inch.

From the front cabin emerged a man about her own age, with dark hair flopping over his eyes, and a tatty red scarf tied around his neck despite the warmth of the summer's day.

'Good morning,' he said, smiling broadly. 'You've wandered a long way from the festival.' He nodded towards the weekend pass hung around her neck, and Posy self-consciously tucked the lanyard inside her summer jacket.

'I was looking for more of a unique bookshop experience,' she said.

'Well, we definitely have that here,' he held out a hand. 'I'm Roger, and yes, sometimes I have been known to be jolly.'

Posy laughed despite herself. 'I'd imagine it's hard to be that unhappy when you live in a floating bookshop with a cat, and what smells like some really good coffee.'

'You make a good point. Can I interest you in a cup?'

Posy nodded. 'That would be lovely, thank you.'

While Roger left to make the coffee, Posy explored the racks of books. She found several Dahlia Lively novels she hadn't quite reached in her exploration of the canon yet. Mostly she'd taken to reading them on her Kindle, but there was something about the older paperbacks that drew her interest. The gaudy covers were a particular joy, and she picked up a few to buy – including one each for Caro and Rosalind, as a small penance for walking out on them earlier.

'You're a Lettice Davenport fan then, I take it?' Roger held out a mug towards her. It was red and covered in white spots, and the coffee in it smelled like the best thing ever.

He didn't seem to recognise her in her off-duty jeans and T-shirt, which was a refreshing change. As Posy wasn't in a hurry to get into the discussion of celebrity, she smiled and nodded. 'I'm a recent convert,' she explained. 'And there're quite a few I haven't read yet.'

'I'm reading the first one myself right now,' Roger said. His gaze flickered towards the cabin again, as if he was trying to decide whether to show her something. Posy didn't know what tipped it in her favour, but after a moment he added, 'Come see this.'

Posy followed him into the small cabin at the front of the boat, surprised to find it slightly more spacious than she'd imagined. The rest of the barge was so full of books, it was hard to imagine there was room to swing even that proverbial cat that was snoozing in the sun up on the roof.

But there in the cabin, Roger had found space to prop up a large magnetic whiteboard, covered in pictures and Post-its and index cards, all held together with magnets and pieces of red string.

Posy began to worry about what might be in the coffee.

'My boyfriend calls it my serial-killer wall,' Roger said with a laugh. 'But I swear I only use it to solve fictional murder mysteries.'

Posy leaned closer, taking in the details on the board. Now she knew what she was looking for, she saw several familiar names and places written on the index cards.

'You're dissecting the plot of *The Lady Detective*!'

'I am.' Roger selected a Post-it note from a stack and added it to the board. 'It's my first Dahlia Lively mystery. I thought I'd better start at the beginning. My boyfriend is frustrated though, because I won't go and see the new movie until I finish trying to solve it myself. I've been stuck on chapter twenty for the last week.'

Posy laughed. 'I won't tell you who did it then.'

She traced a finger along one of the red strings, thinking hard. It was easy, seeing it set up like this, to spot the links between people's motives and their actions, their alibis and the lies they told. The story was stripped away, and all that was left were the facts. Maybe that was what they needed to solve this case.

'I like it,' she said, lightly. 'It's like a TV detective's method, just applied to golden-age crime instead.'

'Exactly!' Roger beamed. 'You understand. Would I be right in guessing you're something of an amateur detective yourself?'

'Oh, I don't know about that,' Posy demurred. Then she grinned. 'But sometimes I play one on TV.'

Chapter Eleven

Never trust a man who says he only did for love something that patently served his best interests.

Dahlia Lively *in* Love Her To Death
***By* Lettice Davenport, 1961**

Caro

By the time the bookshop signing was done it was past lunchtime, and Caro's hand was starting to ache. Rosalind headed back to the hotel for a rest before the evening events – and to see if Posy had found her way back yet. But Caro had been sitting for hours, as she chatted to readers and signed books. She needed to move.

And she needed a decent coffee.

She grabbed a black Americano from the horse-box cafe in the town square, smiling at people who obviously recognised her as she went. As the weekend went on, she felt herself becoming less of a novelty, as the people of Market Foxleigh got used to having celebrities in their midst. It wasn't a large town, after all. If Posy hadn't gone back to the hotel yet, there was a decent chance she'd bump into her sooner or later.

Takeaway cup in hand, she began to wander and, before she really realised she was doing it, found herself walking down towards the river. Rosalind and Posy had told her all about their conversation with Sarah, and now she followed in their footsteps, over the bridge Posy had described and towards the cottages on the other side of the river.

One of which used to belong to Victoria Denby.

She took a seat on a bench and, ignoring the river on her left, looked right and surveyed the cottage on the end of the row. According to the map in Eleanor's file, that was where Victoria had lived. It was part of a short row of three ancient cottages, backed by far more modern homes. The front door of Victoria's cottage sat on the side of the row, as did the door of the cottage on the other end.

She wondered which neighbour had reported seeing Scott running from the scene. Did Eleanor's file even say? She couldn't remember.

Caro spotted a figure moving in the shadows to the side of the cottage, under the sprawling trees. Posy, perhaps, investigating alone. She went to see, but by the time she got there whoever it was had gone.

A small alleyway ran behind the back of Victoria's cottage garden, connecting via a wooden gate. And on the other side of that alleyway, three more houses, these ones side on. Which meant that the kitchen window of the first one looked directly over the alleyway – something she could confirm easily with only a little invasion of privacy. She'd place a bet that the neighbour who saw Scott lived in that house.

Unfortunately, the house in question seemed empty – and a SOLD sign stood in the front garden. Caro ventured closer and confirmed that the other rooms were empty of furniture. Shame. No chance of confirming her suspicions by talking to whoever lived there now.

She continued down the alley, out into a small area with garages and parking spaces behind the second row of houses. This must have been where Scott had parked the car – and where he'd been running to when he was spotted by the neighbour. He'd even hidden the weapon in the boot, which was foolish beyond measure since he'd then driven around with it for two whole days, before the police picked him up.

Unless he hadn't known it was there. Unless someone else *had* put it there, when he'd raced inside and found Victoria dead. He'd been frantic, desperate to get to her before she spoke to his sister, or more likely the police, so it was reasonable that he might have failed to lock the car up.

And if the real killer had been waiting, looking for an opportunity to frame someone . . .

Caro shook her head. Too many maybes. Lettice Davenport could probably have written seven different murderers for this crime. But there was only one truth, and that was the only one that mattered.

She just wished she wasn't more and more convinced that the true killer might *not* have been Scott Baker.

Another figure – or was it the same one? – appeared from around the far side of the row of cottages, and this time Caro had a good enough sightline to identify him easily.

'Hakim,' she called out, smiling her best friendly smile as she approached. 'Out for an afternoon walk, too? Shouldn't you be attending another panel or something?'

He returned her grin. 'I couldn't sit on those plastic chairs for another hour. I decided to take advantage of the afternoon lull to revisit some old haunts. Thought I might even bump into some old friends.' He looked past her to the cottages behind. Caro assumed he was thinking of Victoria, but if he'd come looking for ghosts he was out of luck.

'I'm afraid I'm the only one here,' she said. 'Just . . . familiarising myself with the area.'

'Whereas I am paying something more akin to a pilgrimage, I suppose.' With one last look past her shoulder, he shuddered, ever so slightly, then turned around and offered her his arm. 'It's cooler in the shade, isn't it? Autumn will be with us soon, and the fresh start of the new term.'

'Of course, you're a teacher now, yes?' Caro slipped her arm through his, and allowed him to lead her out of the shadows back into the late-afternoon sunshine beside the river bank.

'That's right.' Hakim took them towards the bridge. 'Some days it feels like a different world.'

They walked in silence for a few minutes as they crossed back to the other side of the river. Along the way, Caro saw a houseboat bobbing colourfully on the water, but Hakim led them back towards the town centre before she could investigate it.

'Can I ask you about Victoria?' she said, after a moment.

Hakim gave a small half-smile. 'I'm honestly surprised you waited this long.'

So was Caro, if she was honest, but she didn't admit it. 'What was your relationship with her like? Were you friends? Or just colleagues?'

He considered his answer before speaking, something she'd noticed him do at dinner the night before. A man who thought before speaking – or one who was being very careful not to say the wrong thing.

The sort of thing that might get him arrested, perhaps.

'I think we were friends, by the end,' he said, eventually. 'She wasn't sure what to make of me, to start. I came late to the writing group, having met Iain at one of the early festivals. He was judging the awards that year – technically it was a panel of judges, but I think it mostly came down to him in the end – and I had entered. He liked my short story, although it didn't win. But he sought me out personally at the festival and suggested I join their writing group. I didn't know then that he hadn't mentioned it to Victoria first.'

Caro had the impression from other conversations that such action wouldn't have gone down well with Victoria, and Hakim's next words confirmed it.

'I think she wanted to make this place, certainly this festival, her own – in her own image, so to speak.' He paused again, his gaze distant. 'She hadn't been divorced for all that long, I believe, and she was building a new identity from scratch. I don't think I saw it then, but with hindsight . . . She wanted everything to be the way she wanted it, because she wanted that control. She always did what was best for the festival, but only for the perfect vision she saw of it in her mind.'

'Interesting.' Caro looked sideways at him. 'But it doesn't tell me much about *your* relationship with her.'

He laughed at that, as if amused at being caught trying to distract her. 'I'm sorry. My students – not to mention my wife and children – would tell you that going off on a tangent is one of my biggest flaws.'

'There are worse flaws to have.' Like being a murderer.

'Victoria . . . I don't think she knew what to make of me. I'd had it all, you see – the big career in the city, the money and status. And I'd given it up to move to Market Foxleigh.'

'You think she was intimidated by you?' Caro guessed. 'Your previous job?'

Hakim frowned a little, as if considering her suggestion, then dismissing it as his brow relaxed. 'Not exactly. The part that confused her was that I also had a wife and kids, a happy family life – a happier one now I'm not involved in organising the festival, I have to say. And I'd chosen to prioritise them as I made my next career move. For

Victoria, everything had to be all or nothing – she was an obsessive that way. It was the balance I valued so highly that she didn't understand.'

Caro nodded. She wasn't sure she'd have understood that before Annie, either. It certainly wasn't something she'd had with her first husband.

'You seem to speak of her more positively than many of the others, though,' she said.

Hakim's smile twisted ironically. 'Well . . . perhaps that's because I owed her. Of course, she knew it, well enough, and held it over me when it suited her. You could say it's my 'motive' if you really thought I could be behind her death.'

He gave her a questioning look, as if waiting for her to dismiss such a possibility as absurd.

She didn't.

Hakim nodded. 'Of course. You have to suspect everyone.'

'Sharing your motive with me *would* make me more trusting though, I imagine,' Caro said. 'How did you owe Victoria?'

'When I was applying for jobs, and especially for the teaching roles, my experience was . . . rather more limited than people were looking for. In particular, I wanted the adult education role for teaching creative writing at the local centre here in Market Foxleigh, seeing it as a stepping stone to a future career – as it turned out to be.'

'She helped you?'

He nodded. 'As is so often the case, I needed the experience of teaching to help with my applications for formal teaching study, but in order to *get* that experience they wanted me to already have some,' he explained. 'Victoria stood as reference for me, and also used her personal contacts to support me, claiming that I'd been acting as teacher for our writing group.'

'But you hadn't?'

He scoffed. 'Victoria would never allow someone else that sort of control over her group. Still, it all worked out. I got the job for the summer classes, and that helped my applications for future roles and teacher training, and now I have a whole new career. But you see, I owe it to Victoria.'

Victoria, who would rather lie than cede control of her little corner of the universe.

'What did she ask in return?'

'Initially, nothing,' Hakim said. 'But as time went on . . . she made it clear that she expected loyalty, in return. For me always to take her side in disputes in the group, to back her up on anything she felt was important. To never support any of the other members above her.'

'Was that hard to do?'

He held up his hand, palm down, and waggled it from side to side. 'Usually, not so much. She had a firm idea of how she wanted the group to run, but she always had its best interests at heart. Not speaking up when she got something wrong, though . . . that was much more difficult.'

'What sort of things did she get wrong?'

For the first time, Hakim seemed to close up a little – as if he were still afraid to betray the confidences of a dead woman. Finally, he said, 'She wasn't always kind. Especially to the other women. Sarah, for instance. And telling Raven she thought she'd stolen her books . . . that was patently ridiculous. But because she'd never *looked* at any of Raven's books online – refused to acknowledge them – she wouldn't know that. Raven didn't need to steal Victoria's work; her own was already doing well.'

'Why wouldn't she acknowledge them, do you think?'

'In her mind, they weren't "real books".' She could hear the air quotes he put around the words. 'Presumably because they weren't the sort her father would have written. In many ways, she was a very troubled woman, with plenty of issues of her own.'

'Danny said he heard someone arguing with her after the meeting that afternoon,' Caro said. 'Do you have any idea who it could have been?'

'Yes.' Hakim looked away. 'It was me.'

'You? Why didn't you tell us that when we asked, back in the library?'

'Because it's not something I'm particularly proud of, and I didn't want everyone else to know.' He gave her an apologetic look. 'It's as simple and as wrong as that.'

'What did you argue about?' Caro asked.

'The chosen winners of the awards,' Hakim said.

'You disagreed with the panel's choices?' It seemed an odd thing for the gentle Hakim to take a stand on.

'No, that wasn't it. I was *on* the panel. We deliberated and discussed and we chose well,' he said. 'But when Victoria gave us the list of winners in that meeting, I realised that one of the winner's names for one of the categories had been changed.'

Caro blinked. 'Why didn't you say something in the meeting?'

'Because the submissions were all anonymous. I wasn't supposed to know *who* had won. But I recognised the writing style and, well, I knew that Victoria must have changed the winner herself, after the panel gave their recommendations. For every other category, the title of the piece was included, but for that particular category the announcement just had the writer's name,' he explained.

'What did she say when you confronted her?'

'She reminded me that she knew my secrets, and could share them whenever she liked.' Hakim gave her a rueful smile. 'You see why I had to confess my own motive first.'

'I do.' Caro's mind was working fast. 'Did you tell anyone else?'

'No. No one at all.' He looked away, a flash of shame colouring his expression. 'The deed was done and, well, I had too much to lose myself. I'm not proud of that.'

They'd reached the town square again, and Hakim released her arm as he gave her another of his gentle smiles, signalling easily the end of her questioning without giving her much of a choice. Instead, he asked his own question. 'I hope you'll be joining us for tonight's special event?'

'That depends. Can you tell me what it is?' The festival programme she'd been handed had a 'spoilers' sticker printed over the evening slot, with just a time and a venue: the town square at eight p.m.

'I'm afraid not. And once you know, you mustn't tell anyone else who might come to the festival in future years,' he said. 'It's a tradition.'

'Hmm.' Caro wasn't sure she was all that fond of tradition – especially the ones that continued for no good reason other than it being the way things were always done. 'Do you know if Iain will be there?'

'I imagine so,' Hakim replied. 'You're still hoping to speak to him, I take it?'

'We are.' But as far as she'd been able to tell, he still had no interest at all in speaking to *them*. 'I don't suppose you could put in a good word for us?'

'I don't think it would help,' he said, apologetically. 'We haven't really stayed in touch. I'm honestly surprised he came – I don't think he's even still writing, anymore. Now, if you'll excuse me, I really must go and prepare for tonight's events.'

Hakim made it a few steps across the square before she stopped him by calling his name.

When he turned back, she asked, 'Who was it you were hoping to see, when you went to Victoria's house this afternoon?'

Hands in his pockets, Hakim looked down at the cobbled streets of the square. 'I'm not sure. Maybe Victoria's ghost. Or maybe . . . yes. I think I hoped to bump into Sarah on my walk today. To apologise.'

'What for?'

'For . . . well. Everything, I suppose. Her brother was the murderer, not her. She didn't deserve the way she was treated afterwards. She didn't deserve any of it.'

He gave her one last, tight smile before he walked away, leaving Caro wondering.

Rosalind

Caro's signing over, Rosalind retired back to her room. Apparently tonight was the big evening event of the whole festival, and she wanted to be well rested for it. After a nap, she ate a club sandwich from room service as an early dinner, surrendering the chips that came with it to Posy when she joined her. When they regrouped with Caro in the hotel bar, they discovered her ensconced in a corner with her agent, Petra, a half-finished bottle of white wine between them.

'Are we interrupting?' Posy asked, sitting down regardless.

'Not at all!' Petra shuffled around in the booth to make more room for Rosalind. 'We were just catching up on Caro's progress with book two, and tossing around some possible titles.'

'*Wales Is Wet And Everyone Dies*?' Rosalind suggested. She did not have fond memories of the events that had taken place in Wales a year and a half ago.

'*Why Does Everyone Want To Kill Rosalind?*' Posy said, smiling impishly.

'We're thinking *A Very Lively Murder*, as a play on the Lettice Davenport title, *A Rather Lively Murder*,' Petra continued, as if she hadn't heard either of them. 'Or we will be, when Caro has a finished draft.'

Caro reached for the bottle of wine and topped up her glass. 'It's not the easiest thing, juggling promoting this book and writing the next one, you realise. Especially now we've got this bloody podcast investigation to do, too.'

'Ah, yes! *Writing A Wrong*.' Petra held out a hand for the wine bottle. Rosalind signalled the waitress to ask for a third glass. 'How's that going so far? Any breakthroughs on whodunnit?'

'We've had some . . . interesting conversations,' Caro said.

'Interesting how?' Petra asked. 'Interesting – might make an article, or interesting – there's a third book in this, Petra, get started on the negotiations now?'

'Not sure yet,' Caro replied, before taking a large gulp of wine.

Rosalind considered her friend. She hadn't seen her writing anything while they'd been away, and as far as she knew she'd been caught up in a case with Ashok for weeks before the book launch and then the film premiere, so she doubted she'd done much then. Was writing losing its appeal already?

'We missed you at the awards last night,' Rosalind said.

Petra rolled her eyes. 'Client having a crisis of confidence, needed talking down. All part of the job. But really, sometimes I feel more like a mother to these authors than their agent.' She patted Caro's arm. 'Not you, of course, darling.'

'Oh, there was one other thing I needed to tell you about,' Caro said, suddenly. 'Will Pollinger was desperate to meet Dexter Rush, but apparently he's been delayed?'

Petra looked taken aback for a moment. 'Uh, right. He had a calendar clash, I think. But he'll be here tonight for the thing. He's doing a reading, actually. Did he say why he wanted to meet him?'

A reading was a big deal for the notoriously reclusive author. Rosalind suspected he was the client with the crisis Petra had needed to deal with the night before, causing her to miss the awards.

'His wife's a fan. Wanted a signed book, that's all,' Caro said. 'And maybe to invite him to lunch.'

'I'm sure we can sort something out.' Petra drained the last of her wine, and gathered up her handbag. 'Now, I'd better go get ready for tonight's entertainment. I'll see you all out there.'

'Do we know what tonight's entertainment is?' Rosalind asked, as they watched Petra head for her room, her mobile phone already in her hand. As she ducked into the stairwell, Rosalind saw Milla approaching.

'The programme just has a big "spoilers" sticker,' Posy said, handing it over. 'Apparently it's one of those "if you know you know" things.'

'And if you don't you're just left looking like an idiot.' With a frown, Caro flagged down Milla. 'I'm not having that.' The festival coordinator smiled a long-suffering smile, and altered her path to head towards them.

'Actually, we still need to talk to Milla,' Rosalind pointed out. 'Perhaps we could ask her some questions about the murder before we get on to top-secret festival celebrations.'

Caro looked mildly put out at the suggestion. 'I suppose.'

'How are the three of you doing?' Milla asked, as Posy waved her into a seat. 'Is the investigation going well?'

Rosalind looked to both her fellow Dahlias before answering. Across the table, Caro was mouthing to the waitress for another wine glass – and probably another bottle of wine, too. 'We've made some progress.'

'We got the others to talk through the day of the murder in the library last night,' Posy said. 'Well, most of them. Iain refused to join us. I don't suppose you could have a word . . .?'

Milla shook her head with an apologetic smile. 'I'm afraid I think I've already used up any influence I had with Iain getting him to show up for the festival in the first place. But he won't miss tonight's event, so you might be able to catch him there.'

'He might be more willing to speak to us alone, I suppose.' Caro tapped a nail against the side of her glass. 'It's worth a try, anyway.'

'I was wondering if you could tell us a little more about how you came to be part of the writing group, and the festival,' Rosalind said. It occurred to her that the jump from Victoria's stand-in cleaner to running the festival after her death wasn't a small one.

The waitress returned and Caro poured the wine. Posy snagged her and asked for a fruit juice – and then pulled out the menu to order some bar bites, which Rosalind had to admit was an excellent idea.

Milla tipped her head from side to side, considering. 'I was late joining the group, you see. I was away at university, and only moved home the third summer, when they were already deep in planning that year's festival.'

'How did you meet Victoria and the others?' Posy's notebook rested on her knee, and Rosalind could just see her making notes under the table.

'My mum was Victoria's cleaner,' Milla explained. 'She owned the cleaning company that cleaned most of the houses around here actually. And my mum *really* likes to talk on the job – which I think Victoria hated, but anyway. I was helping Mum out when they were short-staffed that summer, and Mum told her all about me and how I'd studied creative writing and literature at university, and now I was working part time for her while I looked for a graduate job but really I wanted to be a writer, and I guess one day she was talking about it when the others were there because one of them suggested that I should join the writing group, and Mum wrote down all the details and . . .' Milla shrugged. 'There's not a lot of point arguing with Mum when she gets an idea in her head.'

'You don't know who suggested you join?' Caro asked, but Milla shook her head.

'I expect they got a glare from Victoria, though,' she said. 'I'm not sure she really liked having me there, but I tried to make myself useful during the next year's festival, and did a lot more in the run-up to my second festival – the fifth one – before—'

Before Victoria Denby was murdered on the eve of the festival, and the whole thing was cancelled.

But Milla Kowalski seemed to have enabled the whole thing to rise from the ashes, and become successful in a way far beyond anything Victoria had ever imagined. Rosalind was sure that Milla would say she'd done it in Victoria's memory – all those banners with her name on it ensured that. But still, the project that had been Victoria's baby was now all Milla's, and she seemed to be making a very decent living from it, if her wardrobe was anything to go by. Rosalind knew quality when she saw it, and Milla was wearing it.

'Did you *like* Victoria, Milla?' Rosalind asked. Milla looked rather taken aback, and she clarified, 'It really helps us to get an idea of who the victim was, and of course we never had the chance to meet Victoria, so all we have to go on are the memories of people like you, who knew her.'

Milla nodded slowly as she considered her answer. 'I'm not sure a lot of people *liked* Victoria exactly, but only because she wasn't the sort of person you got to know that way. She wasn't a friend, or someone I'd go out for drinks with or whatever. I mean, she was about fifteen years older than me for a start. We didn't have much in common.'

That hadn't stopped Scott connecting with her though, had it?

'What do you think Victoria thought of you?' Posy asked, her pen stilled against her notebook.

It wasn't a question Rosalind would have thought to ask. What other people thought of her was none of her business, even if she was more privy to their thoughts than most people, given her celebrity status.

But for Posy – and it seemed, Milla – it was a natural next question.

'I don't think she could make sense of me,' Milla said, slowly. 'I mean, I was the daughter of a single mum who worked as a cleaner, but I had a master's degree in English Literature. I was more qualified than she was to be running the group, but my mum scrubbed her toilets – and so did I, sometimes. So, yeah. I don't think Victoria could place me in her little hierarchy that made sense of the world for her. And she didn't like that.'

'Is your mum still living in Market Foxleigh?' Posy asked. Another good question. It would be useful to talk to someone who'd been in and out of Victoria's house regularly before her death. Who knew what she might have seen or heard?

But Milla looked away. 'Sort of. She's in a home, just on the outskirts. Early-onset dementia. I'm afraid she won't be any help to your investigation.'

'I'm sorry.' Posy reached across the table and squeezed Milla's hand. 'That must be unbearably hard.'

Milla gave a brave sort of half-smile.

Time to move away from that topic. Rosalind cast around for something less upsetting, and landed on a new angle. 'Did you ever read any of Victoria's writing? Or any of the rest of the group's?' They were a writing group first and foremost, after all.

Milla nodded. 'We all did. We took turns reading out most weeks when we met, and sometimes we'd use each other as critique partners or beta readers for longer pieces.'

'What was your professional opinion of the others?' Posy asked.

She paused before answering. Did this count as badmouthing festival authors, Rosalind wondered? 'Everyone in the group had talent, Victoria wouldn't have let them in otherwise. But everyone also had a very different style – like Hakim's literary crime short stories, or Danny's hardboiled sci fi. Scott's stories usually ended up more like Dahlia Lively fan fiction, if I'm honest, but they were still well written. He just couldn't see outside that golden-age bubble, I guess. Sarah's were similar, but more original, and they had . . . I don't know, something special about them. The others varied – but if you want to know what Rachel's were like you can just read them, she's indie published like twelve of them now, I think. Victoria hated that – she thought self-publishing was cheating, which is, frankly, a ridiculously old-fashioned view, in my opinion.'

Rosalind nodded along, as if she really had views on the matter, which she didn't. 'And Victoria? What were her stories like?'

'I only ever heard the short snippets she read out in the group,' Milla said. 'She never let any of us read anymore, I don't think. Too paranoid that someone would steal her work, like we talked about last night. But she was good – she had a great writing voice. She just never seemed to actually finish anything. Every week it was something different.'

Which tied up with what Sarah had told them. It painted a familiar picture, to Rosalind's mind. A woman with big dreams held back by a fear of failure, perhaps. One who tried to control everyone else around her, to build other things, because she was too scared to go after what she really wanted.

Or was there something else there? Another secret, hidden in plain sight?

Who was the romantic partner she was arguing with before the meeting? Rosalind had a nagging feeling that he might hold some answers to the woman's personality.

'Was she dating anybody?' Posy asked. 'As far as you know?'

Milla shook her head, but slowly, like she wasn't really sure. 'I don't . . . she never talked about anyone that way. But I was cleaning before the meeting the day she died, and I heard her arguing with someone on the phone and she said, *I know you love me, don't deny it now.* So, I guess the answer is, maybe?'

Or maybe that was the ending of a relationship. If it *was* Danny on the phone and he'd broken things off with her, and she wasn't willing to accept it, how far might he go to keep her from telling his wife?

They would have to pin him down again before the weekend was over, assuming he'd come back for day two of the festival. Otherwise she saw a road trip to Bristol in her future.

But Danny wasn't the only man on the committee – or even the only man she could have been talking to. What about her ex-husband? Rosalind wondered if Posy had missed anything in Eleanor's file about him, beyond the fact that he'd moved overseas and was out of the country at the time of her death.

She'd been thinking too long.

'What's this secret event business about tonight?' Caro, unable to hold in the question she really wanted to ask any longer, shoved the programme under Milla's nose, and the chance to ask her more questions about Victoria was lost.

Milla's lips jumped into a smile, and her eyes brightened. 'Oh, tonight is my *favourite* part of the whole festival. You'll have to wait and see exactly what it's all about, but . . .' She darted across the bar, back to the reception desk, and pulled out three black fabric tote bags with the festival branding on them, and returned to hand them each one. 'You'll need these.'

From the foyer, someone called her name, and she turned to leave with a small wave.

Rosalind reached into her tote bag, and pulled out a plastic skeleton mask, and a cheap black cape. 'What on earth?'

Posy and Caro both returned her blank looks after surveying the contents of their own bags.

'I guess we'll find out soon enough,' Caro said, sounding highly unsatisfied with her own answer.

'I'm not sure I want to,' Posy replied, shoving her mask back in the bag, and pulling out a tiny, battery-powered torch.

Rosalind knew exactly how she felt.

Chapter Twelve

Dahlia raised her glass to clink against Johnnie's. 'To friendship,' she said. 'The one thing that makes everything else bearable.'

Dahlia Lively *in* Look Lively, Dahlia
***By* Lettice Davenport, 1936**

Posy

Darkness had already started to fall before anything happened. Then, suddenly, festival volunteers were everywhere, herding unsuspecting first-timers towards the door, and urging them to put on their masks and capes.

'I'm not sure I like this,' Caro muttered, as she stretched the elastic of the mask over her dark curls. Her familiar face disappeared behind the stark black and bone white of the mask, and Posy shuddered at the sight.

She didn't like putting her own mask on much, either – and not just because of the way the elastic dug in behind her ears.

There was something . . . Dahlia would have called it 'unchancy' about the whole set-up. Skeletons and torches and a whiff of death in a festival where an actual murder had taken place, just a few years ago.

But then, everyone here wrote and read about murder for fun. Probably this was like trick or treating on Halloween for them, and she was just being a big baby about it all.

Telling herself that didn't do anything for the strange weight in her chest, though.

Outside the hotel, the streets were already filled with people – many of them wearing the masks and capes, but not all. Posy guessed that perhaps the locals came out for whatever was about to happen, too. There were even some kids up front holding glow sticks, bouncing with the excitement of staying up late.

Okay, maybe this isn't as creepy as I thought.

'Come on,' Rosalind said, taking Posy's arm in a firm grip. 'If we're going to do this, let's do it properly.'

They jostled their way through the crowds, towards the high street, but since none of them knew what they were there to see, it was hard to figure out where to stand.

Through the mass of people, Posy spotted one she recognised. Danny was just a few metres away, his tall, broad frame standing out among the people around him, and his skeleton mask pushed up over his head, ruffling his carefully styled dark hair. Posy shoved hers aside the same way, then waved until he spotted her.

'The three Dahlias.' The crowds had parted for Danny in a way they hadn't quite for them, as if he just expected that the way would be clear and it was. However he'd managed it, he was standing beside them in a moment. 'Come to see the Skeleton Parade?'

'Is that what this is? What the blazes is actually going on here tonight?' Rosalind asked, genuine confusion in her voice. 'I understood this event was to be the height of the festival, but I admit to being somewhat lost about it all.'

Danny grinned, his teeth bright in the torchlight against his shadowed face. 'This is the Skeleton Parade, Rosalind. And it's exactly what it sounds like. Come on. Follow me, and I'll get you the best view in Market Foxleigh.'

Danny led them along the high street, up towards the bandstand on the slight hill above the town square, which sat in a dip between The Red Fox at one end and the bandstand at the other. They moved behind the crowds as the people thinned out, until they were only standing two or three deep, instead of six or seven.

'Here,' he said, decisively, when they were not far from the bandstand itself. Behind it, Posy spotted a building – the town hall, she thought, from what she could remember from the map in her delegate pack. It also served as the local cinema, somehow, but she hadn't investigated how that worked.

They wiggled through gaps until they were at the front of the crowd, the lower density of people meaning that everyone was reasonably good-natured about it. Danny stood behind them, his superior height meaning he could see everything, anyway. Posy and Caro took the front, while Rosalind waited just behind them.

'From here, you'll get to watch a procession down to the town square, ready for a twilight reading by this year's very special guest – yourself excluded,' Danny added, with a nod to Caro.

'Dexter Rush?' Posy said.

Danny dropped his voice conspiratorially. 'I'm not on the committee this year, but I believe so.'

'Can't keep a secret with a committee,' Caro said, sagely. 'But what's all this about, anyway? Why skeletons?'

'It dates back to the very first festival, ten years ago,' Danny explained. 'It's sort of a mixture of traditions. In this area, there's a strong history of fire festivals, and the communal lighting of fires for occasions. And just over the border in Wales, there's a strange tradition by which a horse's skull is taken around from house to house between Christmas and New Year. When they were looking for something dramatic, something to make the festival stand out, Iain suggested combining the traditions into this – the Skeleton Parade.'

It still felt otherworldly to Posy. Caro leaned closer and whispered. 'Okay, but I'm just saying, this is the perfect night for a murder.'

Suddenly, from nowhere, a drumbeat sounded.

'Here we go,' Danny murmured near Posy's ear, his voice close enough to make the hairs on her neck stand up. 'Just watch.'

The steady thud of the drums kept going, vibrating through the air, through the town. Posy could feel it in her chest, replacing her own heartbeat.

Then, the doors to the town hall were flung open, and dark figures started to emerge, taking up places on the bandstand. Posy turned to ask Danny who they were, but the space where he'd stood was empty.

'Where did he go?' she asked Rosalind, who merely shrugged, without ever taking her eyes off the spectacle building on the bandstand.

There was a moment of stillness; the crowd hushed, the dark, faceless figures motionless, like statues. Only the drumbeat continued.

Posy blinked as a light shone, bright and unexpected, on the tableau on the bandstand. So *that* was where Danny had gone; he was the last one still settling into place, his mask down now, unless she was mistaken.

A voice – low and sonorous and familiar – spoke, and it took Posy a moment to realise it was coming from the front of the bandstand tableau. Hakim, she was sure. With his dark clothing, his skeleton mask firmly in place – and looking a lot more realistically spooky than the plastic ones they'd been given – it was only his voice and his height that gave him away.

'We are gathered here this night to welcome the spirits of the departed, the voices of those seeking justice. Welcome, all those who seek answers!'

A bit too on the nose, given the anniversary of Victoria's death. But maybe that was the point. If you made murder entertainment, in books and stories, you had to honour it too. Respect it. Maybe this was their way of doing that.

Another flash, as torches were lit around them. These weren't the cheap, battery-powered ones that Posy and the others had been given, though. These ones belonged in some medieval movie, and the flames that skipped above them were very real.

Each figure, all dressed in black, with the eerily accurate skull masks hiding their faces, began to move, stepping down from the bandstand and onto the path to the high street.

Through it all, the drumbeat never faltered, although for the life of her Posy couldn't figure out where it was coming from. At the front of the group, one of the figures held, not a torch, but what looked to be a horse's skull, dressed with blood-red ribbons where its mane would be.

'It's like a macabre hobby horse,' Rosalind muttered. 'What does any of this have to do with writing?'

'It's spectacle,' Caro replied. She, at least, seemed to be enjoying the occasion. 'People sitting around talking about books is all well and good in the daytime, but at night I guess they need something more to hook the punters in.'

The creepy group with torches, led by the horse skull, made their way down towards the high street and, without prompting, the crowds they passed fell in behind them. Posy, Rosalind and Caro found themselves swept up in the river of people, without any real choice as to whether they wanted to be there.

The air was filled with whoops and cries, with flashes of light from glow sticks and torches, with cracks and heavy footfall as the mob cascaded down the high street, towards the town square, where the war memorial stood.

As more and more people fell in behind the parade, it became a crush, and Posy wondered if there were meant to be this many people there, if maybe someone had miscalculated, because surely, even with the roads blocked to cars, there was no way all these people could fit safely in the town square . . .

All around, people jostled against her, and she felt her breath coming heavy and harsh in her chest, the air rasping against her lungs and her throat as she struggled to catch it. She reached out, her hands flailing as she tried to find Rosalind's arm, or Caro's, to find the reassurance of her friends. But they were gone, swept away into the crush somewhere, and she couldn't spot them in the sea of black.

Up front, another skeleton – not Hakim this time, they weren't tall enough, and not Danny either, she was pretty sure – hopped up onto the wall surrounding the war memorial, holding their torch aloft. They were joined by the person carrying the horse skull.

They started to speak, both together, a Greek chorus of sorts, but Posy couldn't make out the words. She couldn't make out anything except the crushing weight of the crowd around her, and the sound of her own harsh breathing in her ears.

She needed to get out of here. Away from the crowds. She'd find Rosalind and Caro again later, somehow.

Behind her, she heard Milla's voice announcing their very special guest, but if felt like it was happening miles away.

She pushed blindly past the people around her, all of them more interested in getting closer to the action than letting her get away from it. Eventually, though, she found her way to the outskirts of the square.

The crowd pressed all the way up to the walls of the shops surrounding the square, so Posy made for a gap in the brick – the alleyway they'd walked down that morning, she thought, with the antique shops and such. It was in total darkness; none of the shops had stayed open this late, and there was no street lighting away from the high street.

But even in the dark, it felt safer than the mass of humanity in the square. She tripped on something, and looked down to see a humped form, all in black, a skeleton mask beside it. Blood pounded in her ears as she reached down to touch it. Maybe someone had fallen, hurt themselves. She'd just shake their shoulder, check that they were okay . . .

The black robes on the floor crumpled between her fingers, revealing only pavement beneath. Someone must have dumped them there.

Thank God. For a moment, she'd thought—

Another movement in the crowd pushed bodies into her, and Posy stumbled forward, her knuckles scraping against the brick as she moved deeper into the refuge of the alley. Outside, the noise of the crowd swelled and grew, but everything sounded like she was underwater.

One arm on the wall above her head, she closed her eyes and rested her forehead against the brick, and tried to calm her racing heart.

She managed three whole breaths before somebody slammed into her back, winding her as her entire body hit the wall. She tried to turn, to face her assailant, but the weight of their body against hers held her pinned in place. She got a glimpse of a skeleton mask and an impression of black clothing, but that was all.

Her bag was ripped from her shoulder, and her attacker shoved her against the wall again before the bulk at her back disappeared. Wincing, Posy tried to turn as fast as she could, to see if she could spot the mugger. Forcing her eyes to stay open, she scanned the alley, and the lights of the square beyond. But everything hurt – from the scrapes on her arms and hands, to the bruise she could already feel forming on her forehead, to her chest as she struggled to suck in breaths.

Whoever had attacked her was swallowed up into the crowd in seconds, leaving Posy with no clue as to their identity.

And no bag. That bag had everything in it. Her phone. Her purse. The Dahlia Lively novel she was reading.

Her notebook.

Posy's knees gave way beneath her as she sank down the wall to slump on the pavement. Any moment now, she'd head out and find Caro and Rosalind. They'd be worrying. She'd explain what had happened. Ask for their help finding the person who did it.

She'd do all the things she should have done before now.

She'd call Kit and tell him she was sorry for not taking him to her new flat yet.

Maybe she'd even . . . no. She wasn't doing that. Not even now.

But she'd do something. Move. Get up. Take action.

Just as soon as her ears stopped ringing, and her head stopped pounding.

Caro

Caro had to admit, that was quite some spectacle Milla and the team had put on. While it had started out feeling just a little high-school Halloween party, by the time the torches were lit and the drumbeat had vibrated through her, Caro had been properly swept away by the moment.

She always liked a bit of audience participation.

Rosalind, on the other hand, hadn't even pulled on her skeleton mask properly. Too good to play around with the hoi polloi, probably.

'At least there are proper lights down here,' she said, surveying the square as the crowds began to disperse. 'The torches and the smoke were playing havoc with my varifocals.'

Or maybe she'd just wanted to be able to see. Caro mentally took back all her thoughts about Rosalind feeling superior to the rest of them. Well, some of them, anyway.

Up on the wall surrounding the war memorial, Milla had a microphone in hand, and was announcing the highlight of the evening. 'And we are so lucky to have with us tonight, bestselling author Dexter Rush, to give us a twilight reading from his latest book!'

There was a roar of approval and excitement from the crowd.

'Where's Posy?' Caro glanced around the square, but there was no sign of the third Dahlia in the crowd. Most people had removed their masks by now and, anyway, Posy's slim build and blonde hair usually gave her away.

'I thought she was beside you,' Rosalind said.

Caro shook her head. 'Not after we came down from the bandstand. We got separated.'

Rosalind frowned. 'What's going on over there?'

The roar of the crowd had faded into a confused murmuring, and in the centre of the square, Milla was talking urgently with several other people still in their black cloaks.

'Um, Dexter? If you're here, please come and join us here in the square.' Milla scanned the crowds. 'A round of applause for Dexter Rush!'

The gathered fans dutifully clapped. But nobody joined Milla at the microphone.

Caro had a horrible feeling in her stomach. 'We need to find Posy.'

'Call her. Maybe the crowd got too much for her,' Rosalind suggested. 'She might have headed back to the hotel.'

'Maybe.' She narrowed her eyes as she looked around. No sign of Posy – or Dexter Rush, for that matter.

Caro pulled out her phone and called Posy. Really, modern technology did make so many things easier. Dahlia would be so jealous if she knew.

The phone rang in her hand, but there was no reply, and eventually the call rang out. 'No answer.'

'Try again,' Rosalind said, frowning. 'I thought I heard something.'

This time when she called, Rosalind drifted closer to the shops on one side of the square, and Caro followed. And then she heard it too.

The familiar, beloved strains of *The Dahlia Lively Mysteries* TV theme tune.

'Did you reprogram *all* our phones with that ringtone?' Rosalind asked, wearily.

'Of course.' Rosalind had not been pleased at that discovery, when Caro had called her while she was at Jack's after her last visit to her and Annie's house. 'Posy left her phone undefended at breakfast, so it was fair game.' Of course, Caro had also had to put the volume on, since Posy habitually left her phone on silent and didn't answer anyone who called anyway.

But she'd have answered now, wouldn't she? If only to stop Caro's theme tune playing.

Unless she couldn't get to her phone.

One look at Rosalind's worried face told her that the eldest Dahlia was just as concerned about Posy's whereabouts. Posy might be an adult, but she was still their responsibility, in some ways. Whether she liked it or not.

She was a Dahlia. That made her family.

'Keep calling,' Rosalind said. 'We'll follow the sound.'

The tune that had defined Caro's professional life sounded tinny and small in the vastness of the lamplit town square. People were still milling around, waiting to see if Dexter Rush would appear, but the crowd was definitely thinning, since it seemed like he'd wimped out of this one, too. Milla was on her phone, but nobody seemed to be answering there, either. Caro would have to ask Petra for the full story, later.

'Here!' Rosalind called out, and Caro hurried to her side.

There, in the tiled doorway of a small local pharmacy, sat Posy's bag, abandoned.

The ringtone was still playing from inside it. Caro hung up the call.

'She wouldn't have just left it here.' There was a numbness seeping through her. It was a feeling she recognised. One that meant she'd deal with the emotions later, for now she needed to focus on action. She just had to keep moving. 'She can't be far away.'

Rosalind nodded her agreement. 'I'll search clockwise around the square from here, you go anticlockwise.'

They both called as they searched, but Posy's name just echoed unanswered off the buildings surrounding the square. Caro shivered, despite the warm, August night air.

Nothing about this felt right.

She came to the alleyway they'd walked down the day before, and a shadow in the dimness, darker than the rest, caught her eye, then a flash of light, and Caro realised it was one of those bloody skeleton masks. She moved closer. 'Posy?'

Movement. 'Caro?'

Caro dropped to her knees and eased the mask away from her friend's head. It wasn't covering her face, she realised, just her hair. But she'd pressed her chin so low against her chest the skull had appeared like a face looking out at her.

Caro shuddered, and turned her head over her shoulder to yell, 'Rosalind! Over here.'

She smoothed Posy's wavy blonde hair away from her face, revealing scratches and grazes on her forehead and cheek. 'What happened? Are you okay?'

Posy nodded, then winced, the movement apparently more painful than she'd anticipated. 'I will be. It's just scratches, I think. Nothing broken. I just needed a moment. There was . . . I guess it was a mugger. Someone in one of these damn masks, I think. They shoved me up against the wall face first and snatched my bag from my shoulder. By the time I could turn around, I'd lost them in the crowd. And then my heart was pounding so hard I just sat down here . . .'

'You didn't see who it was? Man? Woman? Anything?' Caro pressed.

'They were all in black. That's all I saw.'

Well, that narrowed it down to a couple of hundred skeletons, then.

'Do you need the hospital?' If she'd lost consciousness she'd need checking out.

'No. Honestly, I'm more shaken up than anything else.'

'We found your bag.' Rosalind loomed over the two of them, dropping Posy's shoulder bag beside her. 'It was just a few doors up on the square. They must have grabbed what they wanted and dumped it.'

Posy dragged the bag into her lap, nodding as she pawed through the contents. 'That was lucky.'

But Caro frowned. Something wasn't right here.

'That's strange.' Posy's brow was furrowed too. 'My purse is still here. And my phone.'

'What kind of mugger doesn't take the phone and the money?' *That* was what had bothered her. No mugger in their right mind would leave the phone behind, but they'd only found the bag because they heard it ringing.

'Is there anything missing at all?' Rosalind crouched down beside Posy at last, as if to verify the lack of stolen objects.

'Just . . .' Posy stopped, and looked up at them, her eyes wide and white in the darkness. 'Just my notebook. The one with all my notes about the case.'

'Eleanor's file?' Caro asked urgently.

'No. I left that in the hotel room. It made my bag too heavy.'

'Let me look.' Rosalind began pulling things out of the bag, and Caro knelt down on the pavement to double check things.

A piece of loose paper fluttered out. A page from the notebook, perhaps? Caro grabbed it and began to unfold it. 'What's this? Is this part of it?'

'No!' Posy reached out to grab it back from her, but not before Caro had seen the signature on the bottom. She handed it over to Posy without a fight.

But not without comment. 'Your mother is writing to you now?'

Posy winced, although whether from pain from the mugging or because of the mention of her parents, Caro wasn't sure. 'She wrote. Once. I . . . saw them at Uncle Sol's funeral. She says she wants to reconcile.'

'And do you?' Yes, Caro knew this wasn't the place for this conversation. But if anything, a head injury made it more likely that Posy would answer. Sol's funeral had been *months* ago, and she hadn't mentioned anything since.

'Kit says it's just guilt, and her own mortality catching up with her.' Now Caro was really worried. Mentioning her mother *and* Kit in the same conversation was surely a sign of a head injury for Posy. 'That I don't have to speak to her if I don't want to.'

'You don't,' Caro said, baldly.

'And Kit's right,' Rosalind added. 'Guilt is a powerful motivation. But don't worry about that now. We need to get you back to the hotel.'

'We *need* to find my notebook.' Posy pushed against the pavement and, leaning against the wall, slowly got to her feet. 'I'm fine. But without my notes—'

Rosalind glanced at Caro and caught her gaze, and Caro knew instantly what her friend was thinking.

'This isn't the place for this conversation.' She reached down to take Posy's hand, helping her up. 'Come on. Let's get you back to the hotel with a nice cup of tea, and we'll patch up those scrapes you've got.'

'Caro's right,' Rosalind said – something Caro never got tired of hearing. 'We can try to figure out who did this and why tomorrow. Tonight you need to rest.'

They each kept an arm around Posy as they made their cautious way back up the hill towards The Red Fox. Across the way, Caro saw Petra, on the phone – probably calling her errant client. Likewise, Milla was halfway to the hotel, telling other volunteers to check the bars and pubs.

She stopped when she saw Posy's banged-up face. 'Oh my goodness! Is she okay?'

'I'm fine,' Posy answered for herself. 'Just got a bit crushed into a wall.'

'No sign of Dexter Rush?' Caro asked.

Frustration flitted across Milla's face. 'No. I'm just going to check with hotel reception, and get his room number. I can't believe he'd do this!'

She stalked on ahead, while Caro and Rosalind followed more slowly behind, supporting Posy between them.

They took the lift to the first floor, rather than the stairs. The corridor leading to the room Rosalind and Posy were sharing was fortunately empty.

'Nearly there,' Caro murmured encouragingly. 'Wait, is that your door?' Halfway down the corridor, one door stood wide open, but there was no sign of the occupant.

'No. Ours is on the other side.' Rosalind stopped walking. 'That's Iain's. The door doesn't shut well.'

'We should check,' Posy said, faintly. 'Someone could have broken into his room while we were all at the parade.'

'Or he could have forgotten to shut it properly because he started on the whisky early,' Caro pointed out.

Still, since it was directly opposite Rosalind and Posy's room, it made sense to glance in, and check everything was okay.

Except it wasn't okay. Not at all.

Chapter Thirteen

'You never forget the smell of death,' Dahlia said. 'And you never get used to it, either.'

Johnnie reached for the teapot. 'I'm not sure this is really appropriate conversation for afternoon tea.'

Dahlia Lively *in* Alibis and Afternoon Tea
***By* Lettice Davenport, 1950**

Caro

She knew something was wrong the moment she stepped into the doorway. The eerie silence told her what she'd find before her eyes did. Posy, leaning against the wall outside Iain's room, shot her a concerned look.

'What is it?' Rosalind said.

Caro stepped inside to let them see for themselves.

There, sprawled across the hotel bed, lay Iain Hardy, eyes wide but unseeing.

'Oh hell.'

'I was going to use stronger words,' Caro said. 'But yes. Oh hell.'

They all stared for a moment, the only sound the curtains flapping in the breeze from the open windows.

He was clearly dead, that much was obvious without even touching him. But what had killed him? Could it possibly be natural causes? And if not, who was responsible?

None of that was clear. If anything, everything was suddenly more *unclear.*

Scott Baker couldn't have done this, because Scott Baker is in jail.

Had Sarah been right all along? Was her brother really innocent? Or was this just a horrible coincidence?

'We need to call the police,' Rosalind said, as Caro crept closer to Iain's prone form. She recognised his face, even from their brief interactions. But why did he have to die?

'What did you know?' she whispered, still keeping a respectful distance from the body.

She might be growing more accustomed to death, but that didn't mean she liked it any more. How long had he been dead? When did bodies start to smell? Iain wasn't, yet. Did that mean he hadn't been dead long?

They'd have to ask Jack.

'Caro,' Rosalind said, more firmly. 'We need to call the police.'

'We do,' she replied. 'But we need to understand this, too.'

She looked up to find Posy hovering half in, half out of the room. Rosalind had her phone in her hand already, and was looking exasperated with Caro, as usual.

'You call,' Caro said. 'I'll just . . . take a look around here.'

'Don't touch *anything*.' Rosalind was already dialling.

'I'm not an amateur, you know,' Caro grumbled. Even though, if she thought about it, that's exactly what she was.

Well, so what? Dahlia had been an amateur too. Hadn't stopped her.

Caro pulled out her own phone, and opened the camera. She didn't need to touch anything to record the scene. Not just the body – although she took a photo of that too, for the record. But the room. Anything that stood out. Anything that told them something they didn't already know.

She might not recognise what any of it meant yet, but if they had the photographic record, maybe it would spark a connection they wouldn't have seen otherwise, when they went back over Posy's notes.

The notes she didn't have anymore. Damn. Well, that just made the photos more important, didn't it?

Caro turned away from the body, her stomach reaching the point where rebellion would become imminent. Rosalind had stepped outside the room to make the call, but from the way Posy's gaze followed Caro as she moved around the room, Caro suspected Rosalind had given her instructions to watch her before she left. Posy leaned against the doorframe, looking grey and tired, the bruise around the graze on her forehead starting to colour. She needed to rest.

Soon. When they were done here.

Unsettled, she moved to capture the whole of the hotel room in a video. There was a small dressing table that he'd clearly been using as a desk, as it still looked like he'd just stepped away to fetch another cup of coffee, not leave his work forever. He must have been writing while he was here. His laptop had put itself to sleep, and she didn't dare touch it to see if it might not be password protected.

The police would do all that. They'd get the cause of death, and any relevant information from the computer files. The Dahlias would just have to hope they could persuade someone to share that information with them, further down the line.

She kept her phone tightly gripped in her hands – partly so she could snap more close-up photos, but mostly to stop her accidentally touching anything she shouldn't. They needed to get out of there, she knew – to preserve the scene for the police. But she just knew there had to be something here, something they needed to see . . .

No earring or cufflink left on the floor by the body. No muddy footprint, or cigarette end.

She took a photo of the contents of the bin under the desk just in case, then glanced up at the door again to see Rosalind beckoning her out of the room. She'd need to be quick, now.

She turned to the desk itself.

There was a stack of paper beside the laptop, and an envelope on top – a very familiar-looking envelope. Iain's letter from Scott. Danny had delivered it, then. Had it been opened? She couldn't tell; it was placed with Iain's name facing up.

She wanted to touch it, but she knew Rosalind would freak. So she satisfied herself by leaning closer, trying to get a peek at the underside . . .

Which was when she noticed something else entirely.

The stack of pages under the envelope weren't just a manuscript print-out as she'd assumed. They were page proofs – typeset and ready for checking for last-minute typos and errors, before sending back to a publisher – just like her own had been before publication.

And the name at the top of the page was Dexter Rush.

Rosalind

Rosalind hung up with the emergency services, then called down to the hotel front desk too, so they could come and deal with the situation while they waited for the police. Then she fished Caro out of the room, and they waited in the hallway with the hotel manager when she arrived, assuring her that they hadn't disturbed anything, just called straight away.

But not disturbing things didn't mean they hadn't learned anything.

Iain was Dexter Rush. Well, at least they knew why he hadn't shown up for his reading, now.

Milla wasn't far behind the hotel manager, looking pale and horrified at this turn of events. Which was when the obvious occurred to Rosalind.

'You knew he was Dexter Rush,' she whispered, as the police made their way along the hallway to the room. 'You must have done.'

Milla winced. 'I knew. That's how I persuaded him to do a reading at the festival this year.'

'You blackmailed him?'

'No!' Her eyes bulged wide. 'I just . . . asked. And he agreed. But he's so protective of his secret identity, he never does events like this. So when he got here, I guess he got cold feet and pulled out of the awards ceremony. But he was still planning to do the reading tonight, as long as he could do it with the mask and the cape.'

'But he never showed up,' Rosalind finished. 'Because he was here. Dead.'

'Why didn't you come straight here when he didn't arrive?' Caro asked.

'Because I knew he'd been down at the parade already,' Milla explained. 'I figured he'd probably stopped for a drink and lost track of time.'

Rosalind frowned. 'You saw him at the parade?'

'We were all there,' Milla replied. 'It was . . . I didn't want to make a big deal about it, but with it being the fifth anniversary of Victoria's death, I thought it would be nice for us all to do the Skeleton Parade together. Iain, Hakim, Danny, Sarah, Raven and me.'

'You *saw* Iain?' Caro pressed. Milla nodded. 'Without his mask on?'

Her face fell. 'Oh. I . . . no. I just assumed. I saw the grey hair and his usual trainers and, well, who else could it have been?'

'I don't know,' Rosalind admitted. 'But I don't think it was Iain.'

Any one of them could have paid someone to stand in for him at the parade. If they didn't know he was Dexter Rush, they wouldn't even have worried about being found out when it came to the time for the reading.

Maybe that was what they needed to find out next – who knew Iain's secret.

Deaths in hotel rooms were, as Rosalind understood from the nervously talkative hotel manager, not uncommon. There were procedures to be followed.

'Probably another hotel suicide,' one of the police officers said, nonchalantly. 'Third here this last year and a half, isn't it?'

The hotel manager nodded, glumly. 'We're trying not to take it personally.'

'Still, no suicide note,' the officer went on, like he was weighing up his options. 'But no forced entry or sign of struggle either . . . Could have been a heart attack. He's the right sort of age.'

The hotel manager perked up at that. 'Obviously we'll close off this room for as long as you deem necessary . . .' She didn't add 'instead of the whole hotel,' but Rosalind was pretty sure that was what she meant.

If they thought it was murder, they'd all be kicked out of here in a heartbeat, and the whole festival would probably be shut down. There'd be crime tape and questions galore.

'It's an important weekend for the town,' the manager went on, wheedling slightly.

The officer still looked uncertain. 'Odds are it'll be suicide or heart attack,' he said. 'But if it turns out to be something else later . . .'

'But what if it doesn't?' the manager countered.

Rosalind decided they were better off staying out of this one.

In the end, they decided that since Iain's room was at the end of the corridor, just closing off the room itself would be sufficient, something the hotel manager looked very relieved about.

For now, they were free to go.

Posy was pale and exhausted, but still refused to go to hospital, claiming she felt fine.

'I didn't lose consciousness, not really. And my memory is fine – I know what day it is and where we are. Nothing is blurry, I don't feel nauseous, I just want to go to bed.'

Rosalind looked at Caro, who pulled a face, but eventually they gave in. Once they'd cleaned the scrapes and cuts she'd sustained from the brick wall, they put her to bed in the second bed in Caro's room, away from the police tape and guard. They kept a small lamp on and her phone charging at her side in case she needed them, then left her to rest.

'Where are we going?' Caro asked, as Rosalind marched back down the landing towards the sweeping staircase that led down to the ground floor.

'To the bar,' Rosalind replied. 'I don't know about you, but I need a drink.'

'Hell, yes,' Caro said, with feeling.

Outside on the lawn behind the hotel, the fairy lights that twirled around the sail tent covering the bar twinkled like stars. The management weren't keen to advertise the news of a death in the hotel, so things had been kept very quiet. Chances were, nobody here had even noticed the two police officers entering the building.

Every table was full, but Rosalind managed to snag a couple of stools placed around a barrel as two people departed, leaving Caro to go and fight her way through the scrum at the bar.

While she waited, Rosalind checked her phone and found a message from Jack – just a loving, supportive text hoping everything was going well. The sort that didn't ask any questions he didn't want the answers to.

It was too much to hope that it would never get back to Jack that she and her friends had stumbled upon *another* dead body. But Rosalind really couldn't face dealing with that revelation tonight. So instead she sent back a photo of Caro and Posy in their skull masks, and another of the torchlit parade as it left the bandstand. For a message, she simply said, *Having a great time with the girls.*

Which she was pretty sure he'd identify as a lie, but Jack was a gentleman, so he probably wouldn't call her on it.

Yet.

One day soon, they were going to have to have a conversation. Just like Posy was going to have to stop carrying around a letter and decide what to do about her mother.

But not tonight.

Caro returned with the drinks, finally, and took a long pull from her gin and tonic before turning to Rosalind and saying, 'Right. What the hell?'

Rosalind sighed. 'I don't know. But we need to figure it out.'

Iain was dead – by natural causes, his own hand or someone else's was still unclear.

Caro was flicking through the photos on her phone, the ones of the crime scene.

Rosalind pulled a face. 'Do you have to? Here?'

'Hang on. There was something I . . . There!'

'What is it?' Rosalind leaned closer. It seemed to be a photo of a portion of skirting board, and a bin. And something tucked behind it . . .

Caro used two fingers to zoom in on the image, and suddenly it became clear.

'A paper dahlia,' Rosalind breathed. 'Why didn't you say?'

'I didn't know!' Caro's eyes widened. 'I didn't really notice it when I took the photo – and if I had, I'd have just thought it was just a piece of paper that had fallen on the floor under the desk. Maybe the breeze from the open windows blew it there.'

'All the way from the bed?' Rosalind didn't think it was likely.

'Maybe it wasn't on the bed. Maybe it was on the desk – with the Dexter Rush manuscript.'

'Could be.'

If the police officers had seen it, they'd probably have shut down the whole hotel – and by extension, their investigation. She suspected that somebody was going to get into a lot of trouble somewhere down the line when someone did a proper search of the crime scene – and realised it *was* a crime scene.

They should tell them – except that would mean admitting that they'd spent rather more time searching the room than they should have done. And the room was sealed now – with an officer standing guard until the body was dealt with. They'd find it eventually, she was sure.

But that paper flower meant Iain's death was probably not natural causes, and definitely linked to Victoria's murder somehow.

And that wasn't even the only thing that had happened tonight. Posy had been attacked; they couldn't minimise that. The fact the only thing missing from her bag was her notebook suggested that it was also by someone connected to the case. The same person? Until they knew exactly when Iain had died, it was hard to say, but Rosalind suspected he'd been dead before the parade started, which meant it was possible. All of their suspects had been part of the skeleton parade, but with the masks hiding their faces it wouldn't have been too hard for one of them to slip away and grab Posy.

And now there was that damn flower. It had been bothering her from the start, the flower left beside Victoria's body. Why would Scott order them online, something so easily traced, if he planned to leave one by a murder victim?

But if someone else had seen them in his house and taken one to frame him . . . but who? And when? Scott said he'd only just opened the package when he saw the message from Victoria. So it was always possible that things had happened exactly as he'd said, and he'd had them with him and left one behind by accident.

Or he was just more of an idiot than anyone thought, so used to reading golden-age crime fiction that he'd forgotten about modern policing. That was always possible too.

And now they had another flower, and another dead body. Rosalind was sure the police would be tracking down where this one came from too – once they found it – but she suspected the killer would have done a better job of hiding their tracks than Scott had.

She'd leave that riddle to the professionals for now. They had enough to worry about here in Market Foxleigh.

'Do you think she'll be okay?' Rosalind glanced up towards the hotel windows, to where she vaguely knew Caro's room was, but there was no sign of a distraught Posy at the window, and her phone remained silent.

Caro wrapped her jacket tighter around her, even though the evening wasn't cold. 'She's probably sleeping.'

'Probably,' Rosalind agreed, but neither of them sounded very convinced.

She wondered if Caro was remembering the same thing she was, how Rosalind had tossed and turned for hours every night, after she was almost stabbed on set in Wales. Or how they'd all stayed in her room together at Aldermere, the night that Caro was attacked, not really sleeping at all.

Some things made sleep hard to find.

'Maybe we should have stayed with her,' she said.

But Caro shook her head. 'She needs space, too.'

'Yes, I suppose.' It just felt wrong. But she knew Posy wouldn't appreciate them fussing over her, either.

Caro let out a big sigh. 'Okay. We can't do anything about Iain's death until we know a bit more. But from a purely practical point of view, we need to try and recreate what was in Posy's notebook,' Caro said. She sounded all business, but Rosalind couldn't help but notice her hand shook a little as she reached for her drink again.

'At least she'd left Eleanor's file in the room, so we still have that.' Rosalind tapped a nail against the side of her glass. 'So what we've really lost is her notes from the conversations with Sarah, Danny, Milla, Hakim and Rachel.'

'Oh, hardly anything, then. That's fine.' Caro glowered at her from under dark brows. 'You know what the real problem is here?'

'That our memories are unreliable and we've got used to having Posy's notes to back us up?' Rosalind guessed.

'That too,' Caro admitted. 'But, no. The biggest problem is that we didn't clock anything explosive in those interviews when they happened, or in Posy's notes afterwards. But someone else obviously did, or why take it? Which means somewhere in them was something vital, and we missed it.'

'Probably something small, then,' Rosalind mused. 'A tiny detail that would only have any meaning at all in context, when we'd put the rest of the clues together.'

'Exactly. And the chances of any of us remembering that tiny detail that didn't seem important?'

'Pretty low, I'd imagine.' Rosalind shifted on her stool, wishing it was a proper chair in a proper pub, not some wooden thing without a back perched on uneven grass. Her back was already aching.

'It's just like in . . . well, any number of Dahlia Lively mysteries, really,' Caro said. 'That one clue that only makes sense later, that Dahlia or Johnnie hung on to just in case. And we've lost it.'

Across the bar, a large group cleared and suddenly Rosalind could see to the table beyond, where Hakim sat with Raven and Danny, all three of them still oblivious, for now, to the events of the night.

Maybe they hadn't lost that clue at all. In fact, it was possible that the culprit had actually opened themselves up to more risk by attacking Posy – and perhaps by killing Iain.

'I don't like admitting that I'm wrong,' Caro said, very slowly. 'Or even accepting there might be a possibility of it.'

'Really? I never would have noticed,' Rosalind deadpanned.

Caro ignored her. 'But that wasn't the only reason I didn't want to take this case.'

She wasn't joking now, Rosalind realised. She stilled, and listened.

'After the trial, even when Scott was in prison, people still wanted to talk about it. Everywhere we went they'd bring it up. And Annie . . . she hated it. Hated the idea that he'd been watching us, lingering outside our home without us knowing. It really freaked her out.'

'I can understand that,' Rosalind murmured.

'We hadn't been married more than a year or so then,' Caro went on. 'And I worried . . . I was scared she'd leave me. That this life would be too much for her. Back then, I was thinking about fame and celebrity. But now . . . the choices I've made, to get involved in murder cases and investigations, to open cans of worms that maybe should stay closed . . . I can't help wondering if I've been fair to her, doing that.'

Only Caro would have these thoughts two full years after starting on the path. Rosalind kept the thought to herself, though.

'Is that why you told Annie not to come this weekend?' she asked instead.

Caro nodded. 'I just didn't want her to have any reminders of that time. Scott's letter . . . maybe that will help, I don't know. I just don't want her to worry anymore. And now, with Iain . . .' She trailed off, her expression unhappy.

She'd been unfair to Caro, Rosalind admitted to herself. Thinking she just didn't want to admit that she could have made a mistake – that her testimony could have sent an innocent man to jail.

But now . . . they had clear signs that she really might have done.

'What do you want to do now?' she asked, and Caro looked up in confusion. 'The weekend is almost over. You gave us until the end of the festival. Are you still sticking to that, or do you want to continue?'

Caro glanced up towards the hotel windows, the same way Rosalind had done a few moments earlier. 'I don't think that answer just depends on me anymore, do you?'

'No, I suppose not.' But Rosalind knew Posy. If anything, she was likely to wake more determined to solve this than ever before.

She'd really liked that notebook.

'I think we need to keep going, though.' Caro's words were soft, but audible. 'There's something here, and . . . you know me. I'm not good at not picking at scabs, or letting sleeping dogs lie, or whatever other cliché you want to throw at it.'

Rosalind smiled. No, she wasn't. But that was part of what made Caro a good detective – and a good friend. She stuck at things, sometimes long past the point where other people might have given up.

'So we keep investigating,' Rosalind said. 'In that case, what's our first move?'

'Going over everything we know so far, and putting it together to figure out what we missed.' Caro frowned. 'No, actually, that's not right. The first thing we need to do is—'

'Buy Posy a new notebook?' Rosalind guessed.

Caro nodded. 'Exactly.'

Posy

The Red Fox was sombre and quiet the following morning. News had clearly got out about Iain's death while Posy slept in, although she hadn't heard anyone mentioning the name Dexter Rush yet. As far as she could tell, people seemed to be assuming that it was a very sad case of death by suicide.

She wondered if the police report would tell them any different. Or if the police had even found that paper flower Caro had told her about excitedly the moment she woke up that morning.

By the time Posy was packed to go back to London, Rosalind and Caro were already waiting for her in the lobby, having claimed they had an errand to run before they left.

'Looks like our suspects have scattered to the winds,' Caro said, as Rosalind checked them out. 'I saw Milla overseeing the marquee crew, but none of the others are anywhere to be found this morning.'

'Not so surprising, I suppose,' Posy said. 'They all did the same after Victoria's death too, remember?' If not quite so fast.

Rosalind turned back to them, tucking her purse into her handbag. 'There you are. We've got something for you.' She pulled out a tissue-paper-wrapped object from a shopping bag and passed it to Posy, who opened it gingerly.

Inside was the most beautiful notebook Posy had ever seen. The cover was decorated with tiny snowdrops and butterflies and swirls of gold leaf, and the edges of the pages were sprayed with a marbling effect. Just looking at it gave her a pang in her chest for the plain black notebook she'd lost.

'It's beautiful,' Posy said. 'You really shouldn't have.'

Rosalind beamed, apparently not realising that Posy really, really meant that she shouldn't have.

It wasn't that it wasn't a beautiful notebook, it was just that she was used to her scruffy old plain black one, with the cardboard cover and a spiral binding that got in the way when she tried to write. The one filled with notes from the last two investigations, as well as her observations on this case.

This new notebook was just too pretty to use. Even if she knew what it was she wanted to write down.

'I know it won't replace the one you lost,' Rosalind said. 'But I hope it'll give you a fresh start for this investigation.'

'Because God knows we need to go right back to the start and go over everything we've learned so far.' Caro shook her car keys, making them rattle. 'So come on. We'd better get moving.'

'What about the flower?' Posy asked. 'Are you going to tell the police?'

Caro grinned. 'I just happened to bump into our friendly local police officer outside Iain's room this morning. I mentioned what a very famous and high-profile man he was . . . and how they'll want to be sure they've done everything by the book on this one because the papers are bound to be interested. If he hasn't found that flower yet, I don't think it'll be long.'

The drive back to London felt like a replay of the drive to Market Foxleigh. Rosalind had even picked up more sherbet lemons when she'd gone out to whatever store she'd found Posy's new notebook in.

Once again, they went through everything they knew, and once again they found no answers.

Posy tried to take notes, but she couldn't bring herself to write on the pristine pages of her new notebook, so instead she scrawled them in the margins of the papers in Eleanor's file. Thank goodness that hadn't been in her bag the night before, or she was sure it would have been stolen too.

Rosalind and Caro had shared their thoughts on why the notebook had been taken. The idea that there was something hidden in those notes that she'd missed – a clue, one that might actually explain everything – worried her.

She'd missed something, but what?

If she couldn't find a way to recreate the notes they might never know.

'So,' Caro said, as they ran out of new information. 'Does Iain's death mean that Victoria's killer must still be at large?'

'Or that someone wants us to *think* they are,' Posy added.

'Or even that someone has taken advantage of the doubt Eleanor's podcast has sown to camouflage a murder committed for another reason by linking it to Victoria's death.' Rosalind picked out another sherbet lemon from the bag.

'That damn flower.' Caro swerved from one lane to the next without indicating. 'If it wasn't for that, there wouldn't be a link.'

'Except that Iain was already one of *our* suspects.' Posy tapped her pen against the file. 'I suppose that the flower could be taken as a confession, even, if it turns out to be suicide? Remorse for killing Victoria?' It was a stretch, but not impossible. If only he'd left a note . . .

'So we're down to six suspects, anyway,' Rosalind said, with a sigh. 'That's one way of narrowing them down, I suppose, but I'd rather we could avoid losing any more that way.'

'Five,' Posy said, suddenly. 'We're down to five suspects.'

Caro frowned. 'How so? Oh! Because Scott *couldn't* have killed Iain because he's locked up.'

'Exactly. Although, I suppose he could have arranged for someone to do it for him?' Posy's pen hesitated above her list of suspects, before just putting a dot beside Scott's name instead of crossing him out.

'And even if he didn't kill Iain, that doesn't mean he didn't kill Victoria,' Rosalind added. 'See earlier observation about camouflage.'

Posy groaned. They were going around in circles.

'We need to know the details of Iain's death,' Caro said, as the countryside sped by even faster outside the car.

'We *saw* the details.' Posy swallowed as she remembered that room. 'What more do you want to know?'

Caro tapped the steering wheel with each item. 'Time of death. *Method* of death, come to that – there was no blood, was there? No blunt instrument to the back of the head like Victoria. Evidence found at the scene – fingerprints, DNA evidence, fibres, hair, all that sort of thing.'

'Things the police are unlikely to be willing to share with us,' Rosalind pointed out. 'I can ask Jack, I suppose, but I don't know how much he'll be able to find out.'

'Perhaps not.' In the rear-view mirror, Posy saw Caro's eyes widen, and her smile grow bright. 'But Iain didn't have any family listed in Eleanor's file, and nobody mentioned calling any last night, either. I don't think he had any family left. The only person they called was—'

'His agent,' Posy said, excitedly. 'Petra! Do you think you can get *her* to tell us what's going on?'

'I can try.' Caro's gaze returned to the road. 'I'm doing that morning cooking show on the BBC this week – that's high-profile, so she'll want to be there. I'll see what I can find out.'

Just telling Petra that they knew Iain Hardy was Dexter Rush might shake something loose. It was a start, at least.

Rosalind hummed her agreement. 'And in the meantime, I'll head to Wales and work on Jack. Then Posy and I will track down all the other suspects. We're going to need to speak to all of them again.'

'That makes sense.' Except it would also just give them more information she didn't know how to process.

Posy settled back into the leather seats of Caro's sports car, and thought about everything she'd seen in Market Foxleigh. And slowly, an idea started to form in her mind.

Chapter Fourteen

It was a case that shook the quiet Cotswolds town of Market Foxleigh. But while many thought it was dead and buried, we now know the murder of Victoria Denby was only just the beginning . . .

Trailer for* Writing A Wrong *Podcast
***By* Eleanor Grey**

Posy

Posy's flat was much as she'd left it.

Empty.

There was a postcard lying on the mat, though, as she opened the door. She crouched down to pick it up, smiling at the image of Budapest on the front before flipping it over.

If you squint, you can almost *see where I'm staying, in the two hours a day we're not filming. Hope the sleuthing is going well, and Caro and Rosalind are behaving themselves. Kit x*

A postcard with an actual foreign stamp on it was old school, Posy decided, ignoring the niggle that said it was also a good way to avoid a conversation, unlike an email or a text message. Or, God forbid, a phone call.

Maybe that was why her mother had written, rather than calling, too.

Posy pushed the thought away. She had more important things to deal with than her love life or her estranged parents. So, once she'd propped the postcard from Kit up on the kitchen counter, resting against the tiles, she got to work.

The WHSmith at the service station they'd pulled in at on the M4 had furnished her with most of what she needed – Post-it notes, index cards, drawing pins, marker pens, and some embroidery threads that came as part of a friendship bracelet-making set. Luckily, Caro and Rosalind had been too busy trying to keep a low profile to notice what she was buying.

The mini-printer she'd ordered online wouldn't be there until tomorrow, but she could get started at least.

She eyed the large, blank wall between the kitchen and living room that she'd always planned to hang some artwork on, but had never got around to.

Just as well, really. It served her purposes perfectly.

She took a moment to picture the murder board Roger the floating bookseller had set up on his houseboat bookshop. Then she picked up the first Post-it note and wrote Victoria Denby's name on it, before sticking it in the middle of the wall.

She smiled. This was going to work.

Two days later, she had all the information from the file, her notes in the car and her memory stuck up in one place on the wall of her flat. The mini-printer had allowed her to add photos from their time in Market Foxleigh, too – as well as copies of some of the photos in Eleanor's file that she didn't want to put up full size.

The red embroidery thread criss-crossed the wall, linking people and thoughts and possible clues and definite facts. But none of it made any sense, yet. She couldn't see the patterns she needed to make sense of it all.

Which meant they needed more information.

Rosalind had been right about them tracking down the rest of the suspects again. But Rosalind was in Wales, having a few days with Jack – and leaning ever so politely on him to see if he could get any information from the local police about Iain Hardy's death.

And Caro had been right about them not knowing the cause of death. Would it even be ruled as murder? Would they have jumped to that conclusion if it wasn't for the paper flower Caro spotted later?

The thought she'd had in the car resurfaced. Could Iain have killed Victoria, then killed himself, leaving the flower as his suicide note when he realised that the reopening of the investigation for the podcast might catch him?

That would be putting an awful lot of faith in the power of a podcast, and the investigative skills of the three Dahlias. It wasn't like they'd been getting anywhere close. Still, not impossible.

She reached for her phone to text the others for their thoughts, but her phone remained silent, her message unread. Phone signal was notoriously awful at Jack's house, and Caro would be preparing for her appearance on *Food Matters* that morning. She'd have to wait to hear from either of them.

But one of their suspects was right here in London . . . Posy pulled a business card from her phone case, then typed in the web address written on it.

If they needed more information, then she was going to go out and find it. Getting out of her empty flat was just an added bonus.

Caro

Food Matters was, according to her publicist, the papers, and at least three other authors she'd spoken to in the green room at the Market Foxleigh festival, *the* show to get. Which was why Caro knew Petra would be there to watch.

She wasn't the only one, of course. Jemima, her publicist from the publisher was there too, running interference between Caro and the show, and making sure she was comfortable with what she was there to do.

Basically, sell the book. That was the main thing. Anything else was a bonus.

Annie was there, too. She *loved Food Matters,* watched it religiously, the same way a more religious woman might watch *Songs of Praise* on a Sunday night. Or, now she thought about it, actually go to church. Regardless, as soon as she was booked for the show, Caro had begged a ticket for Annie too. She'd be out in the audience watching, which just meant Caro had even more incentive than usual not to screw up.

As if the millions of people watching at home weren't enough.

It had been a while since Caro had done the daily shows and last time she'd done them as Dahlia, really, not herself. So she wasn't too proud to admit that she was a little nervous.

Well, still too proud to admit it to Petra or the publicist, or anyone connected with the show, but she'd admitted it to herself. And to Annie, who had just kissed her sweetly and told her to knock their socks off.

No pressure, then.

It didn't help that a new trailer for Eleanor's podcast, *Writing a Wrong,* had dropped the night before, without any prior warning, following the investigation into Victoria's murder, and hinting at a fresh case to study as well as the cold one. She didn't actually use Iain's name, but anyone who'd read the papers in the past few days would know what she was talking about. There'd been no mention of the paper flower, but Caro suspected that was because the police were keeping that detail back to filter out attention-seeking confessors as much as to deter copycats.

Eleanor had even used an audio clip from the video Scott had made them, asking for their help, ensuring that if they pulled out now everyone would know they'd abandoned a probably innocent man in his time of need.

Because as the papers had already been pointing out, the death of another member of that writing group on the fifth anniversary of Victoria's murder, just as a fresh investigation into the case had been launched . . . well, it was a hell of a coincidence.

It made Caro a little nervous about what sort of questions she was likely to get that morning.

But that wasn't the worst part.

Food Matters was, ostensibly, just a nice, gentle, morning chat show, with guests talking about their favourite food memories – and whatever project they were there to promote, of course – while the host chef cooked them breakfast. But this time there was one other, rather more risky element involved.

She had to cook.

She, Caro Hooper, more famous for setting ties ablaze than actually using fire to cook anything, was expected to make – and flip – a pancake. It was a sort of test they set all celebrities, laughing merrily when they failed.

Except Caro hated failing. Especially when her ex-husband had been on the show four months ago and had absolutely nailed it.

She'd been practising in the kitchen at home when she could, but she still only had a fifty-fifty record.

Probably she should be more nervous about the interview than the pancakes, but there you had it.

As she sat in the make-up chair, Petra gave her what Caro expected was meant to be a calming pep talk.

'All you need to do is just not screw up,' she said, cheerily. 'How hard can that be? Just don't say anything stupid and flip the bloody pancake right. Easy.'

'Easy,' Caro echoed. She looked up and met Petra's gaze in the mirror, as the make-up artist swept a brush across her cheeks. 'I'm surprised you're here, you know. Given everything.'

Petra looked away. '*Food Matters* matters. Of course I'm here to support your career.'

'Of course. But given *everything* . . .'

She left it hanging there. Eventually, Petra huffed, and gave the make-up artist a hard look. 'Are you done?'

'Nearly!' Then she caught Petra's eye. She gave one last, perfunctory sweep of the brush, and stepped back. 'All done! And I just need to go and check . . . something.'

'If I have to go on national television with uneven blusher, I'm going to blame you,' Caro said, as she watched the make-up artist hurriedly depart.

'You look fine.' Petra perched on the edge of the counter. In the mirror behind her, Caro could see that the back of Petra's hair was uneven, not perfectly straight in a sharp bob as she usually wore it, but with one section starting to show its natural wave. She supposed it had been an early start; it was understandable that Petra might have missed a spot. But it *was* unlike her to be even slightly ungroomed.

Maybe she was more upset by Iain's death than she'd thought.

'Do you want to talk about it?' Caro asked.

Petra's eyebrows leaped in surprise, not a stray hair out of place there. 'I assume you're talking about Iain?'

'You mean Dexter Rush.' Okay, so Caro might still be a little bit annoyed that Petra hadn't shared that piece of information with them earlier.

Petra sighed. 'As I assume you know by now, they're one and the same. And I can't imagine the press will be far behind you in figuring it out. Pen names aren't uncommon, you realise. Not every author has a celebrity background to cash in on, and not all ordinary writers want their real name out there in public unnecessarily.'

'Perhaps not,' Caro allowed. 'But Dexter – I mean, Iain – took it a bit further than that, didn't he? He didn't appear at any festivals, or do any events, there wasn't even a photo of him on his website.' They'd checked.

Posy had spent part of the car journey home from Market Foxleigh looking for links between Iain Hardy and Dexter Rush on her phone, and coming up with nothing. The only author photo on Dexter's official website and social media platforms showed the silhouette of a man in a hat, standing on a balcony with a city skyline behind. Everything else was photos of books, or reviews.

Iain Hardy's social media was far more open and personal, even as it also promoted the few books he'd released under his own name – all with smaller, digital-first publishers than his Dexter Rush stuff.

There was simply nothing connecting the two personas. Except for Petra.

'He was a very private person.' Petra looked down at her hands, rather than meet Caro's gaze.

'He let someone in though, didn't he?' Caro said, softly, thinking of that open hotel-room door. 'And they killed him.'

Petra jerked her head up at that. 'I know you found the body. The police . . . what were you even doing there?'

'His room was opposite Rosalind and Posy's. Pure coincidence.'

'Funny how often that seems to work out for you,' Petra said, sharply.

She was getting to her. Good. 'Were you close, the two of you?'

'He was my first client.' Suddenly, the edge in her voice was gone, the sharp, quick wit missing entirely. She spoke now as a person, rather than an agent, possibly for the first time since Caro had met her.

'As Iain? Or as Dexter?'

Petra smiled softly. 'Dexter came later. He had the better name, bigger books, wider appeal – and he sold well, of course. But it was Iain's stories I wanted first. They were what I signed him for.'

Caro considered her agent as she sat there, lost in memories. This was a side of Petra she'd never seen before – and she didn't for a moment think that she'd be so upset if it was *Caro* who had died. There was something deeper here.

'The papers said he didn't have any family. Is that right?' Petra nodded. 'So who gets his . . . his legacy, I suppose? The rights to his books? The royalties . . .'

Petra looked surprised at the question. 'Well, I don't know the particulars of his will yet, but last time I spoke to him about it . . . he'd left a lot of different legacies to charities, mostly literacy ones, but some local ones too, and a few health ones that had a personal meaning for him. And, well. The rest . . . I was his oldest and closest friend, as well as his agent, you see.'

Money. Cold hard cash was always the most solid motive, in Caro's view, and it looked like Petra could inherit a lot of it, now.

Especially since in death Dexter Rush stood to become even more famous – and lucrative – than in life.

Well. That changed things, didn't it?

Posy

Posy exited Green Park tube station, pulled her baseball cap a little lower over her eyes, and joined a group gathering around a young woman standing on a podium. A man with a branded hi-vis jacket approached and she held out her phone so he could scan her ticket.

She'd signed up under a fake name, hoping no one noticed her real name on the credit card section, and dressed as inconspicuously as possible, in jeans and a sloppy T-shirt, as well as the cap covering her hair, apart from the short ponytail at the back. There was no make-up on her face, no jewellery besides her watch, and nothing about her at all that screamed 'movie star'. If she was lucky, nobody would even notice she was here at all – until she wanted them to.

Besides, who would expect the star of the latest Dahlia Lively film to be taking a Dahlia Lively Walking Tour, anyway?

'Right! If we're all ready?' At the front, Raven Cassidy looked down at the assistant with the scanner, who nodded. 'Great! Welcome, Dahlia fans all, to London's *only* walking tour dedicated to Lettice Davenport's finest creation, the Lady Detective herself, Dahlia Lively!'

A whoop went up from the small crowd at that. The three women in front of her – sisters, if Posy had to guess – were all American, and *very* excited to tell everyone how much they just *adored* Dahlia. Two of them wore caps just like Posy's, so she stuck close, hoping she might blend in.

'We start our tour here at Green Park, not very far from Buckingham Palace, where Dahlia famously solved a case involving a forged painting in one of Lettice's short-story collections.' Raven hopped down from the box she stood on, and her assistant quickly whisked it away, ready for the next tour guide, it seemed. Posy wondered how many different tours the company did, and whether Raven was the only one doing Lettice Davenport-themed ones.

'But our first real stop is just across the road and down Piccadilly a little way. Follow me!'

She held a vintage sunshade up in the air as she walked, to make it easier for them all to stay together. As they walked, she chatted with those guests nearest to her. Posy stayed back, though. If anyone was going to recognise her out of costume, it would be Raven, so she kept her head dipped whenever their guide glanced back.

They stopped first outside the Ritz. 'And who doesn't recall the time Dahlia solved the case of the Duchess's stolen rubies, and still had time for afternoon tea?'

Posy didn't. She had a feeling that was one of the many Lettice Davenport books she hadn't got to yet. But everyone else on the tour nodded and chattered about the case. These, Posy surmised, were real fans.

Their route took them past the Waterstones on Piccadilly. 'The biggest bookshop in Europe, you know! And it still has its original 1930s hand-rail, which is the perfect height for people of more limited stature, like myself.' Raven smiled self-deprecatingly, as the line got a laugh.

'And do they sell *your* books there? I read about them in your bio on the website.' The young man, who'd been at the front of the group the whole way so far, flushed a little pink as he realised how much he'd given away about his research for the trip. But these were real fans, and no one seemed to care.

Raven even seemed a little pleased, probably to have an organic excuse to plug her books. 'For those of you who *don't* read the tour guide bios on websites, I write murder mysteries myself – about Lettice Davenport in her younger years, solving crimes around London and the Home Counties.'

An impressed hum went up from the crowd at that.

'But to answer your question, sadly Waterstones does not stock my books. But if you want to know how to get hold of them, just grab me at the end and I'll give you a card. Now, moving on!'

There were a few more Dahlia facts on their path up to Leicester Square, but Posy mostly tuned them out. Raven was still self-publishing her books, something Victoria had mocked and looked down on her for. She couldn't be making a full-time living from it, if she was also employed as a tour guide, but according to Caro few writers *could* survive solely on their writing income. How would Raven have felt if she'd learned that another of their group had actually made millions as mainstream author Dexter Rush?

It was a stretch as a motive for murder, but Posy knew people had killed for less.

Leicester Square was bustling as ever, even on a Sunday morning. *The Lady Detective* was showing at the Odeon, of course, and Posy paused for a moment outside the cinema, remembering a different view. One with a red carpet and fancy gowns and flashing lights.

The night when this had all started.

Raven had stopped, too. 'As I'm sure you all know, the new movie version of *The Lady Detective* had its world premiere here just a few weeks ago, and all the stars were in town.'

'Did you go?' someone asked from the crowd.

Raven shook her head with a sad smile. 'I was here in the crowd that night, but I didn't get to actually watch the movie. I did get some great photos of the stars, though!'

In the crowd? Had she seen Sarah, Milla and Eleanor that night? Had she even known about the podcast before the festival? Posy added them to her list of mental questions to ask once she got Raven alone.

Raven moved on to talk about the piano bar that used to be on a side street off the square, and Posy reflected that she hadn't mentioned meeting the actual star of the movie – her – just the week before. Was she just trying to avoid too many questions?

'Have you seen the movie yet?' one of the Americans in front of her asked her companions.

They all shook their heads. 'But I've heard it's great,' one added. Posy dipped her head to hide her smile.

But another of the women scoffed. 'Only if you don't know anything about Dahlia Lively, I heard.'

Posy stopped eavesdropping, and paid attention to their guide, instead.

'And can anyone remember in which book it was that Dahlia took Johnnie to that piano bar for a nightcap?' Raven asked.

Various titles were shouted out in response, but Raven chose to only hear the correct one.

'That's right! It was *Midnight in London,* from 1962.'

They continued up towards Covent Garden, past the statue of Lettice Davenport by Seven Dials, which many of their group posed for photos with. Once they reached Covent Garden market, Raven paused in an area between the many street entertainers and talked a little more about Lettice Davenport's connection to London – moving there in her late teens and finding a writing community where she belonged, the rumoured affair with her first editor in the city, before moving away again during the war, back to Aldermere, all the way up to seeing her plays performed in the theatres and even the premiere of the first of the Dahlia Lively movies, starring Rosalind, in the 1980s.

'Even though many of her more famous mysteries were set in large country houses, often based on her own home of Aldermere, or in English villages of the traditional sort, a surprising number of the short stories, and quite a few full-length novels, were set in London. Like *Why The Lady Sings,* which was set right here at the Royal Opera House in Covent Garden.' Raven pointed towards the entrance – an unobtrusive door from the plaza – and let people wander over to explore for a few moments, before they moved on.

Their next stop was Bloomsbury Square, passing the blue plaque that marked the house where Lettice had lived briefly. The square itself was bursting with green life, with plenty of locals and tourists enjoying the sunshine, or the shade under the trees.

Posy thought about joining them. About abandoning the tour and just enjoying the sunshine for a while and forgetting all about murder.

But two people were dead, and she'd found one of them. How could she walk away, when the memory of Iain Hardy's blank, dead face haunted her whenever she closed her eyes.

She had to talk to Raven and find out what she knew.

'Bloomsbury Square is, of course, the spot where Johnnie proposed to Dahlia, also in *Midnight in London* – sorry, spoilers!' Raven added when a gasp went up from some members of the group. 'But there's a reason that one's a fan favourite. Close your ears if you haven't read this far into the series yet! Dahlia turned him down on that occasion, telling him that good detectives never marry. But we all know how that turned out, don't we!' A knowing chuckle ran through the group.

Posy decided she really had better get on with reading the rest of the books, if she ever wanted to know whether Dahlia married

Johnnie or not. Otherwise she'd have to ask Caro, and she wasn't that desperate.

She could google it, she supposed, but that felt like cheating when it came to Dahlia.

And even though her relationship with Kit was nothing like Dahlia and Johnnie's, not really, she couldn't help but wonder if the Lady Detective might have some dating advice for her, hidden in the pages.

They left Bloomsbury Square by the far exit and turned left onto the street that led them to the British Museum. They stopped before the crowded entrance, so Raven could tell them all about the *Mystery of the Missing Mummy* short story, and how the museum also featured in the investigation for another full-length mystery Posy didn't catch the name of.

She finished by asking them all to complete the short survey that would be emailed to them, and the group gave her resounding applause – along with quite a few tips, Posy noticed. She waited for the last few members of the group – several of whom had stopped to ask Raven for the details of her books – to disperse, then approached Raven directly, as she tucked her tips into her bag.

Raven looked up, did an almost imperceptible double take, then sighed.

'I wondered if you were going to come,' she said.

Posy gave her a tight smile. 'Come on. Let's go inside and talk.'

Chapter Fifteen

Lettice Davenport, author and sometime amateur detective, stepped out of the tube at Green Park into a glorious London summer day. The perfect day, in fact, to solve a murder.

Lettice Davenport *in* The Green Park Murders
***By* Raven Cassidy**

Rosalind

The view over the valley from the window in Jack's breakfast room really was extraordinary, and even after many visits, Rosalind never failed to be charmed by the way the sun hit the river as it raced through Llangollen.

When she'd first envisioned his cottage in the hills, she'd imagined something rather dark and probably a little damp, nestled between mountains and caught in perpetual cloud. Instead, she'd been surprised to discover on her first visit, Jack's cottage was a bright, white building on the edge of the hill looking down on the town, with incredible views over the mountains, and a large, glass-walled breakfast room to enjoy them from. Even the rest of the cottage was decorated in a cheerfully modern, light and airy style. The bedroom, where they'd spent the largest proportion of her early visits together, had a particularly lovely – and fortunately private – view out over a stream that skipped along the edge of the property.

She liked it, and him, rather a lot more than she'd ever expected she might. It felt like an escape from reality. Something she sorely needed just at the moment.

Rosalind sipped at her coffee as she looked out over the valley. Not very far away, she could see the ruins of a Welsh castle on the peak of a hill, looking dramatic in the sunshine. Dinas Bran, it was called, apparently. Jack kept promising – or threatening – to take her for a walk up there one day, but somehow whenever she visited they never seemed to make it past the fabulous Corn Mill pub-cum-restaurant that sat right on the edge of the racing river.

In the corner of the breakfast room, the small telly Jack kept in there to watch the news channel was tuned to a different station than normal, ready for Caro's big turn on *Food Matters*. Behind her, she could hear Jack puttering about the kitchen, preparing some feast or another for breakfast. If she hadn't had to get up for Caro's show, she knew he would have brought it to her in bed.

She should probably feel guilty for not being in London, not forging on with the investigation. But it was hard to feel anything except contentment when she was there.

Besides, this mattered too. Not just rest and recuperation, but being here with Jack. The last couple of years had taught her that much.

Jack appeared with two plates loaded with toasted English muffins, smoked salmon and poached eggs, all drowning in hollandaise sauce. He placed them on the table to her grateful thanks, then disappeared again only to return with fresh coffee.

Really, this definitely mattered too.

He nodded towards the television. 'Not on yet?'

Rosalind, still chewing her first mouthful, shook her head before swallowing. 'After the break.'

'So, you've got a little time to tell me what you want to do today.' Jack cut into his own muffin and egg, the yolk oozing perfectly golden onto his plate. 'Ready to climb Dinas Bran at last?'

'Drat, I forgot my walking boots. Again.' She flashed him a smile, and he rolled his eyes.

'Okay, so what *do* you want to do before we inevitably end up at the Corn Mill for dinner?' Jack asked.

'Well, watch Caro first, obviously.'

'Obviously.'

'And then . . . I was hoping to wander back past that shop with the cushions, you know the one. I think they'd be perfect for Posy's flat.' Along with one of those glorious cashmere throws from that other interiors shop she'd spotted. And maybe some mugs.

'Just as well you brought the car, if you're planning on furnishing Posy's flat this trip,' Jack said, mildly, over the rim of his coffee cup.

'Honestly, Jack, you should see it.' The flat just didn't look like Posy, that was the problem. Their Posy was full of life and humour, sparking with intelligence and insight.

Her flat was just . . . blank. Empty, even.

And not in an up-and-coming designer way. In an . . . unsettled way.

There was no art on the blank white walls. No quirky, personal touches in the glossy white kitchen. No rugs on the hardwood floor, no cushions on the solitary, charcoal grey sofa. No photos of her and Kit, or her and anyone, in nice frames. No flowers on the coffee table, no lamps, no . . . personality.

Rosalind felt a strong pull to do something about that. 'Anyway, I thought a spot of shopping, then I can come back and pack before dinner.'

It only took the space between one breath and the next for the air in the room to change, for Rosalind to feel the tension seeping in.

'You're heading back to London tomorrow?' Jack's voice was still even and calm, but just a fraction cooler than it had been.

Rosalind reached for her coffee. 'That was the plan.' She'd told him as much when she'd called to invite herself up for a few days. 'I need to get back to the investigation.'

And there it was; the frown line between Jack's eyebrows was back, the darkness in his eyes.

Time to have that conversation they'd been dancing around ever since she arrived. Longer, really.

'You want to say something.' Rosalind sipped at her coffee, then placed the cup back on its saucer. 'You might as well say it now, before Caro's spot comes on.'

They could pause it, she supposed. But she had never really liked the idea of having to play catch-up like that. If something was happening, she wanted to see it happen now.

Jack sighed heavily as he put his cup down too. Hands folded, he leaned against the table towards her, breakfast forgotten. 'Another person is dead, Rosalind. Isn't that enough to tell you it's time to stop meddling? To let the police do their job and deal with this properly?'

Her breath caught in her chest. 'I know you're not saying that Iain's death was our fault.'

'No, no. Of course not.' But he didn't meet her eyes. 'I just don't think your involvement is making anything better.'

Is he right? It wasn't as if Rosalind hadn't asked herself the same question.

But when she did, she couldn't help but remember the other cases they'd solved. Remember what might have happened if they hadn't been there. How many more people might have died.

They weren't professionals. They didn't have access to all the forensics and the research the police did.

But they knew people. They saw links where others might not. They ferreted out secrets and made sense of seemingly unconnected events.

'You understand that we were the ones who actually *found* Iain's body, right?'

Jack sighed. 'I *do* understand that. And I know that makes you feel responsible, somehow. But you're *not,* Rosalind.'

She appreciated that he tried to reason with her, rather than make her feel guilty. She was done with that feeling. She'd felt it all through her marriage, and long after – and that was on her, because she had had plenty to feel guilty about.

Now, she didn't. And she wasn't going to spend the rest of her life feeling guilty for doing something that was *right.*

'Do you really think any of us could rest, knowing we didn't at least *try* to find out why and how he died?' She held his gaze across the table, until he swore under his breath and looked away.

'No,' he admitted. 'Which is why I pulled in some favours and spoke to the team on the case.'

Rosalind sat up straighter. 'What did you find out?'

He surveyed her with a steady, searching look. She didn't know what he was looking for, or even if he found it, because he sighed again, even more heavily, before answering her.

'The cause of death I can tell you – that will be public record soon enough,' Jack said. 'Iain Hardy died from an overdose of prescription medication mixed with alcohol, which probably caused cardiac failure. All of which suggests suicide.'

'Except for the flower linking his death to a murder five years ago,' Rosalind pointed out.

Jack wasn't convinced. 'How can you be so sure that it does? Maybe he was a sentimental sod who had a crush on Victoria and kept the flower to remind him of her? You don't know. You never really spoke to him. Or her.'

'Perhaps.' But if it had been a suicide, where was the note? If it had been an overdose, where were the bottles of pills, or booze? A glass, at the least? There had been nothing in Iain's hotel room. Nothing except his dead body, and that flower.

Maybe it *was* suicide, and he'd somehow tidied up the scene. Maybe he'd done it because he killed Victoria, and that flower was his confession, like Posy had suggested.

Or maybe someone else had been there with him – and either killed him, or cleaned up after him.

But why?

Jack reached across the table and took her hand. 'Bottom line, it's not my case. And it's not yours either. So my advice is to let the professionals do their job.' He sat back, then nodded towards the telly again. 'Look, Caro's on.'

Rosalind twisted in her chair to watch. Just in time to hear someone ask Caro a question she was pretty sure wasn't on the approved list . . .

Posy

Inside, the Great Court of the British Museum was flooded with light, filtered through the glass triangles that formed the roof, and reflecting off the white walls and marble floor.

'Did you know that the roof is made of 3,312 panes of glass and no two are the same?' Raven said, as they strolled around the central shop and stairs towards one of the cafes. 'Sorry. Tour guide thing. Hard to switch it off.'

'How did you get started with the Lettice Davenport tours?' Posy joined the end of the queue and eyed up the blueberry muffins. 'I enjoyed it, by the way. It was . . . interesting.'

'When I first moved to London, I got a job doing tours of the usual sights. I learned a lot, but it got a bit boring after a while. I was still working on my *Lettice Davenport, Detective* series at evenings and weekends, and I was exploring a lot of the London she lived in as part of my research,' Raven explained. 'Eventually I found this niche literary walking-tour company, and I convinced them I could do a Dahlia Lively tour. I had to do loads of others too, to start with – learned more about Charles Dickens than I ever wanted to know, but the Arthur Conan Doyle one was interesting. Eventually, though, I built up enough good word about the Dahlia tour, and started making some good money from my books too, so that's the only one I do now.'

They reached the front of the queue and ordered their coffees – and a blueberry muffin or two – then found seats at one of the long, white bench tables. Posy looked around them at the bustle of tourists and day trippers exploring the museum. On the one hand, it seemed foolish to have sensitive discussions about murder where so many people could overhear. On the other, nobody came to the British Museum to people watch – or listen – surely? Not when there were so many other things to see.

'So. What exactly did you want to talk to me about?' Raven asked, once they were seated. 'Dahlia Lively character research? Whether the film rights to my Lettice Davenport books are available?'

'You heard that Iain Hardy is dead?' No point dancing around it, Posy decided.

Raven's shoulders sank, until she was almost curved completely over, her forearms flat on the table. 'Of course it's that. Yeah, I heard, just before I left the festival. People were saying it was suicide?'

Posy dipped her chin to try and get a better look at Raven's face. She looked . . . sad. Genuinely so, as far as she could tell.

'You and Iain were friends?'

Raven shrugged, her shoulders barely lifting her out of the curved C shape she'd formed over the table. 'He was always kind to me. Especially when I first moved to Market Foxleigh. He was the one who talked to me about indie publishing and convinced me it was a valid path for my stories, whatever Victoria thought.'

'But did you know Iain well?' Because that was what they really needed. Someone who could give them insight into Iain's life, his mind. Petra was probably still their best bet for that, but Caro was on that case and, besides, Petra wouldn't be able to tell them about Iain's relationship with Victoria.

Raven finally straightened up, her elbows still on the table as she contemplated her answer. 'Iain was always kind of private. I knew he was Scottish, but I couldn't tell you how he ended up in Market Foxleigh. He didn't have a partner – I don't even know if he liked men, women or both, it just never came up, you know? He didn't seem to have *anyone.* I don't think any of us knew him well.'

'Not even Victoria?' Posy asked.

Raven's brows dipped into a frown. 'I don't know. He'd been part of the group longer than me – longer than anyone except Scott and Sarah, I think. So he had history with her that I didn't. She . . . respected him, I think, more than the others. Certainly more than me.'

Respect didn't seem to be something that Victoria had given easily. Posy made a note to add that observation to the Murder Map on her wall when she got home.

Another thought occurred. 'What brought *you* to Market Foxleigh, and the writing group, in the first place?' As far as she'd been able to tell from Eleanor's file, Raven had just shown up one day, about two years before Victoria's death, and left just as suddenly a month after the murder.

Raven smiled a small, hard smile. 'I suppose I might as well tell you. It was Victoria.'

'Victoria?' Posy blinked. 'How do you mean?'

She studied Posy carefully as she sat back on her stool. 'You know about her father, yeah?'

'Charles Denby. Famous writer,' Posy replied promptly.

'And notorious womaniser,' Raven said. 'Like, probably more famous for that than the writing, really. And one of the women he womanised with was my mother. Before he went back to his wife and *legitimate* child.'

The way she said 'legitimate' – all bitter hatred – told Posy everything she hadn't already guessed.

'Victoria was your half-sister.' It wasn't a question. 'Did she know?'

Raven shook her head. 'That was why I went there – to Market Foxleigh – in the first place. I wanted to meet her. Find out what she was like. I planned to . . . well, I planned to tell her who I was, of course I did. I thought she'd be, I dunno, thrilled to find she still had family, or something. She'd have been fifteen or so when I was born, and I only found out when I turned eighteen who my dad really was – and he was already dead by then. But then I met her. And the more I got to know her, the more I realised she was just like her – our – father. Using people then casting them aside. And suddenly, I didn't *want* her to know anymore. I wanted her to be alone, like he should have been.'

There was a motive in there for murder, Posy was sure. Raven had always been a weak suspect, with only the easily disproven and vague plagiarism accusation as a motive. But this was something far bigger.

Had she resented Victoria for having their father all to herself? For being his heir, presumably, and taking a literary estate that should have at least partially belonged to Raven?

'After her death . . . I'm sorry, I have to ask. Did you inherit your father's estate?'

'No.' Raven stared down into her empty cup. 'There was a complicated legacy thing in the will. I could have contested, but it would have cost a fortune. Still, you never miss what you never had, right?'

They'd finished their coffees, and a group of tourists were lingering, waiting for their seats. Posy wasn't ready to end the conversation just yet, though. She still had more questions about Iain. 'Come on,' she said, clearing their rubbish away. 'We can keep talking in here.'

There were quieter, more private places to have the conversation, but Posy didn't want to lose momentum. Still, the rooms on the ground floor were packed full of people studying mummies and the Rosetta Stone, and other highlights of the museum.

Posy tried to remember the layout from the map by the entrance, but ended up just leading Raven forward, until they found a staircase lined with mosaics on the walls.

Upstairs, things were less crowded. They meandered through an exhibit on Mesopotamia, and Posy stared at the ancient library of Ashurbanipal while she tried to think of how to phrase her next question.

But Raven got there first.

'Is it true that you found the body?' Raven asked, suddenly, her head jerking round, away from the exhibit, as she stared at Posy. 'The three of you, I mean?'

For a moment, Posy's vision clouded, until all she could see was Iain lying there on that hotel bed. 'Yes. We found him.'

'Is it true . . . the papers haven't printed it, but Danny told me that there was another one of those flowers, like by Victoria's body.' Raven looked up at her with wide eyes. Posy couldn't tell if they looked hopeful or scared. Maybe both. '*Is* it true?'

How did *Danny* know that, then? He was a reporter, maybe he had a source at the police. But still . . . it was something to add to the list of questions to ask him. Along with why he called Raven to tell her. 'Yeah. It was . . . there was a flower in the room.'

'Huh.' Raven turned away again, looking back at the ancient tablets as if they held all the answers. 'Maybe he *did* do it, then.'

There was something about the way she said it, as if confirming a thought, or maybe a fear.

'You suspected Iain?'

'No, not . . . well.' She glanced away, towards the door. The room was still mostly empty, just a couple of visitors who looked like students, making notes. 'He just left. Right after the trial, before Scott was sentenced, even. I mean, I know we all scattered – I didn't stay, either. But I kept in touch with everyone. Without me . . . well, you know what men are like. They'd have bumped into each other at the festival every year or two, and that would have been it. Never spoken in between. But I kept us in touch. Email, group WhatsApp, you know. Not long meaningful conversations, sure. But just touching base. We were . . .' She swallowed, hard enough that Posy saw her throat bob. 'We were all friends, once. More than that. We were part of something, together, and we shared parts of ourselves that no one else saw.'

'Your writing,' Posy guessed, and Raven nodded.

'Iain didn't want to stay in touch. He didn't want to be *found* as far as I can tell. None of us knew where he was, until he came back this year.' Raven moved restlessly towards the next display cabinet, and

Posy followed, her footsteps echoing on the floor of the almost empty room. 'He ran away. And maybe that was because everything that happened was so terrible. But I wondered . . .'

'Did you tell Iain? About your father?'

'No. I . . . Danny was the only one I told, and then just because I got drunk on a night out. He kept my secret, though.' She smiled sadly. 'Iain never came on nights out. Said he was too old, and a hangover would stop him writing for weeks.'

'Did you know Iain was also publishing books under another name?'

Raven shrugged, but didn't look away from the exhibit she was staring at. 'So? Most indie-published authors do, and it's not exactly uncommon among traditionally published authors, either.'

'Yeah. But Iain was publishing as Dexter Rush.'

Now Raven looked at her. The shock on her face seemed genuine, but Posy reminded herself not to trust it. Suspects lied – that was part of the game.

'Dexter Rush,' Raven repeated. 'Bestselling – quadrillion copies sold type bestselling – award-winning, six-figure-advances author Dexter Rush was *Iain*?'

'Apparently so,' Posy confirmed.

'Huh.' Raven rocked back on her heels, obviously trying to reconcile this new information with her previous world view. 'Well. Good for him then, I suppose. Apart from the being dead part.'

Posy listened hard for any bitterness in Raven's voice, but if she felt it, she was masking it well. 'You don't feel . . .' No, that was a leading question.

'Betrayed?' Raven finished it for her anyway. 'No. Why should I? There's readers enough for all of us, and the people who read Dexter Rush books probably aren't the same readers who enjoy mine, anyway.' She spread her arms wide, almost knocking against the glass of the nearest exhibit. 'Publishing is a big place these days, and whether the traditionals believe it or not, there's room for us all in it.'

'Yeah, but . . . You told me that Iain talked you into self-publishing—'

'Indie publishing.'

'Your first book. And then he went off and got a huge traditional publishing deal as Dexter Rush.' Posy didn't know much about the publishing industry – only what she'd picked up from Caro, Petra, the festival, and this case. But she knew that someone telling you to do one thing only for them to do the other and be far more successful at it . . . that never felt good.

If Raven was pretending it did, Posy suspected she was lying. So what else might she be lying about?

'Did you know, Dexter Rush indie published his first couple of books? I read it in an article a few years ago. Although I think it might have been under a different name.' Raven looked thoughtful. 'They weren't bestsellers or anything. But they were reissued after he got picked up by one of the big publishers and reached the big time. That's what a lot of indie writers are hoping for, but not me. I like the freedom of doing it my own way – and keeping more of the profits.'

'No. I didn't know that,' Posy admitted. There'd been no sign of that information in her research, but maybe his publishers hadn't liked him to talk about it? 'Was that before Petra became his agent, then?'

'Not sure.' Raven pulled out her phone and tapped at it, searching for something. '*Dead Red Heat* came out four or five years ago, and Petra moved to London to work as an agent's assistant a few years before that, I think – I don't remember when she got made a full agent.'

Something about the way she said it struck Posy as strange. She ran the words back through her head to try and figure out what, but on the face of it they were fine. Except . . .

'I didn't realise you knew Petra so well.'

'I don't, really,' Raven said, with a shrug. 'I've only met her at the festival, briefly. But you know what it's like when everyone else knows someone and you hear their whole history, it's almost like you know them?'

'Everyone else knows her?' Posy asked, puzzled. The premise made sense – she felt like she knew Victoria, and she'd been dead five years before Posy ever heard her name. 'Who?'

Now, Raven looked surprised. 'No one told you? Petra used to live in Market Foxleigh, before she moved to London. In fact, she was one of the founding members of the Market Foxleigh Writing Circle.'

Chapter Sixteen

Celebrity is one thing. Notoriety is something else entirely.

Dahlia Lively *in* The Devil in the Details
***By* Lettice Davenport, 1946**

Caro

Caro pushed the case from her mind as she was led out onto the set of *Food Matters.* For once, there was something more important than murder for her to focus on. She had twenty-five minutes in which she needed to promote her book, talk about the many events she'd be doing around the country over the summer and autumn, eat breakfast without getting it everywhere, not say anything that would make Petra frown at her later – or cause the comments on the show's social media account to blow up too badly – then successfully flip a pancake. That was all.

How hard can that be?

The show's set was bright and cheerful, and from where she stood off camera, it reminded Caro of Little Chef restaurants in days gone by – all red and white check, and colour coded condiment bottles. She suspected they were going more for the American diner look, but no one was really going to believe they were actually in Kansas or wherever, were they?

'Here we go,' the production assistant assigned to her murmured, and Caro took a breath, found her centre, and walked onto the set.

The main host, celebrity chef Ronan Brannigan, welcomed her warmly as the studio audience applauded.

'It's so great to have you on the show! My mam and nan just *loved* you in *The Dahlia Lively Mysteries*. And now you've written a book! I have to admit, I'm more about cookbooks than mysteries usually, but yours really hooked me in! I haven't finished it yet, but I suppose we all know what happens in the end from the papers anyway, don't we? Always the problem with non-fiction! But it's so great to have you here, Caro!'

Ronan turned away, back to the audience, and Caro took her assigned seat on one of the high counter stools. She hopped up carefully, hoping the red leather seat wouldn't squeak too much.

First part of the mission accomplished. I managed to sit down without embarrassing myself.

'My second guest this lovely summer's morning is no stranger to the papers – or the publishing world – either! Felicity Wilmott is a journalist who has worked for some of our best known newspapers, and has now written a book about how the news is reported here in Britain. Felicity, hello!'

There were more welcoming hugs and more applause, as Felicity took her own stool, probably more gracefully than Caro had managed.

They made light chit-chat about their favourite foods, and childhood memories of meals and cooking, while Ronan prepared breakfast for them both. Caro spoke about Annie's culinary prowess, knowing she was blushing somewhere out there in the audience.

In fact, all seemed to be going perfectly smoothly, and Caro had even started to relax a little. She'd managed to mention her book, and her events, and she didn't have egg on her top, so she was close to declaring victory.

Until Ronan said, 'Now, Caro, I understand that you and your two friends – the other two Dahlias in the title of your book – you've been asked to take on a new project, haven't you? A podcast?'

'Uh, yes, that's right.' Caro mentally cursed Eleanor Grey. 'We've been asked to, well, advise, I suppose, on a true crime podcast.'

'I heard it was more than advising. In fact, I think we can hear the latest trailer right now . . .'

Suddenly, Eleanor's voice was echoing around the studio, followed by that clip of Scott, before Eleanor wound it up again.

'Will justice be served this time? You'll have to listen to find out.'

'Ooh, it gives me shivers!' Ronan leaned across the counter, his tone confidential even in a studio set with a live audience. 'You can tell us. Are you calling for the Paper Dahlia case to be reopened? It certainly sounds like it from that clip!'

'We're asking some questions, that's all,' Caro said, firmly enough to put an end to the line of questioning.

Or it would have been enough for Ronan, anyway. But Felicity had other ideas.

'Even though you actually testified against the original convicted killer?' A murmur went up around the studio at Felicity's question.

Caro's mind whirred as she struggled to find the words to turn this around, to get back to talking about eating *pain au chocolat* in Paris on her honeymoon or something.

Ronan tried to help her out, probably because his producer was yelling in his earpiece, she expected. 'And a podcast is new ground for you, isn't it?'

But before Caro could respond, Felicity dove in with another question.

'There are people who claim that your investigations are nothing but publicity stunts, dredging up trouble just to revive your flagging celebrity.' She twisted on her stool to face Caro down, marking her points on her fingers as she spoke. 'Your investigation in Aldermere, detailed in your new book, has been accused of tarnishing the legacy of Lettice Davenport herself, and your more recent case in Wales ended in the deaths of three people, including two beloved celebrities – and almost including your friend Rosalind King, isn't that right?'

'I don't think that's—' Caro stammered, but Felicity kept talking.

'And now, with this podcast, aren't you just causing trouble for the sake of it?' she said. 'The case has already been solved, and tried. And isn't it true, that *another* person has now been killed *because* of your investigation.'

Ronan jumped in, obviously eager to move back onto safer ground. 'You can take the journalist out of the paper, but you can't, um . . .'

'It hasn't been reported in the papers yet, I know,' Felicity went on. 'But I believe in facts. And the fact is that a paper flower – a dahlia, I believe, made from the pages of a Dahlia Lively novel – was found in the room of Iain Hardy, just like the one that was found by Victoria Denby, *proving* the deaths are linked. And more than that – *you* discovered the body, didn't you?'

The audience was aflame with debate now, and Ronan had given up trying to bring things back under control. Felicity sat back, arms crossed over her chest, and a smug smile on her face.

But Caro wasn't going to leave it there.

She'd had enough of being told her motives, her reasons, in her first marriage. Had enough of people telling her she was the wrong person for a job in her career.

The only person who got to decide what she did, and why she chose to do it, was *her*.

And there wasn't a chance in hell she was taking Felicity's

accusations lying down – not when Annie was sitting in the audience watching, and Rosalind and Posy would be viewing at home.

But she wasn't going to lose her cool, either. Wasn't going to give social media a ready-made meme by yelling or setting anything on fire. She'd learned and grown since those days.

So instead, she smiled.

'Honestly, Felicity? I didn't want to get involved with this case, but I am, and if a miscarriage of justice has taken place then someone has to investigate that,' she said. 'But more importantly, I won't be talking about it on this show because, if the police don't want certain details reported yet, I trust that they have a good reason – and if anyone is causing trouble for them, or the victims of crime, it's you.'

Caro spun her stool back to face the audience. 'Now, who wants to watch me flip a pancake?'

Rosalind

They regrouped at Posy's flat the next day. Rosalind had cut short her visit with Jack after watching Caro's TV appearance, and had driven down the night before, trying not to watch Jack's frown in the rear view mirror as she drove away. The uncertain, tight feeling had stayed in her chest all down the M6 though.

Now she arrived first, carrying the cushions and throw she'd bought in Wales in large bags.

'What are those?' Posy asked as she opened the door.

'A housewarming present. Flat warming. Whatever.' Posy looked confused, probably because she'd already been living in the flat for over eight months. 'They're from Jack.'

'Right.' Posy took the bags and pulled out the cushions. 'They're lovely. Um, please thank him for me?'

'Of course.' Rosalind took the cushions from her and began arranging them on the sofa, draping the cashmere throw elegantly over the back. Otherwise she had a feeling they'd sit in bags by the wall for another month.

The buzzer downstairs rang again, and Posy pressed the button to let Caro up.

The papers had all led with the Paper Dahlia murder connection, and most had featured a still of Caro's face from *Food Matters,* looking aghast and a little bit guilty. Another reason to tie this investigation up quickly; none of them needed even more negative press.

Caro looked strangely flat when she arrived at the door, and to Rosalind's surprise Posy pulled her into a hug, even though they weren't usually touchy-feely people. When it was Rosalind's turn to welcome her, she gave her a sympathetic nod, which seemed to satisfy the occasion.

'At least you didn't fall off the stool,' Posy said, making Rosalind think of some of the interviews Posy had done when she was at her lowest point. They still made the rounds on social media regularly, although she never told Posy she saw them.

Rosalind imagined Caro's interview would be doing the same soon enough, even though she'd maintained a remarkable cool. For Caro.

Caro gave a low chuckle. 'And I flipped the hell out of that pancake.'

'You definitely did,' Posy agreed.

'Much better than my ex did.'

'Absolutely,' Rosalind said firmly, even though she had no idea, since she'd never watched the show before, and definitely wouldn't have watched when Caro's ex-husband was on, anyway.

They might not be touchy-feely, but they were loyal.

'Annie sent this for you.' Caro held up a large cool bag. 'She's been on a bit of a batch cooking binge recently and we ran out of room in the freezer.'

'Right.' Posy took the bag with a sceptical look. 'That's very kind of her. Please give her my thanks.'

'Will do.' Caro shoved her hands in the pockets of her trousers as Posy moved to the kitchen to put away the food. 'Think she bought it?' she asked Rosalind, out of the corner of her mouth.

Rosalind shrugged. 'I tried to claim Jack had sent her cushions as an eight-month-late housewarming present.'

'Nice cushions, though,' Caro said. Then she turned to the other side of the flat, and her eyes widened.

Rosalind followed her gaze. Where there had been a large, blank wall that Rosalind had been considering a nice seascape for, there was now a mess of notes, photos and bits of string pinned directly into the paintwork. She'd obviously been too concerned with cushions to notice it straight away, but now Rosalind wondered how on earth she'd missed it.

Well, at least Posy was adding some personal touches to her home at last.

'What's with the serial killer wall?' Caro asked, without a hint of tact.

Posy turned to look from where she was stashing Annie's meals in the tiny freezer compartment of her kitchen fridge-freezer.

'It's a Murder Map. I got the idea from this bookshop on a barge,' Posy said, explaining precisely nothing. 'I just needed a way to see all the information in one place, not on different pages. *That's* how we'll spot what I missed the first time.'

Ah. That explained it. She was still obsessing over the loss of her notes – and Caro's theory that there was something important in them that they'd missed. But still, this seemed a little . . . intense.

For a long moment, Caro and Rosalind studied the mish-mash of red thread, neon Post-it notes, and a few photos from Eleanor's file stuck up on the wall.

'You didn't like the notebook I bought you?' Rosalind asked, eventually.

Posy grinned. 'I love it! Honestly I do. It was just too . . . neat. Murder is messy. I needed to have the space to spread out and consider all the clues.'

'And have you found it yet?' Caro asked. 'The clue we missed?'

'Not yet.' Posy shut the freezer door, and considered her display. 'But I will. Especially now you two are here to help.'

Posy made coffees from the fancy coffee machine – the one thing about the flat that felt like her – and opened a tin of biscuits, and they all turned their attention to the Murder Map, sharing the snippets of information they'd each learned over the past few days and piecing them together, looking for patterns. The news that Raven was actually Victoria's long lost sister came as a bit of a shock, but not as much as the fact that Petra was a founding member of the writing group.

Rosalind still thought the notebook she'd bought Posy was far prettier, but she had to admit that the map did make it easier to see all the details. Posy had even implemented some sort of colour coding system with her Post-it notes, a colour for each of their suspects.

She frowned, as she realised that the purple colour she'd been using for Iain had now been assigned to Petra.

'Wait. So we *still* have seven suspects? Even though one of them is dead?'

'Yup.' Posy stuck on another purple Post-it note with the words 'royalties' written on it, presumably representing Petra's financial motive. 'Just not the same seven we started with.'

And didn't that seem like par for the course with this case? They'd started with a murderer, tried and convicted. But every single thing they learned seemed to take them another two steps back. Give them another month on the case and they'd probably be up to seventeen suspects.

Caro sprawled back against the new cushions and stared up at the map, tapping a finger against her lips. 'So, Petra has a solid motive for killing Iain – money – *and* she knew Victoria.'

'Sarah said she gave her place on that writing retreat where Victoria met Scott to a colleague,' Posy said. 'I'm betting that colleague was Petra – which should be easy enough to double check.'

'And Petra skipped the awards to talk to a client – which could have been Iain – but she was around the night of the Skeleton Festival.' Posy had already scribbled the details down and added another Post-it to the map. 'So Petra had opportunity and motive for Iain's murder. But what about means?'

Rosalind shifted on the sofa. 'Jack said it was an overdose of prescription medication and alcohol, but he didn't say if the medication was Iain's or not. And nobody has explained why there was no sign of them around the body. *Somebody* had to clear up, and I don't think it could have been Iain. If it was suicide, someone else helped.'

'Okay, but . . . say she *did* do it,' Posy said. 'That still doesn't explain Victoria. Unless we think that murder really was Scott and Petra is using the podcast as a smokescreen to do away with Iain and get her hands on his money?'

'Could be.' Caro flopped back down again against the cushions. 'It makes as much sense as anything else right now.'

Too many unknowns, that was the problem. When Eleanor had handed them that file at the premiere, Rosalind had thought they had everything they could possibly need. But none of it seemed to have helped.

'The police will be talking to Petra about Iain, that much we can be certain about,' she said, after a moment. 'But we need to talk to her about Victoria, see if there is a motive there.'

'I can do that,' Caro said. 'I've got three more events this week for the book. She's bound to be there for at least one of them, even with everything that's going on. I'll collar her and find out what we need to know.'

Rosalind nodded. 'Fine. Posy, you've spoken to Raven, so now we need to track down and pay a visit to the other three suspects – Hakim, Danny and Milla.'

'Back to Market Foxleigh, then,' Posy said, with a sigh. 'And . . . Bath, for Hakim, I think. And wherever Danny and his wife ended up.'

'That's not everybody though,' Caro said. 'That's only five suspects. What about Scott and Sarah?'

She was right, Rosalind knew. 'Sarah we can talk to along with the others. And as for Scott . . .' She paused, more for dramatic effect than anything else, if she was honest. Maybe a little bit to postpone the uproar she knew was going to follow – and to try and ensure she sounded convincing as she stretched the truth. She wasn't used to lying to her sister-Dahlias. 'He's agreed to speak with me in person. I'm visiting the prison on Saturday.' She ignored the clamour from the other two and spoke over them to add the lie, 'But *just* me. He'll only do it if I go alone.'

Chapter Seventeen

In fact, Dahlia had to admit to feeling positively down in the mouth about the results of her investigations.

At least, until she put them together with what Johnnie had learned, later that night, and suddenly things began to make sense at last.

Dahlia Lively *in* Impossible Crimes for Impossible Times
***By* Lettice Davenport, 1972**

Posy

With Caro busy promoting her book, Rosalind and Posy had been left to decide their own travel arrangements for this round of the investigation. Posy had suggested the conversations could have been had by video call, but Rosalind refused to believe that they could get the same level of nuance over the internet. But having just returned from her sojourn to Wales, she didn't fancy spending more time driving herself. She also refused to get on a train, or to, in her words, 'go careening around half of England with you behind the wheel'. Which, since Posy didn't own a car, was probably just as well. She didn't even suggest that she drive Rosalind's.

All of which meant that Posy had left Rosalind to make the arrangements for their transport. And so, when a long, black car with tinted windows appeared outside her flat the next morning, and the driver stepped out wearing an honest-to-God peaked cap, she really only had herself to blame.

'We're going incognito and low-profile for this, then?' Posy said, as she slid into the back seat beside Rosalind, and the driver slammed the door before putting her overnight bag in the boot.

Rosalind shrugged her elegant shoulders. 'Why should we? The podcast is public knowledge. Everyone knows we're investigating, and if we haven't spooked our suspects yet, we're hardly likely to start now. So we might as well travel in comfort.'

'Hard to argue with that,' Posy agreed.

Rosalind gave her a superior nod, then pulled her eye mask down over her face, popped in her earplugs, and promptly went to sleep for most of the journey west.

Posy watched London pass and turn into motorway and eventually green fields beyond, turning the case over and over in her mind. After what had happened to Caro on *Food Matters,* it felt like they were reaching their last chance to solve this case before their reputations were in complete tatters. Which meant they *had* to ask their seven suspects the right questions this time around.

Market Foxleigh was quieter, less celebratory, without the bunting and banners for the festival. Still, Posy saw at least three signs for other upcoming events as their driver weaved through the streets, before parking near the town hall.

They found Milla at her desk in the offices behind the main hall, studying two slightly different posters for an upcoming concert in the park. She looked surprised to see them, but happy enough to take a break while they asked her some questions.

Outside, the sun was still gloriously warm, so they walked across to the bandstand while they talked. Posy remembered it in the dark, with the torches and the skeletons, and marvelled at how one place could feel so different under different light.

'I'm glad you're here, actually,' Milla said. 'There was something I wasn't quite honest with you about when we spoke last.'

'Oh?' Posy's fingers itched for her notebook. She'd brought the fancy one Rosalind had bought her, but stuck Post-it notes on the pages to write on, so she could add them straight to the Murder Map when she got home.

'You asked what Victoria yelled at me about that day, and I claimed I couldn't remember,' Milla said. 'But I did. It was a little statuette of a shepherd girl. It belonged to her father, I think. And my mother . . . I told you she has early-onset dementia? Well, one of her early symptoms was taking things that didn't belong to her, when she was cleaning houses. She'd just . . . forget they weren't hers, or that she was holding them, and then where she found them, I think.'

'And so you'd follow behind and put them back,' Posy guessed. 'That's why you were really working for your mum's cleaning company.'

Milla nodded. 'That day, Mum had taken the shepherdess again – it seemed a particular favourite, for some reason – and I hadn't found it at home, so I thought she must have left it somewhere else in the house. I'd hoped to find it before Victoria noticed, but I wasn't fast enough. Sarah arrived early, and she and I hunted high and low for it while Victoria was on that phone call we heard snatches of. We must have gone all over the house. When Victoria realised we were there, it only made her angrier – and she took her phone upstairs to the bedroom. Sarah found the damn statuette in Victoria's top drawer, but I didn't have time to put it back where it was supposed to be, so I just put it on her desk. Victoria was yelling at me for moving it when the others arrived.' She shrugged. 'I know it doesn't matter now. I just wanted to tell you the truth. But that's not what you came here for. You want to talk about Iain. What do you want to know?'

'You knew he was Dexter Rush,' Rosalind replied. 'You told us that's how you got him to promise to appear at the festival this year. How did you find out?'

With a sigh, Milla dropped to sit on the bandstand steps, and Posy followed suit. Rosalind remained standing, looming over them. 'He gave himself away – just last year, actually. Iain had stayed a patron of the festival, you see, although I only had his email. Everything else went through his agent. But then he responded from the wrong email address once, and emailed me as Dexter Rush. It didn't take much to get him to confirm.'

'Did you tell anyone else?'

'No one,' Milla replied, firmly. 'Well, not until we started talking to Eleanor about the podcast. She was looking for new angles on the story, public interest, celebrity, that sort of thing.'

'So you gave her Iain.' Posy had to admit, it made sense. If Eleanor had thought she could get the three Dahlias *and* Dexter Rush on board for her story, that would be quite the coup.

And it explained why Iain's death had sped things up with the podcast plans, too. Eleanor wanted to break the news about Dexter Rush's less assuming but murder-adjacent alter ego, but now he was dead the chances were the press would be on it too. Hence the sudden trailer.

'When you were looking for Iain that night, did you see anybody else at the hotel? Or were any of the other members of the writing group missing?'

Milla spread her hands helplessly. 'Honestly, I don't know. It was dark, and with all the masks . . . I know that Danny and Raven disappeared to hunt for Dexter Rush together, but obviously they didn't know they were looking for Iain, so God knows how they thought they were going to find him. Other than that, I *thought* everyone was there, but then I thought *Iain* was there too, and obviously he wasn't—' She broke off with a small sob.

Posy thought back over the events of the weekend. 'When Iain told you he wouldn't do the awards, what did you do?'

'I tried to reason with him,' Milla said. 'Pointed out that his incognito thing wasn't going to work forever and that, really, would it be so bad if people knew? No dice, though. And then he started talking about not doing the reading at the parade either, even though I'd *told* him he could wear the mask. That was when I asked Petra to go and talk to him.'

'Which was why *she* missed the awards,' Posy surmised. 'She was with Iain.'

She tried to picture in her head the events of that night. They didn't have a firm time of death from the police yet, but apart from the probably phony Iain at the parade, nobody so far had mentioned seeing him since he blew off their questioning session in the library. Could he have been killed the night before, when they were all at the awards ceremony?

Danny had taken up his letter though – they knew that, because it had been on his desk. And Petra had spent time with him later that night.

'Do you know Petra well?' Rosalind asked.

'Petra?' Milla frowned at the question. 'No, I don't know her well at all, really. I only met her this year because of the festival.'

'She hadn't been to the previous ones?' Posy asked.

Milla shook her head. 'No, I don't think so. I know she used to live locally, though – I think she started the group with Victoria?'

'That's right,' Posy said, encouragingly.

'Yes. I'd seen photos of her in the files from the very first festival. And I think she must still have had family locally, because I saw her in town once, after she'd left.'

Pin pricks spiked up the back of Posy's neck. 'When was that, exactly? Can you remember?'

'I can, actually.' Milla gave a wry grin. 'Because it was just after I'd finished giving my statement to the police about Victoria's murder. I walked out of the police station, and saw her getting into her car.'

Posy looked up at Rosalind. So Petra had been in Market Foxleigh around the time of Victoria's murder. That was a start.

Now they needed to find out why.

Milla needed to get back to work, so Posy and Rosalind climbed back into their ridiculously obvious car, and headed out to the new estate on the outskirts of town where Sarah Baker and her husband lived.

'Nice house,' Posy observed, as the driver opened the door for them and they got out.

Rosalind made a dismissive noise at the back of her throat. Posy suspected her standards for property were rather higher than hers.

But it *was* a nice house, in objective terms, if you liked modern-build homes. Detached, with a drive and garage, a navy blue front door and bay windows, and so new that other parts of the estate were still being built. It suited Sarah, Posy decided. Maybe that was why she liked it.

Posy rang the bell by the front door, and heard the chimes echoing through the rooms inside, followed by footsteps on the stairs.

The door opened to reveal a tall man in shorts and a polo shirt, his dark hair damp. He looked slightly taken aback to find Rosalind King and Posy Starling on his doorstep, but he covered it with a broad smile, then stepped back to let them inside.

'Well, hello. I imagine you're here to see Sarah? I'm her husband, Eric. Come on in.' He led them through to a well-proportioned sitting room with an enormous TV over the fireplace, and motioned for them to take a seat. Then, ducking back into the hallway, he yelled, 'Sarah? Babe? Visitors!'

Posy sat on the nearest sofa, looking out of the French doors to a long lawn with a shed at the bottom.

'She'll be right down,' Eric said. 'Can I get you ladies anything to drink?'

Rosalind and Posy both demurred, and Eric hovered uncertainly in the doorway as they waited for Sarah.

'I— I wanted to thank you both, for doing this,' Eric said, suddenly. 'The podcast, I mean. For so long, this thing with Scott . . . it's been a huge stumbling block for us, as a couple. It's always been between us, you know what I mean? And I just hope . . . I hope that this will put it to rest, one way or another, and we can all move on. So I just . . . thank you.'

Posy glanced again at the garden, and realised what she'd really thought, arriving at this house. It was a family home. A place people bought because they wanted kids, wanted to move into that next phase of life.

Had campaigning for Scott taken up so much of Sarah's life that she thought she couldn't have that? Looking at the relieved smile on Eric's face, Posy suspected it had.

Sarah joined them a moment later, settling onto the armchair opposite Posy. The sun caught in her blonde hair as she settled the skirts of her sundress around her thighs.

'Not that it's not lovely to see you both,' she said. 'But I'm assuming this means you have something you want to talk to me about. Is it Iain? It was so terrible, his death. The police think suicide, I hear? Do you think . . . I always liked Iain, but . . . it's suspicious, don't you think? Him dying now?'

There was a strange hopefulness in Sarah's voice. Posy supposed that if it emerged that Iain *had* killed himself, and that it was out of guilt for killing Victoria, it would achieve everything Sarah had been working for over the past five years.

But without a suicide note, Posy didn't know how likely that was.

'We do want to talk about Iain, yes,' Rosalind said, ignoring Sarah's questions. 'But also Petra.'

'Petra?' Sarah frowned. 'What about Petra? She left town years before Victoria's death.'

'Yes. But she was Iain's agent, and a founding member of the writing group, so . . . we're just trying to get a full picture,' Posy explained. 'Maybe you could start with how you met? And how she met Victoria?'

'Okay. Well . . .' Sarah still looked a little puzzled, but continued all the same. 'Let's see. Um, I met Petra when I was working for an estate agent in town. I was just the admin assistant, but she was much higher up – I think her brother owned the business, and she basically ran it. The whole family seemed to have investments and businesses everywhere. We got to talking on a work night out and she told me she was looking for a fresh start – a new challenge. She had the money, that much was for sure. She just hadn't quite decided yet what direction she wanted to go in. Anyway, we started a book group together, and that's when we got to know each other a little better. I told her about this writing retreat my brother and I were going on together – I'd talked about Scott to her a lot, so she knew how things stood there. She was really interested, but the place was fully booked.'

'But you had to drop out because of work, right?' Posy remembered.

'Yeah. There was some kind of screw-up with the rotas, and suddenly I had to work that weekend and nobody else could swap with me. I was kind of gutted, because it wasn't cheap either. But Petra offered to buy my place from me, so that worked out.'

Posy glanced across at Rosalind, whose tight nod told her she was wondering the same thing Posy was.

'Do you remember . . . who was in charge of the staff rotas at the office?' Posy asked.

'Oh, um, it was the office manager,' Sarah said. 'But I think Petra had the final say.'

Of course she did. 'So Petra went on the retreat and met Victoria with Scott?'

Sarah nodded. 'By the time they came back, they had all these plans for a writing group and everything.'

'How did that make you feel?' Rosalind asked.

'A little left out,' Sarah admitted. 'At least, to start with. But then I joined too, and, well, it didn't really matter who'd been there at the start, then.'

Rosalind pressed the point. 'Then why didn't you tell us it was Petra who took your place on the writing retreat?'

Sarah's blue eyes were wide. 'Honestly, it didn't occur to me that you'd know who Petra was. I didn't realise she was Caro's agent until later.'

'How did Petra and Victoria get on?' Posy had her notebook out on her lap, and had already filled a page and a half with notes. 'I imagine they were both . . . strong personalities.'

'You imagine right.' Sarah pulled a wry face. 'Victoria wanted everything to be done her way and, since we held the club at her house, she got her way a lot of the time, which Petra didn't like. In the end, I don't think any of us were very surprised when Petra said she was leaving. I guess the only surprising part was that she'd got a job working for a literary agent, through some family connection or other I think. She said she'd decided she'd rather be on the business side of things than the creative one.'

'She left after the first festival, is that right?' Rosalind leaned forward a little towards Sarah's chair. 'Did you see her again after that?'

'Not really.' Sarah screwed up her forehead as if trying to remember. 'I think she came back for the festival for the first couple of years. She was probably supposed to be there the year Victoria died, but obviously it all got cancelled – although I think I saw her with Iain around then, or just after, having coffee together. After that, I didn't see her again until this year's festival – and even then, not really to speak to.'

'She didn't stay in touch, then?' Posy asked.

'Not with me,' Sarah said. 'No one did, after everything that happened. But she might have stayed in touch with the others – Rachel, or Danny, or Hakim.'

'Or Iain,' Rosalind said.

'Yes, probably. They were close.'

Well, they already knew that much.

Caro

Caro had long since stopped trying to keep track of the details of every event she was signed up to for book promotion over the summer. Instead, she'd simply given her publicist, Jemima, access to a shared calendar, and now all the details pinged up on her phone just before she needed them.

Today, apparently, she was at a large and popular independent bookshop in south London, along with a couple of other authors she'd never heard of. Petra hadn't been planning on joining them – Caro had her publicist along, after all, so she didn't really need her agent too. But Caro was growing impatient waiting to get Petra alone to talk to her about Victoria, so she played the needy client card – something she didn't entirely like but justified to herself as being necessary for the greater good.

'I just feel like I need the extra moral support today,' she told Petra on the phone, the morning of the event. 'After everything that happened on *Food Matters* . . . if someone starts something like that again, it would be good to have you there.'

Not that Petra had been able to do anything to stop some jumped-up journo attacking Caro live on air, but still. Petra had sighed, promised to have her assistant move some calls, and meet her at the bookshop.

'The thing to remember,' Petra murmured now, as they sat together off to the side of the event, while another author took the microphone and addressed the rows of readers in plastic chairs down the middle of the bookstore. 'Is that all publicity is good publicity.'

From what she'd seen of Posy's reported past, Caro knew that most definitely wasn't true.

'What doesn't help is that we don't seem to be getting anywhere with this case,' Caro whispered back. 'Nobody seems to be telling us everything. For instance, you didn't tell us about Iain being Dexter Rush. *Or,'* she went on, over Petra's mumbled objections, 'that you knew Victoria and Scott. More than knew – you founded the writing group with them.'

Petra rolled her eyes. 'Because I left years before her death, and I didn't stay in touch with anyone there, so what did it matter?'

'You didn't stay in touch with *anyone*?' Caro pressed. 'Apart from Iain, you mean.'

'Yes, well. That was different. He came to me as an agent. And that was later, anyway.'

Caro made a mental note to check the timeline on that. 'So you didn't go back to Market Foxleigh once you'd left?'

Petra pulled a face. 'Why would I? Nothing but bad memories there. I'm sure you've heard by now what Victoria was like – it wasn't exactly a welcoming place.'

'What exactly *was* Victoria like?' Caro asked. 'I mean, you're right – we've heard from the others. But I trust your judgement of people over theirs. I'd be interested to hear your opinion.'

It was just the right amount of flattery. Petra settled back in her chair, arms folded, and considered.

'She liked to be in control, that much is for sure,' she said, after a moment. 'I think she had a massive chip on her shoulder about never being the writer that her father was. It felt like she was still reaching for his approval, even though he was dead. Her relationships with the men in the group – especially Danny – were kind of twisted, sometimes. You know? Like she wanted to boss them about *and* make them love her for it.'

'Danny in particular?' Caro pressed. 'Were they having an affair? Sarah said she heard her arguing with someone on the phone . . .'

'Possibly.' Petra tilted her head to the side, considering. 'I don't think they were when I was there. But they might have done, later. Danny . . . I think, from scraps I overheard between them, that he wanted something from Victoria. I'm not sure what. Something to do with her father perhaps? And I don't know how far he might have gone to get it.' She shook her head. 'I don't know. If they were, his wife would have killed *him* if she found out. Anyway. None of it felt right, I can tell you that much.'

'And that's why you left?'

Petra shrugged. 'One of the reasons. But I had much bigger dreams than a tiny writing group in a provincial market town. I was ready to get out – and I had no desire to go back. In fact, I wouldn't even have gone for the festival this year if I hadn't had such an important client taking part.' She nudged Caro meaningfully in the ribs. 'The things I do for you . . . come on, you're up.'

Caro suddenly realised that the applause for the last author was dying down and it was, in fact, her turn at the microphone. Steeling herself, she took to the stage, launching into her prepared chat about *The Three Dahlias* and how it came to be, before taking questions.

To her relief, all the questions today seemed to be about the book, rather than the real-world effect of their more recent investigation. From the way the bookshop staff were keeping a firm hold of the microphones as people stood to ask their questions, Caro figured that might not just be luck.

Still, the event went well. As she stepped down, she saw Petra's seat empty – except for a scrawled note telling Caro she had to run, but would see her at Will Pollinger's book launch.

Caro screwed up the note, and prepared to join the other authors signing books.

Back home that evening, with a glass of wine in hand, she leaned against the kitchen counter and watched Annie making a stir-fry while she listened to the latest updates from Market Foxleigh.

Posy obviously had her phone on speaker, as every time she

recounted a conversation from their day, Rosalind would jump in to add to or qualify it. Caro filled them in on what Petra had had to say – and told them to make sure they asked Danny again about his relationship with Victoria when they spoke to him tomorrow.

'Are you guys staying at The Red Fox again tonight?' Caro asked.

'Yep,' Posy replied. 'But we've got our own rooms this time, thankfully.'

'Thankfully?' Rosalind repeated, her voice getting higher towards the end.

At the hob, Annie smirked, and Caro felt grateful that she was in London and not Market Foxleigh. This splitting up to investigate thing was working well for her. Look how much more ground they could cover in half the time, for a start.

The fact that Posy got to deal with Rosalind's tired snippiness was just a bonus.

'Anyway, the point is that mostly we just got a better idea of how Petra became involved in the group, but nothing concrete on a motive for Victoria's death,' Posy said. 'The most interesting part is that both Sarah and Milla told us that Petra had been in town around the time of Victoria's death – definitely the week after it, anyway.'

Caro froze, glass of wine halfway to her mouth.

I had no desire to go back. That's what Petra had said.

But she had.

Caro slammed the wine glass down. '*This* is why we need to investigate *together!*'

Chapter Eighteen

'What could you possibly know about it?' The policeman looked Lettice up and down with disdain. 'Shouldn't you be writing your silly little stories? Not getting in the way of a real *investigation.'*

Lettice Davenport *in* Lettice Saves The Day
***By* Raven Cassidy**

Rosalind

The offices of the *Bristol Chronicle* were bustling when Rosalind and Posy arrived the next morning, their driver still circling the streets for somewhere to park after dropping them off. A few polite questions had them directed to Danny's desk in no time, and they wove their way between workstations to find him.

His desk chair leaned so far back he was almost horizontal, his feet propped up on a stool beside his workstation, and he had his phone clamped to his ear, nodding as he scribbled down notes in a book that looked not unlike Posy's old one, except the spiral binding was on the top instead of the side.

After a moment or two, he looked up and spotted them waiting. His face froze for a second, then fell back into a resigned frown.

'All right, mate. I'll call back later for updates. Cheers.' He ended the call, then dropped his feet to the floor, the chair springing back into a more normal, upright position. 'Not here, okay?'

'Then where?' Posy asked.

Danny grabbed a file from his desk, then got to his feet. 'Follow me.'

He led them past more workstations, a small kitchen and a few storage rooms, before they reached a private meeting room. He opened the door and beckoned them to enter, shutting it tight behind the three of them.

Posy took a seat at the conference table in the centre of the room, but Rosalind took a moment to admire the view – and the decoration. The walls were lined with framed copies of famous front pages from the Chronicle's history. Was Danny hoping to get his byline up on these walls? Was that why he'd moved to the city from Market Foxleigh?

Or was there another reason?

'You're here about Iain, I suppose.' Danny had dropped into the chair at the head of the table, sprawling across it. Rosalind took a seat opposite him, sitting as straight as she could in defiance.

'You saw about the paper flower?' Posy asked. They knew he had. He'd told Raven.

He nodded. 'I have a mate on the local force, as it happens. He'd already given me the details, off the record. I can tell you, someone got a right bollocking for missing that the first time and not sealing off the whole hotel then and there to preserve evidence.'

Just as Rosalind had suspected they would.

'Can you think of a reason why anyone would want both Victoria and Iain dead? Or a link between Iain and the original murder?' She watched Danny closely as he considered his answer. For a relaxed, almost aggressively casual man, he was careful with his words. Perhaps because he knew how much harm the wrong ones could do.

'I'm sure you've come up with all the same theories I have,' he said. 'Same murderer, covering their tracks now you're investigating. A different killer, using the paper dahlia to throw the police off the trail. Or suicide, because Iain did it, but someone is covering it up.'

'Those are our three main options,' Posy agreed. 'We just need a way to figure out which it is.'

Danny flipped open the file he'd taken from his desk and pushed it towards Posy. 'You're not the only one who's interested in getting the right person for this, you know. I made a lot of notes, not just for the book, but before. When it happened, I mean, and before the police arrested Scott. I was . . . I needed to know, to solve it. But the police got there first. Or so I thought.' He nodded at the file. 'It's all in there, and you're welcome to look through it. But I'd rather it didn't leave the building.'

Posy took the file and started flipping through, adding notes to her own notebook as she read. Rosalind knew that as soon as they got back to London, there were going to be a number of new Post-it notes added to the Murder Map.

But that was Posy's problem. Right now, Rosalind still had some things she wanted to ask Danny.

She covered Petra, first, and Danny gave her almost exactly the same answers that Milla had, the day before. Then she moved on to what she really wanted to know.

'You were obviously close to Victoria. Cared about her.' She eyed Danny with meaning, and watched him squirm.

'Look, I don't know what you've heard—'

'Yes, you do,' Rosalind said. 'You know exactly what we've heard, because it's the truth.'

It wasn't like she hadn't heard what people said about her and Hugh over the years, when they'd been spotted together at a function, whether their spouses were there or not.

She'd heard it and chosen to ignore it. Or not take it seriously. And she'd convinced her husband not to, either.

That was something she had to live with. The same way Danny was living with this.

She didn't release him from her gaze, and eventually he slumped further down in his chair, breaking away from their staring contest.

'When you're working closely with people, like we were on the festival, you grow, well, close. Connected.' He gave a pathetic shrug. 'And when you're sharing your writing too . . . that's an intimate thing to do. You know?'

'I've worked on a lot of film sets,' Rosalind said, drily. 'I know exactly what you mean. But that wasn't all it was with you and Victoria, was it?'

His face took on a pinched, hunted expression. 'Don't know what you mean.'

'There was something you wanted from Victoria, wasn't there? Something of her father's?' Caro had told them what Petra had said about Danny, and another piece of the puzzle of this case had slipped into place in Rosalind's mind. Danny and Victoria had never quite made sense to her as a couple. But if she had something he wanted, she could see it easily.

She stared him down until he looked away. 'You know who her father was, right? Charles Denby. She has all his papers, all his unpublished words . . . so yeah. I wanted to take a look at them. That's what drew me to the group in the first place. I've always been more about fact than fiction, but the writing group was a good way in. But not . . . I'm not so callous as to sleep with a woman just to get a look at some files.'

'And did you? Get a look at the files?'

'As it happens, I didn't.' He sounded rather put out about that even so many years later.

'But that was why your wife wanted to move away? To Bristol? Because of your relationship with Victoria?' Passion was always a good motive. Had the police ever looked at Danny's wife, she wondered.

'It wasn't like that,' Danny protested. Rosalind gave him a disbelieving look. 'No, really. The . . . I don't like to call it an affair. But whatever it was between us, it didn't turn physical until *after* I told her we were looking at moving. It was her way of trying to keep me close, I think. Tying me to her, and to that place. Holding her dad's papers over me wasn't enough anymore, so she had to try something else. And I . . . I've always been weak. I don't deny that. And things were bad with my wife right then.'

'Because she thought you were moving, and suddenly you wanted to stay?' Rosalind guessed.

Danny nodded. 'I don't know if she knew, or suspected, or what. But she started getting grumpy when I was doing things with the group or for the festival. We started arguing more. She blamed the town – said it was too small, that my talent was wasted at that paper. But . . . yeah. By the end I think she just wanted to get me away from Victoria, and everyone.'

Posy looked up suddenly from the file. 'You told the police your wife was out of town, visiting her parents, when Victoria died. Is that true?'

'It is. I'd swear it up and down. Her parents would, too. They live, like, two hundred miles away. There's no way.'

'Just checking.' Posy went back to her notes. Rosalind grinned; she might look like she was engrossed in the file Danny had given her, but Posy was more than capable of concentrating on two things at once. From the speculative look on Danny's face, he was just realising how foolish it would be to underestimate her.

Good.

'Besides, I ended things with Victoria before she was killed,' Danny went on. 'It was already over.'

'And how did Victoria take that news?' Rosalind decided the grimace she got in response to her question was answer enough. 'That was the phone call before the meeting, then. The argument that Sarah overheard – it was you and Victoria?'

Danny grimaced. 'Yeah. We broke up, like, three days earlier, but she wasn't having it. But I wasn't the only one who argued with her that day, you know? I told you I heard someone else getting into it with her about something or other on the way out.'

It was an obvious attempt to redirect their attention from him as a suspect. But Caro had already told them what Hakim had to say about that argument after the meeting, so Rosalind pressed on.

'You took Iain's letter from Scott to him, didn't you? How did he seem that evening? Was he alone?'

'He was. He seemed fine.' Danny shrugged, as if unsure what they wanted to hear. 'If you're asking me if I thought he was about to die by suicide, no. He seemed . . . grumpy, and halfway through a bottle of whisky, but that was all. He took the letter and I left.'

'Did you see anything on his desk?' Posy asked.

'Anything like a paper dahlia? No. I told you. It was all normal.'

'What about the evening of the Skeleton Parade?' Rosalind glanced at Posy as she asked. Danny had been keeping notes on this case for a long time. Maybe he'd been the one who wanted Posy's notebook, for his own reasons. 'You and Raven went together to look for Dexter Rush when he didn't appear for his reading. Given how reclusive the author is, how did you expect to recognise him if you found him?'

Was it possible that Danny had seen the same page proofs in Iain's room that Caro had, and guessed his identity?

But Danny pulled a face. 'That was just an excuse. I actually just wanted to talk to Raven alone, and she'd been avoiding my calls before the festival. I . . . have you spoken to her?'

'You mean, has she told us that she was Victoria's half-sister?' Posy raised an eyebrow. 'She has.'

'I thought she might have access to their father's papers now. Or at least put a good word in for me with the estate, now that I'm a credentialed writer. I knew she'd been trying to find ways to be acknowledged as his legal heir. That was all.'

'What did she say?' Posy pressed.

'That she didn't have the papers, and she didn't have the money to fight in court to try and get them.' Danny gave them a wry smile. 'It was a short conversation.'

He'd still called Raven again, to tell her about the flower in Iain's room, though. Maybe he hadn't totally given up, just yet. And if their conversation hadn't lasted long, either one of them could have been responsible for stealing Posy's notebook.

They just still didn't know why.

Posy

It wasn't a long journey from Bristol to Bath, where Hakim was working, but it was long enough for Posy to start overthinking things.

She didn't trust Danny – given the things they'd learned about him just that afternoon, she'd have been a fool to. But did that mean he'd attacked her in the alley? No.

But he could have. She just wasn't sure why.

There were no answers in his notes, either. She'd gone through his file as quickly as she could, and made her own scribbles about things he'd found out. But there wasn't much she didn't already know.

Still, it was interesting to see what Danny thought might have been going on, back then in the heat of the investigation, rather than with the cold light of hindsight colouring events.

The car slowed outside a leafy, well-manicured campus with a discreet sign identifying it as the location of St Thomas's Independent School, Bath. They turned into the driveway and stopped outside the main, pale stone building.

It was around the end of the school day, but the receptionist was happy to help them, calling through to Hakim and telling them he was in his office. She then collared a student to take them to him, after they'd given their names and been issued with visitor passes.

'So much for the element of surprise,' Rosalind grumbled.

The school was impressive; old enough to instil a proper feeling of awe for the history and gravitas of the place in any visitor, but well maintained and appointed enough to feel modern and effective, too. Posy imagined the fees were astronomical.

Hakim had landed on his feet here, that was for sure. This job he'd got on true merit, not because of Victoria's lies. But if they found out he'd lied on a previous job application, what would that do to his reputation? Posy made a quick note to check *exactly* when Hakim had moved to this school. If he'd been in the process of applying when Victoria died, that might be worth checking out.

Hakim's office was up a small staircase, in the English department. The preternaturally polite student left them there with a nod, and Rosalind knocked on the door. Hakim's voice bid them enter from inside.

'Ms King, Ms Starling.' Hakim stood to greet them, beckoning them towards comfortable visitors chairs. 'How lovely to see you again – in spite of the circumstances. You've come to talk about Iain, I assume?'

'I'm afraid so,' Rosalind said. 'You've heard all about the circumstances of his death, I'm sure?'

Hakim pulled a distasteful face. 'The papers don't leave much to the imagination, do they?'

Posy didn't think that any description in a newspaper could match the shuddering cold that had flooded through her when they discovered the body.

But she nodded politely all the same. She was British again now, after so many years in America, and she never felt it more than at moments like this.

Besides, it was what Dahlia would do.

'Iain brought you into the writing group, didn't he?' Posy asked instead. 'Can you tell us a bit about his relationship with the other members – especially Victoria?'

'Iain . . . he got along with everybody, as far as I know. And he liked to smooth things over for everyone too. But mostly because he never really . . . he never ruffled any feathers, never troubled the water. Never seemed to really *care* as deeply as the others. Do you know what I mean?' Hakim looked up anxiously, as if worried he wasn't making sense.

'I think so.' Posy leafed back through her pages of notes. 'The impression I got from the other members of the writing group was that it was an intense thing to belong to. Everyone was very invested in their writing, in the festival, everything. Is that right?'

'Most certainly. I think, perhaps, many of us joined when we were looking for a new direction in our lives. Something to revitalise us, even. Whether that was publication, a new career, or just an opportunity to make new friends or try new things. Give back to the community, too, in the form of the festival.'

'Which was it for you?' Rosalind asked, eyebrows arched.

Hakim gave a self-deprecating laugh. 'I think I was maybe the most lost of all. When I met Iain at that first festival, I'd just left my job – I'd been working in the City, you see, in banking, and I'd burned out. Completely. My wife and I had just had our first child, and she was taking a career break too – she is a medical writer, and her job involved a lot of travel to conferences, which didn't work for our new lifestyle, either. So we moved out to Market Foxleigh to, well, get away from it all. We had savings, and we sold up our London townhouse, and bought a cottage out here.'

'But you didn't stay?' By Posy's reckoning, they could only have lived in that cottage for a couple of years or so before relocating again to Bath. 'Was that because of your work?'

'It was a fairly extreme move,' Hakim said, carefully. 'Market Foxleigh is a lovely town, but it wasn't a good fit for us. I joined the writing group and the festival committee as part of my search for a new purpose, but I soon realised my new direction would be teaching.'

'Yes, Caro told us about how Victoria helped you with that,' Rosalind said, diplomatically.

Hakim gave a stiff nod. 'Quite so. And, well, especially after Victoria's death . . . I knew for sure I wasn't in the right place.'

Posy supposed murder would put anyone off a town.

'Iain moved away too,' Rosalind said. 'Before any of the rest of you. Did he give you any indication why?'

'He didn't need to,' Hakim replied. 'I mean, we were all thinking about leaving. Nobody was surprised when we woke up one morning to find him gone.'

'So you didn't know that Iain was Dexter Rush, then?' Posy threw it out there casually, eager to get his unguarded response.

She scrutinised his reaction carefully. His mouth fell open, just a tiny bit, like he was waiting for words to fall out but didn't know what they were yet. Then he blinked, very slowly, as if adjusting his whole world view before he looked at it again.

Hakim moistened his lips. 'I didn't know that. No. But I should have guessed.'

'How, exactly?' Rosalind crossed her legs and sat back in her usual 'convince me' pose.

'I only read the first Dexter Rush novel. But the voice . . . I remember thinking that the ending sounded just like something Iain would write.'

'The voice?' Posy asked. 'You can tell who wrote something just by reading it?' Like he'd done for the short story competition, according to Caro.

'Oh yes!' Hakim reached for a stack of essays from the filing cabinet behind him. 'I've just had some of my adult students – I teach creative writing evening classes here too – writing about the authorial voice. Every writer has, well, their tells, I suppose. Something that gives them away when they write. And voice is the hardest thing to fake.'

He handed Posy the stack of printed essays, and she glanced through them, spotting references to Jonathan Swift and Shakespeare alongside more familiar, modern authors who'd written under pen names after they were famous.

'It's why plagiarists get caught,' Hakim went on. 'Someone recognises the voice and goes looking.'

Posy thought about Raven's indie-published books about Lettice Davenport as a private investigator. She'd only read the first few chapters of the first book, and maybe they got better, but it was clear that in the beginning, at least, Raven had been trying to copy Lettice Davenport's style of writing – and failing. Maybe she'd do better just writing in her own voice.

'Victoria thought that someone had been plagiarising her work, didn't she?' Rosalind said, slowly, and in a flash Posy saw exactly where her fellow Dahlia's thoughts were taking her. 'You're the voice expert. Is it possible?'

'It's always possible,' Hakim replied. 'Although, honestly, I don't see how anyone could have been. She never shared enough of her work with us for someone to copy.'

'But her work was all backed up on the festival cloud drive, wasn't it?' Posy said, suddenly. Things were starting to come together now, even if she couldn't make complete sense of it all just yet . . . 'Any of you could have accessed it from there, if you had the passwords.' Milla hadn't been sure who had those passwords, but Posy suspected they wouldn't have been too hard to come by.

Hakim blinked. 'Well, yes. I suppose we could. But who—'

'You said the *ending* sounded like Iain,' Posy reminded him. 'Only the ending?'

'I . . . I'd have to read it again to check, but . . . yes. As I recall.' Hakim had paled slightly as he slumped in his desk chair. 'You think . . .'

'Victoria never finished her stories,' Rosalind said, softly. 'And Iain went to great lengths to prevent the world from finding out that he was Dexter Rush. Yes, Hakim. We *do* think.'

Chapter Nineteen

It was hard to imagine that the three of us – so different in so many ways – would have to work together to solve this case. But solve it we would.

Caro Hooper *in* The Three Dahlias
***By* Caro Hooper**

Caro

Caro was running late for Will's book launch when the call came through, but she stopped outside the tube station at Baker Street and leaned against the wall to take it, all the same.

'What have you found out?' She stared out past the crowds, the statue of Sherlock Holmes, and the traffic, not really seeing any of it as she listened to Posy and Rosalind recount their day of interviews, both talking over each other on speakerphone in the back of the car.

'None of it is proof,' Rosalind cautioned.

'We're five years past the first murder,' Caro replied. 'Proof is going to be hard to come by. We need a confession.'

They didn't contradict her. Not even Rosalind, who *always* contradicted Caro if she could.

All she said now was, 'We need to know how much Petra knew. Did she know Iain had stolen the Dexter Rush manuscripts – or the first one, at least?'

'He self-published his first couple of books,' Posy put in. 'So Petra might not have known. I'm guessing he was banking on Victoria never checking for indie-published books online, because she had such a snobbish attitude to them. And we don't know yet whether the ones published after Victoria's death were written by him or Victoria.'

'Can we get access to the cloud drives?' Caro asked.

'We tried,' Posy said. 'Hakim logged in, but there's nothing there. They've been wiped.'

'Damn.' That would make proving things all the harder.

'We've got Hakim on the case,' Rosalind reassured her.

'We're trusting Hakim?' Caro interrupted. 'Are we sure that's wise?'

There was a pause on the other end. 'We've got to trust someone, I think,' Posy said, eventually. It sounded like a revelation. 'And he's the one who put us on to the similarity in writing style.'

'Which is why we've got Hakim reading Dexter Rush's back catalogue instead of student essays, looking for connections to what he can remember of Victoria's work,' Rosalind said. 'But until he's done . . .'

'Petra's our best source of information,' Caro finished for her. 'Got it.'

'Caro, be careful.' Posy sounded scared, Caro realised. She wasn't sure she'd heard her sound like that before, not really. Nervous, yes. Worried, certainly. But scared? Not so much. 'If Petra found out that Iain had stolen Victoria's work, and she thought he was about to confess – to plagiarism or murder – that could have been a reason for her to kill him herself, to save her reputation and career.'

'I'm not sure I see Petra as a killer,' Rosalind put in.

'Then you haven't seen her in contract negotiations.' Caro pushed away from the wall, and began walking towards Daunt Books. 'Leave it with me. I'll see what I can find out at the launch.'

She hung up before Rosalind and Posy could get their inevitable objections to her plan out. Really, what else was she supposed to do?

Caro had been somewhat surprised to learn that Will's books were published by a different imprint of her own publisher, and he was represented by another agent at Petra's firm; it seemed that almost all of publishing was linked one way or another, in the sort of way she'd assumed only applied to acting, before she started her new life as a writer.

As a result, not only was Petra in attendance – Petra got invited everywhere, as far as Caro could tell – but Caro's editor and publicist, Charlotte and Jemima, too. In fact, they were already downstairs in the glorious surroundings of Daunt Books, helping themselves to glasses of wine and chatting business, when Caro joined them.

'Caro!' Charlotte beamed as she spotted her, and there was the usual round of awkward hugs around wine glasses.

'Sorry I'm late,' Caro apologised as she reached for her own glass from the well-supplied table. Will knew what was important at these events. 'Had to take a phone call.'

The three of them brushed off her concern.

'Don't worry. Will is up there giving a media interview, anyway.' Petra waved a hand towards the galleried balcony. 'He won't have missed you.'

'We were just talking about how thrilled we are by the success of *The Three Dahlias*,' Jemima said.

Charlotte took a sip of wine. 'So, now the book is really out there, I can ask – how are you finding the switch from the screen to the page? Has publishing lived up to all your expectations?'

'Well, I've discovered there's always more booze than food at any publishing events,' Caro joked, getting the expected laugh as everyone acknowledged the truth of her words. 'Other than that . . . in lots of ways it's very similar. The same expectations and attention. The same cliques and gangs, you know? Except here it's the traditional versus the indies, the celebrity authors against the jobbing ones. Debate about awards and who was overlooked, or who didn't deserve this accolade or another. Representation and diversity and how to get it. Who gets overpaid and who barely gets paid at all. The talk about who's phoning it in these days, who got a ghost to cover them – and who outright stole their work.'

She caught a couple of people standing nearby glancing over at her words as she was talking, and wondered if she should keep her voice down. But she wasn't talking to them, anyway.

Instead, she looked straight at Petra as she reached her last phrase, still aware of how Charlotte and Jemima's nodding heads stopped bobbing when she said 'stole'. Petra merely stared back, unmoved.

Charlotte gave a nervy chuckle, tossing her long dark plait over her shoulder. 'Obviously in publishing stealing – or plagiarism – is taken very seriously . . .'

'Oh, I'm sure,' Caro said, flashing her a quick smile. 'By agents as well as publishers, I'd imagine. Isn't that right, Petra?'

Petra jerked into life. 'Of course. Nobody wants that sort of thing in our business. Now, has Will finished that interview? I really think we ought to go and say hello and congratulations.'

But Caro wasn't letting the conversation go that easily.

'I'm curious, Petra. What would you do if you discovered a client of yours had been plagiarising someone else's work?'

'I hope you're not trying to confess to something here, Caro,' Petra joked, but the answering giggles from the others were more nervous than amused.

'Of course not.' Caro leaned towards her agent. 'But really. What would you do?'

'I'd hope to never be in that position.' Petra kept her eyes trained firmly on the balcony, refusing to say anything further.

Caro glanced up to see Will shaking hands with the guy holding the microphone. He'd be coming down to greet people soon. She had to work fast.

Petra had been in Market Foxleigh shortly after Victoria's murder, meeting with Iain. And she'd had access to the cloud drive where Victoria stored her books, assuming Victoria hadn't changed the passwords after she left.

What if Iain hadn't stolen Victoria's work alone?

'What if you'd helped that client plagiarise another writer?' Caro asked. 'What would you do then?'

Charlotte and Jemima were exchanging concerned glances, but Petra looked unperturbed.

'Caro, I have no idea what you're talking about. And I don't think you realise what a sensitive subject plagiarism is in the publishing community.'

'That's right,' Charlotte jumped in. 'Now, can anyone remember the name of that show Will was in back in—?'

'Come on, now,' Caro said. 'I always thought that boozy, scandalous launch parties were the hallmark of the publishing industry? Well, here's a scandal for you. We have reason to believe that bestselling author Dexter Rush – your client, Petra – stole his books from the murdered writer, Victoria Denby.'

There were the requisite gasps from Charlotte and Jemima – along with the couple standing nearby who were obviously listening in – but Petra's schooled look of surprise didn't quite ring true.

'And you knew it, didn't you?' Caro accused Petra.

Charlotte jumped in before Petra could reply. 'Caro, I'm sure all this is just a funny joke, but I do need to point out that these aren't humorous accusations. They're very, very serious. And, well, I need to say that these are the sort of things that people could sue over, if they were repeated.'

'Charlotte's right, Caro.' Petra lifted her glass and took a sip before she spoke again. 'This is too serious for jokes. Now, come on, it looks like Will is about to make a speech up there.'

Caro had never really felt taken seriously in the TV world. And she knew she was something of a novelty as a detective, even when she was working with Ashok instead of Rosalind and Posy.

But she'd thought that publishing was somewhere she could be treated as a grown-up. She'd written her own book, herself, about her own experiences. She'd worked with editors, checked proofs, done promotion and events. She was an author, whatever anyone said.

She might be new to the publishing world, but she wasn't a fool.

And she wasn't about to be dismissed as a joke by Petra, or anyone else.

Caro placed her glass of wine back down on the nearest table, and turned her back on the gallery to face Petra fully, just as she heard someone tapping a microphone.

'We know that you and Iain were involved in plagiarism,' she told Petra, her voice calm and even, but deadly serious – and not particularly quiet. Which was unfortunate, as everyone else had stopped talking as Will took the microphone. 'What we don't know yet is whether you were also involved in one, maybe two, murders. But I intend to find out.'

Her words rang out around the galleried bookshop, drawing stares and murmurs from Will's friends, family, colleagues and professional acquaintances in attendance. Ignoring the wide eyes and death looks, Caro swung her handbag over her shoulder and headed for the stairs, and then the door.

Behind her, she heard Will begin to address the crowd.

'Caro Hooper, ladies and gentlemen – always one to steal a scene!'

'And solve a murder,' Caro muttered to herself.

Rosalind

The fallout from Caro's outburst started early the next morning, with a voicemail from Eleanor Grey on Rosalind's phone.

Rosalind, who was avoiding Jack's calls, stared at the number as the phone rang and waited for the tone that told her she had a message. She listened to it through twice before she rang Caro.

'So, Will's launch last night. How did it go?'

The silence on the other end of the phone told her everything she needed to know.

'You accused Petra of . . . what? Plagiarism? Murder? Both?' Rosalind asked.

More silence.

Then, 'Both. But I said we didn't *know* if she was involved in murder yet,' Caro added, mulishly.

'Without any evidence at all. What were you thinking?'

'I was thinking . . . I don't know. That it all made sense at last, and she couldn't get away with it. Even if she isn't a murderer – and I'm really not sure about that just yet – I'm almost certain she helped to steal someone else's work. And it's just *wrong,* Rosalind.'

Rosalind sighed. She couldn't even pretend to be properly surprised at this turn of events. 'I just got a voicemail from Eleanor. I think we need to all talk. Meet you at Posy's?'

'Are we going to tell her we're coming?' Caro asked.

'If she got the same voicemail I did, she'll be expecting us.'

Posy *was* expecting them, if the spread of pastries and the hum of the coffee machine in action were any indication.

'Eleanor called you too, then?' Rosalind handed Posy a bag with the logo of a local interiors shop, then turned away before she opened it.

'Left a message last night,' Posy confirmed. She opened the bag and peered inside. 'Plates?'

'Cake plates. And forks, actually. We can use them for the pastries.' Rosalind eyed the selection and nodded in satisfaction. 'I'd give them a quick rinse first.'

'Oh, and we can use these for the coffee!' Caro handed over a cardboard box. 'They arrived this morning. Now, what did Eleanor *say*?' Caro followed them both into the kitchen as Posy unpacked the plates and washed them.

'They don't want us for the podcast anymore,' Rosalind said, deciding to pull off the plaster in one quick swoop. 'We're off the case.'

Caro leaned against the counter, mouth slightly open. 'But . . . they can't.'

'You didn't want us to investigate in the first place,' Posy reminded her. She turned to Caro's box as Rosalind dried the plates. 'I'd have thought you'd be glad.'

'But things have changed!' Caro's outrage was clear. 'We've uncovered things the original investigation didn't even know to look for. And a man is dead, for heaven's sake! How can they stop now?'

Posy pulled a mug out of the box and stared at it before placing it on the counter and pulling out the next one. Then she reached for a third, and lined it up too, stepping back to let Rosalind see.

Rosalind blinked. The mugs had clearly been specially ordered, and personalised to each of them. Posy put the first – a delicate bone china one with a photo of Rosalind as Dahlia in the first rendition of *The Lady Detective* movie on it – under the coffee machine to fill, before handing it to her.

'Do you like them?' Caro asked, as Posy made her coffee – in a rather more sturdy cup with Caro's own Dahlia on, of course.

'They're wonderful,' Posy replied, sounding sincere. Her modern, angular mug had a promotional still of her from the new movie on, to round out the set. Rosalind had no idea where Caro had found the blasted things, but she couldn't deny they added some personalisation to Posy's flat at last. 'And it's not that I don't appreciate all the housewarming gifts . . . but you do both realise that it's not your job to look after me, don't you? You're not actually my mothers.'

'Of course we know that,' Rosalind replied, brusquely.

'We might just be feeling a tiny bit guilty about letting you get hurt, I suppose.' Caro held up her mug as Posy handed it to her and stared – a little wistfully, in Rosalind's opinion – at the picture of herself on it. 'But we're done now, I'm sure.'

'Right.' Posy didn't sound like she believed them. 'Anyway. Back to the matter at hand . . .'

'Yes! How can they stop the podcast?' Caro asked again, surprisingly vehemently for someone who'd been so opposed to it a mere week and a half ago.

Posy took her own coffee from the machine. 'They didn't say that *they're* stopping the investigation. Just that they don't want us to help anymore.'

They headed back to the pastries on the coffee table, and Rosalind took a moment to admire the tasteful cushions and throw she'd chosen for the space before dealing with Caro's inevitable meltdown.

'Why? Do they think they can do better than us?' Caro demanded. 'Or are they just going to take everything we've found out and pretend it's their own work? Take credit for our discoveries?' She turned to Posy, pointing with her coffee cup. 'Maybe this was their plan all along. Maybe Sarah stole your notebook.'

'Or perhaps they just feel that we've become more of a liability than an asset,' Rosalind said, sharply. It was important to stop Caro's rants before she got too much wind in her sails.

Caro sank back down onto the sofa. 'You think this is because of what I said to Petra?'

'I think that's almost a certainty,' Rosalind replied.

'You'd think it would be good for publicity,' Caro said, mulishly. 'All they've done is drop that stupid trailer. We've practically solved the case for them!'

'Yes, but apparently the parent company who owns the podcast also owns the publishing house responsible for Dexter Rush's novels,' Posy said. 'Rumours about plagiarism are, as you can imagine, not going down well there.'

'So perhaps you'd better tell us exactly what you *did* say,' Rosalind finished, then braced herself for the full story.

Caro's recollection of the launch party seemed complete, and without too much embellishment – it didn't need it. It was damning enough as it was.

'This is exactly the sort of thing Jack hates,' Rosalind muttered.

She'd been avoiding his calls for three days now, because she already knew what he was going to say. Had known since she'd rushed out on their quiet week at the cottage to get back to Caro, in London, stopping only to pick up the cushions for Posy before jumping in the car.

She just didn't want the argument. Especially when part of her agreed with him, some of the time.

'Okay, so you accused Petra of plagiarism and maybe being involved in a murder or two, and Eleanor called to take us off the case,' Posy summarised. 'So, are we assuming that Petra told Eleanor?'

'Petra, or maybe my publisher,' Caro replied. 'Or anyone else who was at that party last night . . . oh, what does it matter? The only real question here is: are we going to do as we're told?'

Rosalind looked between Posy and Caro, knowing that, on past evidence, the answer was fairly obvious. On the wall behind them, the Murder Map loomed. The answers were somewhere on there, Rosalind was certain. They just had to find them.

'Of course we're not,' she said, crisply. 'We've come too far to stop now. Besides, I don't trust anyone else to get it right.'

'Naturally,' Caro said, but she was smiling.

'Then it's back to Plan A, I guess.' Posy put down her coffee cup, picked up her notebook, and moved towards the Murder Map. 'Find the evidence we need to convict a killer.'

'That's going to be on you two.' Rosalind drained the rest of her coffee. 'In case you've forgotten, it's Saturday. And I've got an appointment with Scott Baker.' The weight of her lie about that still sat on her heart.

'You'll meet us back here afterwards to fill us in?' Caro was on her feet already, hovering anxiously between Rosalind and the door.

She'd taken a knock last night, Rosalind could see that even if Caro wasn't willing to admit it yet. She was always so certain in her convictions – for Caro, it would have been a no-brainer to confront Petra immediately. She'd never really mastered patience, or tact.

But Rosalind also knew how much she'd hate everyone talking about her, again. From the appearance on *Food Matters* to the gossip after the launch, Caro would be feeling foolish, and that was the last thing they wanted.

She needed a boost in confidence – and in support. And Rosalind and Posy were the only people likely to give it to her, besides Annie.

'No, not back here,' Rosalind said, decisively. She'd done the right thing, lying about Scott. And this was the right thing, too. 'Meet me at Langans at eight. I'll book us a table.'

'Langans?' Posy asked. 'Why?'

'Because the three Dahlias don't hide away from anything, or anyone,' Rosalind replied.

Posy

An hour later, Caro and Posy had gone through all the pastries, plus several coffees each – but they still didn't have the answers they needed.

They had to have missed something. Rosalind was right – knowing wasn't enough; they needed proof. And it would be there, somewhere. It always was.

Nobody could commit such a perfect crime that it wouldn't leave a trail somewhere. And they were the only people really looking for it, so it was up to them to find it.

Hands on her hips, Posy stared up at the Murder Map until her vision blurred. That was okay, though. She wasn't looking for details. She was looking for patterns.

Except there weren't any.

With a sigh, she opened up her notebook and focused again to read her notes from Danny's file.

'I'm certain now that Iain's death, and the plagiarism, has to be linked to Victoria's murder,' Caro said.

'Why? And how?' Posy asked. 'I'm not doubting you, I'm genuinely asking. Why are you so sure that Petra didn't just use the cover of the flower to link her murder to the one Scott committed? She could have ordered one under another name before she even came to Market Foxleigh, knowing that we'd be investigating and that Iain was wavering. She could have had it all planned out.'

Posy turned to watch Caro puzzle out the answer to her question. Caro had been the one of them most certain that Scott had committed the crime he'd been imprisoned for.

'I . . . damn it, I can't put my finger on it. It's something you said, or maybe it was Rosalind.' Caro's frown deepened. 'It wasn't a smoking gun or anything. But it was something that made me think. Then I got distracted and now I can't for the life of me remember what it was.'

'All right. Well, I think we need to start back at the beginning. Go through all of our suspect's stories about the night Victoria died.' Posy grabbed a rogue chopstick from last night's Chinese takeaway and used it as a pointer as she talked through the Murder Map again. Who was where, when – and why. That was what mattered.

'We know all this,' Caro said. 'Do we really have to go over it again?'

'Somewhere in here the answer is hiding.' Posy stared at the end of her chopstick as it moved around the map.

Map.

Wait.

Maybe the answer wasn't in there at all.

She reached for Eleanor's file. 'Caro, check that stack of papers on the coffee table for the map of Market Foxleigh, will you?'

Caro rifled through Posy's post – mostly discount vouchers for the local pizza place – and pulled out the small tourist map they'd been given at the start of the festival. Posy opened it up and scanned it for what she needed to see.

The map didn't show everything – just the festival sites, mostly, and other points of interest to attendees. Like bookshops. Including one on a canal boat, just down from Victoria Denby's old house.

Which meant it showed her exactly what she was looking for.

She double checked her instincts with Danny's list of alibis, then spread the map out over the coffee table to show Caro what she'd found. One piece of evidence in Danny's notes that hadn't shown up in Eleanor's file stood out.

'It doesn't necessarily mean anything,' Caro said. 'In fact, if it does, then that means we must be wrong about something else. Unless . . .'

'Exactly,' Posy said. 'We always said it didn't have to be either or. It could be both.'

'Which means they were all in this up to their necks.' Caro shook her head. 'At least it means I won't have to apologise to Petra. Much.'

'It wasn't that we were wrong,' Posy said. 'Just that our theory was incomplete. *If* I'm right.'

There was always the chance that she wasn't. That they'd got everything wrong, right from the start.

But Posy didn't think that was the case. And looking at Caro's face, neither did she.

'Quick. Call Rosalind. This can't wait until dinner. We might be able to catch her before she goes in to speak to Scott. There are some questions we need her to ask . . .'

Rosalind

Rosalind had never been to a prison before. None of the roles she'd ever undertaken had required it. Still, she'd watched enough crime dramas over the years to have a vague idea what to expect.

But nothing had quite prepared her for the intense feeling of claustrophobia that settled on her skin the moment she passed through the gates.

The officer who checked her ID did a double take at seeing her name and photo, but the one who performed the search of her person didn't seem to recognise her at all. The other visitors attending were far more concerned with seeing their own loved ones than celebrity spotting, fortunately.

Scott was already seated in the visiting room when they were led in, and Rosalind would have recognised him instantly from the photos in the file, despite him being five years older, thinner, and possibly wiser, even if she hadn't seen his video.

She'd told Caro and Posy that he'd only agreed to see her, alone. In truth, she hadn't given Scott any choice. She was sure he'd have preferred to talk to Caro, but the last thing Caro needed was to be confronted with the man she'd believed for years to be her stalker, and she'd wanted Posy with Caro to keep her distracted while the visit took place. But now, taking her plastic seat in front of a convicted killer, Rosalind wished she wasn't on her own.

Together, the three of them had power. Security, too. They 'had each other's backs' as Caro would say.

Without the other two Dahlias, she suddenly felt very alone.

'Rosalind King.' Scott didn't stand to greet her. 'You know, I had a strange message from my sister this morning, telling me to cancel this visit.'

More fallout from Will's launch party, then. 'You didn't, though. Why?'

'Because I'm curious, I suppose,' Scott said. 'I always was.'

He looked younger than Rosalind had imagined. More tired, too.

She didn't know, still, if he'd killed Victoria Denby. But she hoped by the end of this visit she would.

If she could just ask the right questions. Including the ones Caro and Posy had sent through, just before her phone was confiscated.

'I'm curious, too,' Rosalind said. 'That's why I came.'

Scott sat back in the red plastic chair, folded his arms across his narrow chest, and nodded. 'Go on, then. What do you want to know?'

Posy

Langan's Brasserie in Mayfair was elegant, old-school, classic and expensive – so it made total sense that Rosalind would have picked it. With its gentle green velvet chairs, and the perfectly starched white table linens, Posy could see Dahlia Lively ordering the cheese soufflé here any day of the week.

Posy spotted a group or two of diners talking about them as they waited to be shown to their table, but hopefully the news about the blowout at Will's book launch wouldn't have reached beyond the publishing circuit just yet. Chances were, the other diners were gossiping about any one of Caro or Posy's previous indiscretions.

She ignored them all, and concentrated on distracting Caro with the menu instead, until Rosalind finally joined them.

'It's the only way it all makes sense,' Rosalind said, later, after they pushed their plates aside and Caro and Posy had finished sharing their theories, trying to keep their voices down and not talking over each other too much. 'And it fits with what Scott told me, too.'

Posy knew she'd have been running the scenario through in her head the whole time they were talking. Testing it for holes, inconsistencies or problems.

If she hadn't found any . . .

'Well, if we're going to fill in the last few gaps in our theory, we're going to need proof. This time.' Caro added the last bit with a rueful smile.

'Then we'll get it.' There was a certainty flowing through Posy, now. The knowledge that they were closing in on the end of this case. That justice would be served after all.

'Yes, but how?' Rosalind asked. 'Who can prove *this*?'

'We need them all,' Posy said, calmly. 'They were all a part of it, in their own way. We need all seven of them together – well, okay, minus Scott for now, but Rosalind, you can use his testimony from earlier.'

'Do you think they'll do it?' Rosalind asked, and Posy shrugged.

'Tell them each what we know, up to a point, and it might tip it. Tell them whatever it takes. It's the only way this is going to work.'

They all shared a look – one filled with an excited sort of hope, and a sense of nervous anticipation. There were still so many ways this could all go wrong. And always the chance that they were jumping to the wrong conclusion, again, and their next dinner out would result in countless papped photos and negative stories to go with it.

But Posy felt in her bones that they'd got this one right.

And soon, they'd be able to prove it.

Chapter Twenty

'We can't let him know we're onto him, not yet,' Dahlia said.

'Why not, Miss?' Bess asked, with a frown.

'Because we don't yet know how much more he has to teach us.'

Dahlia Lively *in* Lies and Lilacs
***By* Lettice Davenport, 1966**

Caro

It was only to be expected, Caro supposed, that their investigation – and the death of Iain Hardy, recently outed in the press as Dexter Rush, as they'd predicted – had caught the interest of the nation.

With that interest came a renewed focus on the writing group Victoria Denby had founded, the festival that continued in her memory and, of course, the new podcast that re-examined her murder.

Eleanor was rushing the podcast into production, by all accounts – and had even called Rosalind to see if they might still be able to contribute 'off the record'. Rosalind had told her she didn't think Eleanor – or her bosses – would like what they had to contribute, and Caro had done a little silent cheer off to one side.

Coincidentally, all this new interest was exactly what Caro needed to prove their case, which was handy. They'd spent all of Sunday setting things up, cajoling their suspects into place, and now it was time.

'Are you sure you're ready for this?' Rosalind asked, just off to the side of the *Britain Now* set, as Caro was fitted with her microphone. Across the way, she could see Eleanor, Petra and Sarah also waiting for their moment in the spotlight. And in the front row of the audience, she knew, Danny, Hakim, Milla and Raven were already watching.

'I'm ready,' she said, her voice calm and even. 'I'll get it right this time.' She didn't like to admit to making mistakes, but she'd made one with Petra the night of Will's launch. She wouldn't repeat that error today.

Not to mention the bigger error she still needed to redress.

'And we'll be right here if you need us,' Posy added. 'Rosalind's got Jack on speed dial.'

Not that he'd do them much good if he was still in Wales, but Caro didn't point that out.

They'd talked, of course, about bringing in the police. As they'd put together all the final evidence they'd gathered, over their table in Langan's, Posy had asked if it was time to call them. To give them a heads-up on what they had planned.

They'd decided against it, in the end, for a couple of reasons. Rosalind's reason, which was the most sensible, was that even with all the clues and evidence they'd put together, it wasn't conclusive. There wasn't enough for the police to close the case, even if they took them seriously enough to consider it. They needed their killer to incriminate themselves. To put them in a position where they couldn't lie their way out of it again.

Caro's reason wasn't quite so mature. For her, it was simply that their way of doing things made a much better story – and looked a hell of a lot better on TV.

It had all come together when Jemima the publicist had emailed to say that *Britain Now* wanted her for the week-night evening show, along with Eleanor, Petra and Sarah, to talk about 'the people behind the story' of Iain's and Victoria's deaths. Or, as Caro interpreted it, to get all the gossip.

'It's the perfect opportunity,' Caro had told the others, gleefully. 'Pin them down on live TV. There's no way they'll be able to wriggle out of it after that!'

'Unless we're wrong.' Posy had worried at her lower lip with her perfect white teeth.

'We're not,' Caro had told her, firmly.

'Or they're expecting us,' Rosalind had added.

That one had given Caro more pause. 'I don't think they are,' she'd said, eventually. 'I think they've got away with this for so long, and been so clever about it all, they don't believe they'll ever be caught.'

And she still believed that now, preparing to go on camera. It took a certain sort of confidence to believe you could get away with murder. She just wished that the memories of accusing Petra at the launch, of the incredulous stares and the whispers, would stop playing on a loop in her mind. She hadn't meant to do it, exactly. It was just that it had all come together in her mind in that moment and she couldn't stop herself from blurting it out.

This time, she was more prepared. This time, she'd do it right.

She had a job to do. She couldn't afford to be distracted. Even if Petra was standing just a few feet away, ready to represent Iain's memory and estate, smoothing down her hair before their entrance.

The presenters – a sweet young woman with a Scottish accent, and a guy from Yorkshire who used to be some sort of sports star – turned to camera and began their introduction. All solemn faces and just a hint of salacious anticipation. Just what their audience wanted.

Then they were ushered on, ready to take their places on that famous red sofa, before the camera turned back onto it. Caro made sure she was sitting with Sarah between her and Petra, and Eleanor on her other side. She risked a glance over at the audience, just about able to see Posy taking her seat in the front row with Rosalind and their other suspects.

It hadn't been easy to persuade everyone to be there. But the promise of unmasking Petra as the mastermind behind Iain's plagiarism seemed to have reassured the rest of them that they were safe – and refusing to get involved only made them look more suspicious. Nobody else wanted to be implemented in this mess.

And if they'd leaned a little heavily on the idea that Iain had killed himself out of guilt, well . . . The end justified the means on this one, as far as Caro was concerned.

Petra and Eleanor, of course, had been thoroughly reassured by Rosalind that Caro had no intention of revisiting her past accusations on air. She just hadn't mentioned that it was because she had new ones. And she hadn't promised that she or Posy wouldn't do it, either.

The interview started smoothly enough – a brief, non-graphic recap of the founding of the writing group and festival, Victoria's murder and Scott's arrest. Petra spoke briefly about the early days of the group, and Victoria herself.

Then the host, Stephanie, turned to Sarah. 'But you never believed your brother was guilty, did you, Sarah?'

From there, it was a bit of a spiel about the new podcast, of course. Eleanor and Sarah spoke about that, making it sound like a righteous cause for social justice, rather than a publicity grab. Caro straightened her spine and settled her face into a camera-ready expression. They'd be coming to her next.

'This is where you came in, isn't that right, Caro?' Jason, the male host, gave her a warm smile. 'Would you like to tell us how that came about?'

Now. This was her chance. Her heart pounding in her chest and the blood whooshing past her ears was distracting, but she forced herself to slow her breathing. After so many years in show business, appearing on camera was old hat. But accusing someone of murder on live TV was still new – and terrifying.

'Actually, Jason, I was part of this from almost the start. You see, I testified at Scott's trial – against him, as it happens. So, as you can imagine, I was pretty surprised when Eleanor and Sarah came to me asking for help getting him acquitted!'

She placed a hand on Sarah's knee as she said it, setting everyone at ease with the joke. The murmur of noise around the audience was half unsure laughter, half question, but that was okay.

It would all make sense to them very soon.

'But Sarah appealed to our better natures, and the case piqued our interest, so we agreed,' Caro said, glossing over the part where Eleanor had announced their involvement before they'd even signed on – or the part where she'd now fired them.

'You say "we",' Stephanie interjected quickly. 'That's you and the other two . . . well, I guess you call them Dahlias? Rosalind King and Posy Starling.'

'That's right.' Caro motioned towards the audience. 'They're my best friends, and the only people I'd want to investigate a murder with. They're also here today, if they want to give us a wave?'

Rosalind and Posy dutifully stood and waved at the audience, a camera swinging round quickly to catch the moment, Caro had no doubt.

This was good. Nobody even suspected that they were about to witness the *J'Accuse* moment of this murder investigation.

Not even the murderer.

'So, can you tell us much about the investigation so far?' Jason asked. 'Without tipping off your suspects, of course!'

He laughed, but no one else did.

'That would be difficult, as all our initial suspects are right here in your studio,' Caro replied, with a wry smile. 'You see, if Scott was innocent, and we discounted the possibility of a random attack by a stranger, it seemed that one of seven people must be responsible – and except for Scott, who's in prison, and Iain, who's sadly no longer with us, they're all here today.'

'Does that mean you *do* know who the killer was?' Stephanie asked, sounding slightly incredulous. That hum of uncertain curiosity in the audience had risen in volume, too. This wasn't what they expected from their early-evening chat shows. But they'd probably been queuing for hours to be there. Caro figured they deserved a show.

At the end of the sofa, Petra shifted awkwardly. Caro smiled.

'We think we do, yes. Although we still have one or two questions left to answer – perhaps you won't mind me asking them now?' She kept her tone polite, as if she were asking for nothing more than a cup of tea.

From the way Jason's eyes widened, Caro suspected his producer was having words in his ear. She just wasn't sure which way they were going.

Jason reached up and touched his ear. 'Well, if we can help catch a murderer, we'd definitely want to do that, in the name of public safety, right, Stephanie?'

Stephanie looked less convinced, and her strained expression suggested that the producer talking in her ear wasn't entirely on board either. But she nodded, all the same.

'Fantastic, thank you.' Caro clapped her hands, and jumped to her feet. She always explained things better when she was pacing. Maybe that was what had gone wrong at the launch.

'Okay, so as I said, at the start it seemed like any one of seven suspects could have committed the murder. They were all part of the same writing group, and all attended the festival planning meeting the day of the murder, which the police file and all the evidence suggested was the start of things. As our investigation progressed, it also became clear that Victoria was not the kind, generous pillar of the community that her legacy, and newspaper reports at the time, suggested. But I'm getting ahead of myself.'

Caro paced to one end of the sofa, until she was facing Milla, in the front row of the audience. 'Obviously our first port of call was to speak to all of them individually. And since it happened that I was in Market Foxleigh that weekend for the annual Crime Writing Festival, we were able to do just that. Starting with the festival coordinator, Milla.'

Milla looked rather like a startled rabbit, so Caro gave her an encouraging smile and motioned for her to stand up. Hopefully the camera would follow. 'Milla, you told us many interesting things about Victoria. How she looked down on you within the writing group, because you were a cleaner – even though you held a master's degree. It was obvious that you'd taken the festival to heights Victoria hadn't dreamed of, and you wouldn't have had that opportunity if she'd lived.'

'That doesn't mean I killed her!' Milla protested, eyes wide.

'Of course not,' Caro said, soothingly. 'But you also gave us a key insight into Victoria's behaviour – how she hid her own writing while talking down everyone else's, and – crucially, it turned out – how she never finished writing anything.'

Milla – and the rest of the audience – looked puzzled as to why that was crucial, but Caro was already moving on.

'We talked too to Danny, and it quickly became apparent that he had plenty of motive for killing Victoria.' She hoped he'd talked to his wife before he came on this show, but whether he had or not, the secrets were all coming out today. She didn't have much patience with adulterers. 'He'd been having an affair with the victim and, when he tried to end it, she threatened to tell his wife everything. Surely that was enough to cause him to kill?'

A murmur went up around the audience at that – nothing like a bit of illicit sex to get people interested. In the front row, she saw that Hakim had his hand on Danny's arm, keeping him in his seat.

Caro kept going. 'But it wasn't the affair that really caught our interest. Danny told us something else – that he'd heard Hakim arguing with Victoria after the meeting that day. Isn't that right?'

At the front of the seats, Posy took a microphone from a stand meant for audience participation later in the show, and held it out to Hakim, who leaned forward to talk into it.

'It is. I was on the judging committee, and so I knew the story she had printed as having won in the programme for the awards night wasn't the one that the panel had chosen.'

'And do you know who wrote the story that *should* have won?' Posy pressed.

'The entries were all anonymous.' Hakim glanced sideways along the line of suspects. 'But like I told you, I'm very good at identifying authorial voice. And, well, the writing of the winning story was definitely familiar.'

'Whose was it?' Caro asked, bored of the sidelines already.

'Sarah Baker's,' Hakim said, and the crowd gasped. Sarah looked outraged, and Eleanor was whispering furiously in her ear.

Stephanie, the host, frowned. 'Wait a moment. You're not saying you think Victoria Denby was killed because of a short-story competition, surely?'

'Not at all,' Caro said, reassuringly. 'In fact, Hakim told us he never shared that knowledge with anyone – even Sarah herself. But it was important, because it told us something else about Victoria. She was terrified of being outshone by the other members of the group, wasn't she, Raven?'

Raven looked slightly startled that it was her turn, but she nodded all the same, as Hakim handed her the microphone. Caro really hoped they'd managed to swing a camera round to show all this. It was TV gold.

'She was,' Raven said. 'She hated anyone going the indie route – publishing their books themselves, I mean – because that meant they had actual books out in the world, which she'd never do.'

'Only imagine how she'd have felt if she'd witnessed *your* success, knowing you were actually her half-sister.' Caro said it mostly for the gasp from the crowd, which was gratifyingly astonished. The other suspects – except Danny – also looked amazed. None of them had a clue where this was going. It was perfect!

Posy rolled her eyes at her, before taking the microphone herself and addressing Raven again. 'Before she died, Victoria accused you of plagiarism, didn't she? Of stealing her work?'

Raven nodded. 'But she was wrong. All my work is my own.'

'It most certainly is,' Posy agreed.

'You can check it out at my website—' Raven started, talking to the audience, but Caro cut her off. If she was right, there'd be plenty of time for Raven to indulge in self-promotion after today.

'But even though she was wrong about *you* stealing her work, she wasn't entirely mistaken that she was being plagiarised.' She looked just off camera and gave Rosalind, who'd left her seat to move to the edge of the stage set, the nod. 'And my friend, Rosalind King, is going to explain to you all exactly how.'

Rosalind

Rosalind smiled politely at the audience's applause as she took the stage, accepting the microphone that was handed to her, and greeting the hosts. She was amazed they – or their producer – had let this go on as long as it had already, especially given how Caro was hamming it up. The green room must be filled with other guests impatiently waiting their turn – or already knowing they'd been bumped to tomorrow's show.

But she had admit, this made good telly. She couldn't blame Stephanie or Jason for wanting it to happen on their airwaves. On the other hand, somewhere her agent was probably spitting feathers. National treasures didn't do this sort of thing – even ones who used to be Dahlia Lively, a lifetime ago.

She turned to the audience and let her smile fall away. Murder was not a smiling matter.

'Our investigation had started as a cold-case enquiry,' she said, studying the suspects in the front row intently. 'Looking into a case we thought had been settled five years before, thinking that no one could get hurt. But this was where it took a more dangerous turn.'

She stepped forward, looking up at the rest of the audience as she explained. 'There were seven suspects to start with, but they weren't the same seven we ended up with. The final member of the original writing group was a man called Iain Hardy, but before we could persuade him to talk to us, he was dead.'

The audience gasped again at this, even though they had to have all read about it in the papers already. You really just couldn't beat a bit of theatre.

'Upon stumbling over his body, we discovered another secret this group had been hiding. Iain Hardy had reinvented himself – as Dexter Rush.' Rosalind waited for another gasp and murmur from the crowd, even though this, too, was public knowledge now. Stephanie, she noticed, was looking eager for them to move it on, so she did.

'That wasn't the only surprise, though,' Rosalind went on. 'We asked Hakim to check the books Dexter Rush had published to see if he recognised the style – and he did. As Victoria Denby's.'

That titbit hadn't made any of the papers yet, since they hadn't shared it with anyone – excepting Caro's outburst at Petra at the launch party. It was enough of a revelation to buy them a little more airtime, anyway.

Caro stepped up to continue the story. 'Iain might have been acting alone when he stole those books originally – but we know he had help building his publishing career. While he indie published the first two under another name, he soon scored a literary agent and a big publishing deal. The deal would have risked exposing his crime of course, so we reasoned he would have had to at least confess all to his agent, Petra Wren.'

She didn't mention that Petra was also *her* agent, Rosalind noticed with amusement.

'But Petra wasn't just a stranger who stumbled into this,' Caro went on. 'We discovered that she was actually a founding member of the Market Foxleigh Writing Group – meaning she could have been in on this from the very beginning.'

'This definitely gave Petra a motive for both murders. First, to stop Victoria realising it was them who had plagiarised her, and then to stop Iain confessing all,' Posy said, joining them up on the stage set. 'After all, if we'd found the connection, so might someone else. And Petra's career would be ruined if the story got out.'

Petra leaped to her feet. 'I could sue you, you realise? This is defamation. Or libel. Or something!'

'Not if it's true,' Rosalind said, calmly. 'And right now, I believe the police have a specialist team checking Dexter Rush's books against Victoria's drafts to establish that. If they find what we expect them to find, you're going to have a lot of questions to answer.'

'But I deleted—' Petra cut herself off, but it was too late. She'd already given herself away. Which was just as well, as they didn't actually have any of Victoria's drafts for anyone to check against.

'You came back to Market Foxleigh just after Victoria's murder, didn't you? So you could delete not just the cloud files – you could have done that from anywhere – but destroy the originals you knew Victoria would have printed out, too.'

Petra slumped back down onto the sofa. She seemed defeated, broken even, as she nodded. 'The house was still a crime scene, but I knew she kept the print-outs in her filing cabinet in her writing shed in the garden. It was easy enough to break in there and take them and shred them.'

Caro looked delighted that she finally had confirmation that she'd been right about Petra. Rosalind was more interested in where that led them next.

'Nearly there,' she murmured to Jason and Stephanie, away from the microphone, before she stepped forward again, closer to Petra this time. She knew the part she needed to play now. Someone ready to listen while she shared her secrets. 'Tell us what happened when you went up to talk to Iain, the night of the Skeleton Parade.'

'I . . . he was already dead when I got there.' Petra's voice was stilted, her face white under the lights. 'I'd talked to him the night before, and he was scared about the truth coming out. He said that someone knew, but he wouldn't tell me who. I don't know, maybe he thought . . . maybe *he* thought I killed Victoria, and he was trying to protect whoever had uncovered his secret. I told him to sit tight, not to do anything – that I'd get someone to cover for him at the parade. But he wanted to do the reading, so I said I'd fetch him before that.

'I already had a copy of his hotel room key. He was terrible for losing them. So I let myself in . . . I walked in there and saw him dead on the bed, pill bottles and whisky everywhere, and . . .'

'He'd killed himself?' Posy asked, softly.

Petra nodded. 'There was a note. He'd confessed everything. Said he was confessing before it all came out, since he knew it was going to. And I knew that would be the end of me. So . . . so I cleared it up. I used the shower cap to cover my hands before I touched anything, then I washed up the toothbrush glasses with the whisky in and put them away. Took all the other evidence with me and hid it in a skip a few streets over. Then I hurried back down to the parade and burned the note, so there'd be no proof that he did it himself.'

Rosalind allowed herself a small smile – and saw her sister Dahlias do the same. There it was. The last piece of information they'd needed.

Oh, not the suicide. They'd already guessed that.

'What about the flower?' Rosalind asked. 'There was a paper flower made from a Dahlia Lively novel in the room. We think it must have blown off the desk onto the floor. Did you leave that there?'

'No. I never even saw it. If I had I'd have taken it with the note and burned it. The last thing I wanted was anything linking Iain's death to Victoria's – not just because of the books. Because he didn't kill her – and neither did I!'

Caro asked the next obvious question. 'How did Iain know it was all going to come out – the plagiarism, I mean?'

Petra blinked. 'I assumed you'd told him. I knew you were asking too many questions, I just hoped if you couldn't confirm your suspicions . . .'

'And that's why burning the note wasn't the only thing you did at the parade, was it?' Posy said, joining them on the set. 'You also cornered me in a dark alley, and stole my notes. So you could be sure about what we knew. I only figured it out later, but . . . there *wasn't* anything earth shattering in my notebook at that point. Nothing that any of the suspects should be afraid of, anyway. Only someone who didn't know that – someone who hadn't sat in on any of the conversations we'd had with them – would want to steal it. Which left us with you.'

'Unfortunately for you, when you were clearing up his room, you missed the page proofs on the desk,' Caro added, with a small grin. Rosalind couldn't really blame her. 'The ones that told us that Iain Hardy was Dexter Rush.'

'But who else knew that?' Rosalind said. 'As far as we could tell, only Milla Kowalski, who found out and used it to persuade Dexter to appear at this year's festival as a special guest. And that was all – until she told Eleanor Grey to try and use the celebrity angle to persuade her to use her podcast to reinvestigate the murder her best friend's brother had been imprisoned for.'

'Which brings us right back to where all this started,' Caro whispered – in a stage whisper meant to carry, because this was still Caro, after all. 'Sarah Baker.'

Chapter Twenty-One

The handcuffs clinked closed, and Dahlia felt relief seep through her whole body. Another murderer would soon be behind bars, and her work here was done.

'Come on.' Johnnie took her arm. 'Let's go home.'

Dahlia Lively *in* Dahlia Saves The Day
***By* Lettice Davenport, 1971**

Posy

Sarah looked pale and shaky. 'What? Why me?'

'You warned Iain that his secret was about to come out. Didn't you?' Rosalind said. 'Milla told you when she told Eleanor.' They couldn't be sure if Sarah had ever read any of Victoria's drafts before her death – she'd had access to the files, and might have been curious enough. But they'd realised she didn't need to. Just a cryptic warning that the truth was coming out, referring to his pen name, would have been enough to spook the already nervy Iain – probably to the point where he confessed all.

Posy watched as emotions and thoughts flickered across Sarah's face. She saw her debating whether to deny it or admit it, unsure which would get her into most trouble.

She didn't realise yet that she was already in all the trouble there was.

'I . . . Iain was a friend,' she said, finally. 'I thought I owed him a heads-up. I didn't know about the plagiarism stuff until he told me. He'd already had quite a lot to drink.'

'Of course.' Rosalind gave her a friendly smile that Sarah apparently didn't know well enough not to trust, as her shoulders seemed to relax as Rosalind moved on again.

Posy kept her gaze mostly on Sarah, though.

'Hakim.' The man sat up very straight at the sound of Caro saying his name. He knew what was coming, though. Posy thought he might even have begun to suspect before she called him yesterday. 'The day before we left Market Foxleigh after the festival this year, I found you walking by Victoria Denby's house. You were hoping to bump into Sarah. Why did you think that might happen there?'

'Uh, because I knew that her husband, Eric, used to live in the house behind Victoria's, before they were married, and I hoped they might still live there.'

And that was it. The one detail they'd needed to tie it all together – and they hadn't even seen it until it was almost too late. Until Posy had stared at the map of Market Foxleigh pinned at the centre of the Murder Map, and remembered two things: Hakim looking for Sarah there, and how Eric had said that the investigation had always been between them. Not the murder, the investigation.

Because Eric, they'd confirmed from the address in Danny's notes, was the neighbour who'd witnessed Scott fleeing the scene. A small detail Eleanor – or more likely Sarah and Milla – had left out of the file.

It had all started to unravel, once they'd realised that.

'Sarah,' Posy said, and she turned her wide, frightened eyes on her. 'You were with Eric the night of the murder, watching a movie, right?' A cautious nod. 'Except you told me, the night we met, that Eric always falls asleep during films. So you were on the scene, with plenty of opportunity to sneak out and confront Victoria about any of your grievances, plus the murder weapon was found in your car – a car you shared with Scott, but that *you* were using that night, as we know Scott fled on foot. Eleanor, did she tell you any of this when she approached you about the podcast?'

'No.' Eleanor was staring at her business partner with an expression somewhere between wariness and rising horror. 'Milla just said . . . she said Sarah knew her brother was innocent, and that together we could prove it.'

'And maybe that was true,' Rosalind said. 'But possibly only because she knew the real murderer was herself.'

'No!' Sarah cried out, wringing her hands together. 'You've got it all wrong.'

With her fluffy blonde hair and wide blue eyes, Posy knew Sarah would have at least some of the audience on side. The ones who believed a woman wasn't capable of such cold-blooded things.

The three Dahlias knew better, though.

'Actually, Eleanor, you've just answered my next question,' Caro said. 'Because you see, we couldn't figure out why Sarah would want to reopen the investigation if she was the murderer herself, or if she knew that Scott really had done it. But she didn't, did she? It was *Milla* who approached you, trying to do something nice for her best friend.'

'Of course, Sarah couldn't object once that ball was rolling – she'd spent years claiming her brother was innocent,' Posy said, picking up the story. 'So she had to go along with it – and she decided to use the opportunity to frame someone else for Victoria's murder. Someone with a perfect, ready-made motive. Iain Hardy.'

'The way we see it, things happened one of two ways.' Posy turned towards the audience as she lifted the hand not holding the microphone and held up her index finger. 'One, Victoria's murder happened exactly as the police said it did. Scott argued with her over the embezzlement, hit her over the head with the trophy, accidentally dropped or purposefully left a paper flower, stashed the trophy in the boot of his car, and then ran. In which case, Sarah went along with this whole podcast investigation to try and get him acquitted and, when there was no evidence to support that, decided to make some.'

'So you went up to Iain's room and put the fear of God into him,' Caro continued. 'And then you either poisoned him and made it look like a suicide, or drove him to kill himself while you sat there sipping whisky with him – don't forget, Petra told us she washed up the glasses, plural, and I don't think he'd have needed two if he was alone, do you?'

'Either way, you brought about his death,' Rosalind said, her voice low and heavy. 'And the fact you had that paper flower ready means you must have planned this in advance. If you're telling the truth about not knowing about Iain's plagiarism before that night, I imagine you hoped that people would jump to the conclusion that this meant the killer was still at large. But when Iain confessed to stealing Victoria's work, well, that gave you a handy scapegoat, didn't it? You goaded him into writing that confession and made sure that paper flower pointed everyone to exactly why he'd done it by leaving it on top of Dexter Rush's own manuscript, and a letter from Scott.'

Caro took over. 'It wouldn't take a huge leap in logic to conclude that Iain had killed Victoria so he could keep publishing her writing as his own, then killed himself because the truth was about to come out. And if it hadn't been for Petra clearing up the room and burning the confession, and a breeze blowing that flower out of sight, that's probably what would have happened.'

'It's all pretty horrible. But option two is even worse.' Posy held up a second finger. 'Because in this scenario, *you* murdered Victoria Denby. Not because of a short-story competition, or even because she'd been belittling you and taking advantage of you for so long. But because you went to confront her about one thing and instead found she was expecting you.'

'Wait. How did she know about the short-story competition? Hakim said he didn't tell her.' Stephanie, the host, was leaning forward with eyes wide and curious.

'We think she found the original panel results in Victoria's desk drawer earlier that day, while helping Milla search for a missing shepherdess statuette,' Caro said, as an aside. 'It was a whole thing.'

Posy tried to get them back on track, facing Sarah again. 'Victoria had sent you a message, about Scott – one Scott would intercept as you'd left your phone at home. She thought you were there to talk about how your brother had been embezzling funds, and she was about to call the police on him.'

'You'd always protected your brother, you told us that,' Rosalind said. 'It's not so much of a stretch to imagine that, when faced with this woman who'd already cheated you and was now about to destroy Scott's life, you acted to protect him again. You lifted that trophy that should have been yours and hit her with it. Maybe you only wanted to stall her, maybe you meant to kill. Either way, she dropped like a stone.'

'You're a smart woman. Maybe you had a plan to get away with it. Perhaps you intended to dispose of the weapon, firm up your alibi, I don't know.' Caro had her arms folded over her chest as she stared dispassionately at Sarah. 'In the end it didn't matter. Because Scott came to visit Victoria – accidentally dropping one of the paper flowers he'd just received in the post – and Eric, awake again, saw him running away from a crime scene and told the police. Scott took the car before you could remove the trophy and dispose of it. And Scott had a very solid motive.'

'You couldn't protect him this time,' Posy said. 'Not without incriminating yourself. And when it came down to it, you still cared about yourself more than him, it turned out.'

Rosalind came to stand beside her, the three Dahlias together, facing down their prime suspect. 'But you had to live with that guilt. And maybe this podcast was your way of trying to make amends.'

That was what Caro had finally put her finger on, late into the night after their dinner at Langans. *You said we weren't your mothers, and I said we were feeling guilty. And it reminded me of Sarah, but I couldn't figure out why.* They knew now, though.

The studio was hushed, everyone hanging on their words. Posy bit back a smile. They had them in the palm of their hands.

Caro waited a moment, of course, for the showmanship of it all. Then she asked their final question. 'So? Which is it, Sarah?'

The question hung in the air, possibilities hanging with it.

Then Sarah gave an anguished cry and bolted from the sofa – only to be stopped by a security guard standing at the edge of the set. As she turned to watch, Posy saw uniformed police officers trooping down the aisles in the audience seating; Rosalind must have called them after all.

Good.

'I saw Scott yesterday, Sarah.' Rosalind's voice rang out around the hushed studio. 'I told him everything we'd discovered. You can't protect him anymore. You can't even protect yourself. Because it was you, wasn't it?'

Then the police reached her and began to read Sarah her rights.

And behind them, a stunned Stephanie announced that they'd be right back, after this break . . .

Chapter Twenty-Two

And that's the story of how we became the three Dahlias. But I promise you, it's only the start of the adventure.

Caro Hooper *in* The Three Dahlias
_By_ Caro Hooper

Caro

Getting someone released from prison, even if they were innocent, wasn't as easy as setting up a murderer on live TV, it turned out. And Sarah hadn't even confessed to Victoria's murder yet as far as they knew. So Scott Baker was still in prison when Rosalind took Caro and Posy to visit him a few days later. She'd confessed about the small deception that meant she'd visited him alone the first time, and seemed stunned when Caro had actually hugged her in thanks.

Even now, knowing the truth of it all, Caro was glad she wasn't there at the prison alone. Or just alone with him – a man she'd been afraid of for so long, but now looked so small and broken.

'I suppose I should thank you all,' he said, his expression rueful as he stood to greet them. 'You did exactly what I asked you to do – found enough evidence to throw doubt on my conviction. I just wish . . .'

'We're sorry it had to be this way,' Rosalind said. 'But we were only ever after the truth.'

It wasn't their fault that his big sister was a murderer, anyway.

'My lawyers are talking with the police,' Scott went on. 'They're hopeful they can get me released this time.'

'We hope so,' Posy said. Then she looked at Caro, obviously waiting for her to say something.

But what was she supposed to say?

'I read your letter,' were the words that came out. 'You really weren't stalking me?'

Scott shook his head. 'I promise I was only ever a loyal fan.'

Well. She supposed that was all right, then.

Even if she still couldn't wait to just get home to Annie.

'So which one of them *did* do it?' Annie asked the next Sunday, as she pulled the tray of perfectly crispy roast potatoes from the oven. Caro felt hungrier just looking at them, but Annie was adamant they couldn't eat until Posy arrived. Not even to taste test. 'Do you really know for sure?'

On the counter, a newspaper with a punny headline and a photo of the three of them on the set of *Britain Now* was being used as a mat for the waiting gravy boat, not least because the accompanying article focused more on their appearances than their sleuthing abilities.

Sitting next to it at the kitchen counter, and looking rather incongruous perched on a bar stool in the glass-roofed extension, Rosalind sipped her glass of white wine before answering. 'I know. I knew when I sat with Scott and watched his face as I told him everything we'd found out.'

'It was Sarah,' Caro said, and Rosalind nodded.

'I imagine there'll be a new trial, and it will all come out,' Rosalind said. 'I suspect the police will find enough evidence to charge her with Iain's murder too.'

'It wasn't suicide?' Annie put her hands on her hips, one single oven glove on each of them. 'I thought it was suicide.'

'It was supposed to *look* like suicide, and Petra certainly thought it was,' Caro explained. 'But I'm not so sure. Petra burned the note he left, so it's hard to be certain. But from what she said, it sounded less like a suicide note, more like a signed confession. My guess is that Sarah told him it was all going to come out, and it would be better for him if he confessed upfront. Then she encouraged him to write down what he'd done, and used that to make it look like he'd decided to end things.'

Annie shook her head. 'Honestly. I should have known that going to a crime writing festival could only end badly for you three.'

Rosalind twisted on her stool, looking over her shoulder towards the front door. 'Where *is* Posy, anyway? Shouldn't she be here by now?

'She knows that Sunday dinner is served at three, right?' Annie asked, anxiously. 'She did spend a long time in America . . .'

'She knows. She said she had to pick something up on her way.' Caro leaned over to pluck the gloves from Annie's hands. 'Sit down and have a drink while we wait.' She passed her a glass, and kissed Annie's temple as she took it.

'So, what's next for the three of you?' Annie settled onto the stool on her side of the counter. 'Finding out the identity of Jack the Ripper?'

'Back to the day job,' Rosalind said, with a wry smile. 'I've got a project filming out in Ireland for a month or two, then I'm hoping to spend some time in Llangollen with Jack. And Posy will have the second Dahlia Lively movie starting filming before too long . . .'

'And *I've* got a new book to write. Two, in fact. I had a call with my editor, Charlotte, yesterday, and apparently sales of *The Three*

Dahlias are really taking off after our live TV *J'accuse* moment. She thinks they won't just want our Welsh adventure chronicled, but this mess too.' Caro paused, as something occurred to her. 'I'll need to get a new agent, though.' It didn't seem likely that Petra would be holding onto her position at the agency now everything had come out. Oh well. Someone would come along who was the right fit, she was sure.

Maybe a writer's first agent was like a woman's first spouse – sort of a trial run, until they knew better what they needed.

She smiled softly at Annie, who raised a curious eyebrow at her.

The sound of the doorbell stopped her having to explain. Caro placed her wineglass on the counter and disappeared into the hallway to answer it.

The hall was dark after the brightness of the kitchen, with its glass roof and view of Annie's carefully maintained garden. But the darkness only allowed her to see that there were *two* figures silhouetted against the frosted glass of the top arch of the door.

Caro allowed herself a small smile as she guessed the identity of the interloper. 'Had to pick something up, indeed.'

She pulled open the door suddenly enough to surprise the pair on the doorstep, as Kit looked up from kissing the top of Posy's head and grinned at her.

'Room for one more for dinner?' he asked hopefully.

'Lucky for you, Annie always cooks enough for an entire film set. Come on, come in.'

She ushered them through to the kitchen, where she heard delighted exclamations, demands for hugs, and everyone talking over each other. And she paused for a moment, just to listen.

Sarah Baker had thought that family was about protecting each other above all else – except when it really came down to it, she hadn't. She'd saved herself. Maybe trying to atone for that was what had sent her off kilter, and started a chain of events that had ended with two people dead, not just one.

Caro was protective of her loved ones, too – of Annie, and Rosalind and Posy. She'd want to help them – whether that was making sure Annie took breaks when work was too much, or stocking Posy's empty fridge from time to time, or . . . well, she couldn't imagine Rosalind needing her help. Apart from that thing with the death threats in Wales.

The point was, she loved them, cared for them – but she knew they had to make their own choices, live their own lives, and make their own mistakes.

Would Posy and Kit live happily ever after, despite the vagaries of their work schedules and everything else that separated them for months at a time? She didn't know. Would Rosalind find happiness in a cottage in Wales with Jack, even though they fundamentally disagreed every time Rosalind got caught up in a case? Only time would tell.

But one thing Caro was absolutely sure of.

This was what family looked like.

And she'd never take it for granted.

Three Months Later

Mr and Mrs William Douglas

Request the honour of your presence at the wedding of their son

Duncan Graham Alexander

To

Libby Alice McKinley

At

The family chapel at Dunwick Castle, Argyllshire

On the 24th December at half after two in the afternoon

Reception to follow at the family residence

Dear Rosalind, Caro and Posy

Duncan and I do so hope you'll be able to join us for our special day! It'll be so festive and beautiful up at Dunwick Castle. Of course, Jack, Annie and Kit are welcome too.

Actually . . . there's going to be a rehearsal dinner and other 'getting to know you' things happening for close family in the days before the wedding. As I'm somewhat lacking in actual family these days, I wondered if you would consider coming early to make up my side of things?

Okay, fine, I have to confess – there's another reason I want you there.

Ever since I moved in here at the castle, after we got engaged, I can't shake the feeling that there's something . . . wrong. More than that . . . well. I'll tell you when you get here. If you agree to come.

Please come.

Love,
Libby xxx

Acknowledgements

I couldn't have written *Seven Lively Suspects* without my brilliant agent, Gemma Cooper, who more than deserves to have this book dedicated to her, because none of it would have happened without her *Midsomer Murders* and *Murder She Wrote* obsession.

Huge thanks too, to the fantastic team at Constable: my editor Krystyna Green, my publicist Beth Wright, my marketing guru Brionee Fenlon, not to mention Amanda Keats for wrestling the manuscript into shape, Tara Loder for a fab copy-edit, Christopher Sturtivant for ably assisting, and everyone else there who has had a hand in bringing my Dahlias to life.

Grateful thanks to crime advisor extraordinaire, Dave Carter, for always telling me when things just wouldn't work that way in his perfectly policed world – and also understanding when, for the good of the story, we need to find a way that they just might . . . needless to say, any errors in investigation that remain after he's had a go at the manuscript are entirely my own.

I also want to thank Theakston's Old Peculier Crime Writing Festival in Harrogate, and the Bloody Scotland Festival in Stirling – not just for inviting me to take part in their brilliant festivals, but also giving me the idea for the setting of *Seven Lively Suspects* . . .

Special thanks goes, as always, to my family – especially Simon, Holly and Sam, who've put up with the Dahlias taking over our lives a bit this year, and me being here, there and everywhere talking about them. Also to my parents, in-laws, aunts, uncles and cousins, and many friends, for sending me encouraging photos of my book wherever they spotted it in the wild!

I'm hugely grateful to all the bookshops and booksellers who have got behind this series and supported it, gleefully pressing it into the hands of readers they think will enjoy the sort of hijinks the Dahlias get up to. Super special thanks goes to Waterstones, for making the first in the series their Thriller of the Month, and making my whole year in the process.

But most of all, I'd like to thank all the readers, book bloggers and reviewers who have celebrated the books online or come to events to meet me and tell me how much they enjoyed reading about the Dahlias. It's thanks to all of you that I now get to write another three adventures for the Dahlias after this one! I don't know about you, but I can't wait to see what they get up to next . . .

It wouldn't be a country house weekend without a little murder . . .

Three rival actresses team up to solve a murder at the stately home of Lettice Davenport, the author whose sleuthing creation of the 1930s, Dahlia Lively, had made each of them famous to a new generation.

In attendance at Aldermere: the VIP fans, staying at the house; the fan club president turned convention organiser; the team behind the newest movie adaptation of Davenport's books; the Davenport family themselves; and the three actresses famous for portraying Dahlia Lively through the decades.

There is national treasure Rosalind King, from the original movies, who's feeling sensitive that she's past her prime, TV Dahlia for thirteen seasons, Caro Hooper, who believes she really IS Dahlia Lively, and ex-child star Posy Starling, fresh out of the fame wilderness (and rehab) to take on the Dahlia mantle for the new movie – but feeling outclassed by her predecessors.

Each actress has her own interpretation of the character and her own secrets to hide – but this English summer weekend they will have to put aside their differences as the crimes at Aldermere turn anything but cosy.

Available now.

One murder mystery movie. Three Dahlias. And a whole cast of suspects . . .

Ex-child star Posy Starling is finally filming her dream role – Dahlia Lively in *The Lady Detective* movie. But things take a nightmare turn when a prop weapon is replaced with the real thing – with almost fatal consequences for her fellow Dahlia, Rosalind King. There's something very wrong on the set of *The Lady Detective* – which means it's time to call in Caro Hooper, so the three Dahlias can investigate.

In between filming scenes, signing autographs for locals, photoshoots on set and jetting off to France for an impromptu party, the three Dahlias do what they do best – surreptitiously sleuth. And very soon the evidence starts to point towards one particular co-star . . .

But before they can prove it, a murder rocks the production. And this time, with a storm raging, the river flooded and the bridge washed out, there are no police to rely on so it's up to the three Dahlias to stop a murderer in their tracks . . . before another victim is claimed.

Available now.